Always Ella

SOFIA SAWYER

Always, Ella

Copyright © 2020 by Sofia Sawyer

Printed in the United States

First Printing, 2020

ISBN: 978-1-7332090-2-1

Editor: Jen Graybeal Editing Services

Proofreader: Salt & Sage Books

Cover Design: Qamber Designs and Media

❀ Created with Vellum

ALSO BY SOFIA SAWYER

No Place to Hide

Saving the Winchester Inn

One Stormy Night

Stay updated about new releases. Subscribe to Sofia's
mailing list at **www.sofiasawyer.com**.

To anyone who's felt they couldn't be themselves. I hope you find the courage to show the world all the amazing things you have to offer.

1

ELENA

Elena Lucia watched as the train wreck unfolded, weeks' worth of hard work slowly burning up car by car. She sat at the conference table with a stiff smile, eye twitching in irritation, while her work nemesis derailed her client pitch in one fell swoop. Brittany, smiled broadly as she made her final point, convincing the men sitting across from them to consider a new direction for their advertising campaign.

What's it say in the professional etiquette manuals about slapping your coworker in the middle of a meeting?

Of course, the clients would listen to Brittany Hale, as if she had the answers to all their problems. The holder of the mysterious silver bullet they'd been looking for. She was one of them, after all. A Southern belle through and through, a voice as sweet as the tea they served. Cute as a button with her silky blonde waves and pastel dress that flared at the knee. She could almost pass for a Stepford wife, had Elena not known her for the snake that she was.

Brittany was a junior copywriter working under Elena and was supposed to be observing this pitch. *Just* observing.

Learning the ropes. But in her usual fashion, she came to the meeting with a trick up her sleeve. Her tactics had been more subtle these last few months, but today she took the cake. She didn't come to this meeting with side quips and "helpful" suggestions. Oh, no. She came with a fully formed pitch, ready to take this client by force.

However, she did it with manners that would make her mama proud. She didn't shoot down Elena's pitch outright —a pitch Elena had spent weeks agonizing over every single detail—but she did it in an undermining way and a not-so-subtle "nice fucking try, loser" tone.

And there they had it. Again. Brittany was everything that Elena could never be. As a transplant from the Northeast, it was near impossible to wiggle her way into the inner circle of the born and bred Charlestonians, even after twenty years. Sure, the beautiful southern city was very metropolitan with people from all over and a booming tourist industry. But business was about relationships. Around here, if your parents didn't go to grade school together, you weren't part of the "in" crowd.

Elena realized she was now extraneous as she watched her clients smile at Brittany with entranced nods. Their minds were made up. The partnership was no longer hers. And all the insecurities she'd felt since she first arrived in South Carolina as an impressionable ten-year-old came rushing back.

She wasn't enough. Never would be.

The thought was confirmed the second Brittany shook the men's hands, sealing the deal. She looked Elena up and down smugly as she walked the gentlemen through the posh lobby and out to the bustling streets of downtown. Feeling defeated, Elena stopped by her desk and stuffed her laptop into her oversized purse so she could make her own quick escape. There was nothing more for her to do at work today now that her clients had chosen their lead writer.

Elena pushed through the advertising firm's front doors and stepped out to East Bay Street, the warm air thawing her after sitting in the freezing office all day. She slipped off her cardigan and tossed it into her purse, taking a moment to enjoy the fresh air laced with scents from all the amazing restaurants lining the quaint, historic roads. She closed her eyes and took a deep breath, conjuring up images of world-famous fried chicken and a glass of wine while sitting across from Brad.

Brad. He'll make this better.

Adjusting the heavy purse on her shoulder, she set out to Brad's apartment a few blocks away. The early evening sun washed the cobblestone roads and colorful buildings in a golden glow. Elena hadn't expected to wrap up the meeting this early, but it was just as well. Another three minutes in the room with Brittany, and she would have screamed. The clients had said they wanted something "distinctive" in the discovery calls, so Elena had poured her heart into writing their upcoming advertising copy.

Stupid.

Of course, they nixed it and agreed to a knock-off of what their competitors were doing. How could they not see through Brittany's copycat version? It was insulting and exhausting.

The sweet scent of confederate jasmine enveloped Elena as she rounded the corner, briefly pulling her from her sour mood. Spring in Charleston was always her favorite, and the soothing smells would normally have raised her spirits, but it was hard getting past another letdown. This disappointment was eating her alive.

A quiet night with Brad was just what Elena needed. A

bright spot in her crappy day. She would say to him—very dramatically, of course—"They sucked my creative mojo dry." And Brad would tell her it was their loss.

She hustled down a side alley, careful to not catch her heel on the uneven stones like she'd done one too many times before and turned onto his street. A sense of relief washed over her as his house came into view.

Elena trudged up the historic Georgian-styled home's humidity-warped steps and used a copy of his key to let herself into the converted upstairs apartment. She paused in the doorway to admire the man in front of her—the man she was hopelessly in love with.

But she couldn't do that. Not now.

Not while his head was between another woman's legs.

She stood in shock, the keys to the apartment slipping from her fingers. Her boyfriend, completely oblivious she was there, continued to lick the woman with all the gusto he could manage. The girl—a perfect, tiny blonde thing—was sprawled out on the table with her skirt to her hips. One pert breast fell freely from the top of her shirt. Her eyes were closed with lazy passion, and her lips parted, allowing the blissful moans to escape.

After a speechless moment, Elena found her voice. "What the hell?" she screamed.

Brad shot up in surprise, his mouth still glistening from things she didn't want to think about. The woman, who looked no older than her early twenties, scrambled off the table and covered herself.

"Who the hell is she?" the girl asked as if she had every right to be angry.

"I'm his girlfriend."

"No one," he answered simultaneously while wiping his

mouth with the back of his hand and straightening his button-up.

"No one? *No one!* We've been together for two years." Elena snatched the keys from the floor and threw them at him like a pitcher for the Riverdogs. "Do you often give your key to strangers? Do you tell them you want them to move in when their lease is up in a few months? Or do you just go down on them and send them on their way?"

"A girlfriend, Brad?" the blonde screeched and slapped him before pushing past Elena and toward the front door.

Elena stared at Brad. She was reeling, her heart fracturing into painful shards, cutting her deep. Yet, he stared back without an ounce of remorse in his eyes.

"We're done," Elena stated as evenly as she could, fighting the quiver in her throat.

"Don't be like that," he pleaded, his face red, most likely from the heat of passion rather than guilt. "It was just one time. We can work past that."

"No, it wasn't!" the girl screamed from the stairs, which only transformed Elena's hurt into rage.

Heat warmed Elena's skin, and her nostrils flared as she tried to keep herself from spinning out. "Goodbye." She whispered, barely believing she said it.

How could so much go so wrong so quickly?

She spun on her heel—fighting the urge to cry, scream, and plead—and left his apartment with as much dignity as she could muster. She turned down the next street, and once safely out of view, she let the tears fall. Two knives had been twisted in her back today, and it hurt like hell.

Wow. Ugly crying in public. This is a new low, even for me.

She wiped her eyes with the heel of her palm, not caring how smudged her mascara was. What was she supposed to do now? The future she had been planning for was suddenly gone, leaving a gaping void.

They were supposed to move in together. She had already bookmarked a bunch of cute stuff online to transform his bachelor pad into a home they could share. To show him how much better life could be once they were together. She wanted him to see how happy he'd be coming home to her each night.

Elena was almost certain that was the next step before he was going to propose. She hadn't gone and made a vision board or anything, but she couldn't help her mind from considering what life with Brad would look like. On more than one occasion, she'd stopped and admired the gowns in bridal shop windows she'd walk by on the way to work, mentally noting the styles she preferred.

God, I'm going to die alone, she thought as she zoomed through the streets of downtown, the world a blur around her.

Elena was angry. Broken. Confused.

She could call her mom, but she didn't feel like being coddled. She could go to her best friend's place but wasn't ready for over-the-top, loyal angst.

She needed time to process. Make sense of it all. Her life had taken a jarring turn, and she wasn't sure what to do next.

Almost without realizing it she headed up the stairs to her small apartment, shaving off a few minutes from her usual twenty-minute stroll. It was small. Simple. Way more expensive than it needed to be—thanks to the influx of people moving to Charleston these last few years—but it was nice. Maybe a little creaky in some areas. Likely haunted. But it was hers. A safe place filled with all her favorite things: books, fluffy blankets, and her lovable golden retriever, Marley.

Dropping her keys on the side table and giving her dog a quick pat, she went straight to the photos of her and Brad sitting on the media center. Elena pulled the pictures from their frames, ripped them in tiny pieces, and tossed them into the fireplace along with a lit match. She poured herself a glass of red wine and sipped it while watching the flames lick up the last of the pictures—the shards of a broken dream. And although cathartic, she still felt unsettled.

She wanted to throw things. Break things. She needed a release but was paralyzed by the sinking feeling deep inside. What did she do wrong? How could she have been more? Better?

How could I have been so stupid to think I was enough?

The large pine floors creaked loudly as she paced her living room. Anxiety bubbled in her stomach, mixing with the burning acidity from the wine. She shook her arms to relieve the tension, but nothing eased the sharp pain in her heart.

How did I miss all the signs? Was he good at hiding things, or was I so stupidly in love that I ignored them?

Love *really* was blind. Elena prided herself on her smarts, but today had her wondering if the joke was on her. She'd worked so hard and was one-upped by a junior copywriter. She'd devoted herself to Brad and the life they had planned to share, only to be replaced by someone else.

Maybe it wasn't that he had cheated that stung so much but rather that he felt so confident they could work through it. It wasn't a question. It wasn't a plea for forgiveness. It was more like a command. An expectation. Like it was his right to cheat, and she'd just better deal with it.

Did he really value me so little?

Elena gulped down the rest of her wine and picked up the bottle, a slight tremor to her hand as she poured. It had been a while since she'd had her heart broken like this, she forgot how bad it physically felt. She took another sip of wine, trying to push past the clenching of her stomach and the tightness in her chest. She needed a way to make sense of everything that had happened.

Elena scanned the room. Her laptop sat idly on the table.

Of course.

Putting fingers to keyboard and letting her stream of consciousness take over always made a dark day seem less grim, and always gave her some clarity to her feelings. And sometimes, if she was lucky, an action plan, too. It had worked for her while growing up when she felt like an outcast all those years. And it sure as hell was going to help now.

I hope.

She had fallen in love with writing when her mother gave her her first journal. Her mother, a children's therapist, had seen Elena's struggle while adjusting to life in the South. But rather than pry for details, she placed the journal on Elena's nightstand and let her work it out herself.

Writing served as both therapy and an escape. And right now, being anywhere but here was appealing.

Fueled by emotions, she flopped onto the couch and pulled her computer into her lap. Marley hopped up and rested her warm body against Elena's leg, providing the kind of comfort only a dog can give.

She let out a breath and pulled up her web browser as she decided how she wanted to tackle it. Did she just need to vent? Should she write a letter to Brad about how he hurt her? Or maybe create a ten-step action plan for how to get over life's disappointment? A pep talk?

A pep talk. Advice. "Dear Abby."

"Yessss," she whispered under her breath as she pulled up a blog site. "No one really uses this anymore anyway, right?" she asked Marley, who looked up with her big brown eyes. "Social media made these online journals obsolete now that everyone airs their dirty laundry on Facebook." She snorted and took a big gulp of wine.

She signed up and made a few adjustments to her account before she pulled up a new post. She stared at the white space, the cursor blinking, taunting her to stop stalling. With the *Dear Abby* advice column still in mind, she put her fingers to the keyboard.

Dear—

She paused. Dear who? She couldn't write to herself. That was weird.

Looking at it critically, she had to be the "Abby," a person who wasn't involved but eager to help. Someone to be objective. They had to provide tough love with a compassionate flair. She had to be a better, stronger version of herself to offer the advice she really needed.

Ella.

The name popped into her head as clear as day. She hadn't been called by her nickname since the first week she had arrived in Charleston when the other Ella in her class backed her into a corner with her posse of friends—friends Elena would never make—and told her there could only be one.

The kids in her class had grown up together. Their parents had grown up together. And *their* parents' parents had grown up together. Their bonds went back generations, and they had made it clear how out of place she truly was that day.

It had never felt like that in New York. There were always new kids joining her class at odd times throughout the year. If you were the new kid, you wouldn't be for long. Maybe that's why things had seemed easier for her back then and why it was a shock to her system when they first came to Charleston.

Elena rubbed her eyes and shook her head. Maybe that's where it all went wrong. When ten-year-old Elena let other people define her. The old, pre-Charleston Ella would never have allowed that. She had spunk. She was brave.

The old Ella would have dusted herself off and gotten back on the playground already, not wallowed on the sidelines.

The old Ella knew who she was and wouldn't bend to anyone.

Until one day, she did.

Elena wished she hadn't given in all those years ago. Maybe things would have been different.

Every once in a while, she could feel the old Ella stirring about. But Elena knew better. She learned early on that side of her wasn't tolerated or accepted. If she wanted to fit in here, she needed to play by their rules.

Yeah, that had worked out great. Maybe it's time to make my own rules for a change.

Putting her fingers to the keyboard, she began to type.

Dear Ella,

Where do I start? Is there ever really a starting point when you're lost? Truthfully, I've felt out of place for...a while now.

But I brushed it off, telling myself that everyone my age feels that way.

But today I realized how wrong I was, and now I'm wondering if that feeling influenced all my decisions, including my boyfriend, Brad.

I loved him. Love him.

I don't know.

Catching him with another woman should have shocked me to the core. And it did, a little. But there's this nagging in the back of my mind that keeps saying I shouldn't be surprised.

That's what's bothering me.

The cheating hurts like hell, but it's the voice repeating over and over that I should have seen it coming.

I just don't know how I would have.

We were happy for two years. He made me feel like I belonged for the first time in a long time. We were about to move in together. How could I have known he would hurt me like this?

Elena's eyes filled with tears as she stared at the screen, not truly seeing it. Why was her gut telling her this was expected? Hadn't he been supportive? Loving? There?

No. No. And no.

She pushed back in her seat. Where did those thoughts come from?

Without thinking, she clicked the button to start a bulleted list and let her heart take the keyboard.

Red flags:

- *Dismissing dream of writing novel*
- *Never truly supportive when people like Brittany ruined work for me*

- *Reluctant to introduce me to certain groups of friends*
- *His parents never warmed up to me, acted like I was temporary;*

She paused before she listed more bullets that were itching to be typed. These weren't just red flags, these were *really* red flags. And yet she had ignored them all this time. She continued writing.

The signs were subtle, he hid them well and played them off, but they were there. What do I do now that I know my relationship was a lie? How do I trust myself again?

Sincerely,
Dazed and Confused

Elena took a sip of her wine as she reread what she'd written. There it was. Out in the open. She'd stuck with a man who didn't respect her. Who—depending on his situation—would *hide* her. All those horrible things she thought about herself came rushing back. All the self-doubt. The self-image issues. Her foolish hope that she finally fit in blinded her to what was right in front of her.

She wouldn't fall back into that pattern of self-loathing. She pushed those thoughts aside.

What would Ella do?

Dear Dazed and Confused,

It can be hard to come to terms with something like this. You put your trust in someone and loved them, yet they couldn't do the same. But you need to know this isn't your fault. Would it have been nice to know he wasn't treating you the way you deserve sooner? Sure.

That's not on you, though. He made you believe one thing

but did the opposite. If there's a lesson here, it's to trust the actions and not the words.

More importantly, you need to trust your gut. Judging by what you wrote, it looks like you had a subconscious clue something was off.

When you have that reaction, pay attention to it. It could save you from a world of hurt and a lot of wasted time.

In the meantime, embrace the pain. Let it all out. And then find a way to do something positive with your life. You alone control your future. That may seem sad as your heart heals, but when you get past that initial ache, you'll see a lot is waiting for you.

I see a bright future ahead for you. All you have to do is reach out and grab it.

Always,
Ella

After an hour of cathartic writing, Elena sucked in a deep, cleansing breath and started to feel a little better. The tears had dried into a crusty mess on her cheeks. She felt gross and restless, but a little less hopeless.

Walking to her bathroom, she eased her way into the shower and let the hot water wash away the day. She stood there for far too long, her fingers pruning in the process and the water running lukewarm. After, she threw on comfortable clothes and opted to towel-dry her long, thick, dark hair. It would be a disaster when it dried—not quite straight, not quite wavy—but she didn't care.

Little things like that didn't matter when you had no one to impress anymore. She sighed, shaking the negative thought away. She needed a break from her pity party.

Shuffling back into the kitchen, the worse for wear, she

poured herself another glass of wine and guzzled it in a very unladylike way.

Not a Southern Belle at all, that's for damn sure.

Her laptop dinged from the coffee table, pulling her attention from the wine bottle. Her eyebrows knitted in confusion, trying to place the notification noise. It definitely wasn't for an email.

Another ding.

What is that?

She crossed the living room in three strides and woke the computer, the screen a bright, blinding light in her dim apartment.

You've been mentioned. Click here to see the post.

Elena scanned the list of notifications on the blog site, another handful saying the same thing. With a shaky finger, she clicked the first message.

Dear Ella,

I love my girlfriend, but our families don't approve because we're not the same religion. I want to spend the rest of my life with her, but she thinks we should break up because she sees no way around this.

Elena sucked in a breath, her heart racing. She clicked another message.

Dear Ella,

I want to do something grand and romantic for my promposal, but my girlfriend is scared because she hasn't officially come out yet. How do I help her feel ready to embrace who she is?

"Oh my God," Elena hissed. Frantically, she clicked her account details and pulled up her privacy settings. "Shit. Shit. Shit."

"Set to Private" remained unchecked in her settings. She could have sworn she did it first thing.

Another ding indicating a new notification made her blood pressure spike.

All of these people were desperate for help. All of them waiting for her to respond.

2

ELENA

"Open up!" Elena shouted as she pounded on the door. "I'm coming! Jesus," she heard a muffled voice from the other side. Seconds later, the door swung open to reveal her best friend, Mae St. Julien. Looking confused, she ran a hand through her wild hair, which was a shocking shade of pink this week. "What's wrong with you?"

Elena and Marley pushed inside the swanky apartment of the new complex built on upper King Street. She unhooked Marley's leash, who immediately sniffed around with curiosity despite having been there a bunch of times.

"Are you drunk? On a *Wednesday?*" Mae feigned shock. She was probably enjoying this far too much.

Elena dropped Marley's leash on the quartz countertop and ran a hand through her mess of thick waves. "Kinda. That's not the point."

"Celebrating your new client?" Mae guessed.

Elena rolled her eyes. "No. That's a story for another time—"

"Brittany strikes again?" Mae guessed.

Elena grabbed her friend's shoulders and shook. "Listen to me! We have a situation."

Mae smirked. "What is it this time? Your Lilly Pulitzer pals said your shirt was offseason?" she jabbed.

Mae was a free spirit. Although born and raised in Charleston to a well-off, well-respected family, she was anything but the Southern angel she was destined to be. A graphic artist, Mae liked to express herself any way she could: colorful hair, provocative tattoos, and an ever-changing wardrobe. Her current phase was some form of nineties grunge.

On more than one occasion, Elena had seen Mae's mom clutch her pearls. Literally.

She had been trying to get Elena to let loose since they became friends in the fourth grade. Mae didn't understand how hard it was for Elena to fit in, and she had tried hard.

Elena wasn't one of them. Mae didn't get what it was like to be an outsider, and even if she had been one, she likely wouldn't have cared. That's just how she was.

"Brad and I broke up."

"Wait, what? You finally got rid of the Ken-doll?" Mae had never been shy about her opinion of Brad.

Elena nodded quickly. "More on that later. The issue is this." She shoved her phone in Mae's face.

She took the phone and held it away, adjusting her gaze to see what Elena had thrust at her. "Okay. It's a blog site. So what?" She shook her head in confusion.

Elena paced back and forth, Marley following along, likely wondering where all this pacing was leading to. "I had this stupid idea to write a letter to myself to help me work out my feelings."

"Writing always helps you, though."

She paused and pinned Mae down with an exasperated

look. "I know." She paced again. "I thought I set it to private, but it must not have saved, and now people are writing in like I'm the new *Dear Abby*. I have no idea how they found me."

"Looks like someone with a big following reblogged your original post. It has a ton of shares, comments, and likes." Mae handed back her phone and shrugged. "You can still shut it down. It's not that big of a deal."

"But it is." She grabbed the phone and scrolled. "These people...they're all going through something. Just like me. They're looking for someone to help them."

"Doesn't mean it has to be you. You don't have to answer."

Elena bit her bottom lip. "I kinda already did."

"You w*hat*?" Mae snatched the phone back and looked at the posts, sucking in a deep breath. "I have to admit, your responses are pretty amazing. But really? It's not like you to put yourself out there like that."

"I'm not. *Ella* is."

Mae rolled her eyes. "You don't think someone will find out eventually?"

"No one has called me Ella in years. Plus, none of my account information even hints at who I am or where I'm from. I don't even have an avatar loaded."

"So..."

"So, I can be Ella. I can help people. In helping them, it'll also help me deal with the Brad stuff."

"I know you loved him, but it isn't a big loss. He never deserved you."

Elena paused at that but tried to keep her facial expression even, as she'd learned to do over the years. Deep down, she never felt like *she* deserved *him*. She had always waited for the day he would realize it.

I guess it was today.

"Maybe so. And maybe one day I'll see that. But right now, I don't. And right now, I'm hurt. And sad. And feeling pretty shitty about myself. But answering those people? I felt a little better."

Mae leaned in and sniffed. "You sure you're not feeling a little better because of the wine? What is that? The pinot noir we like from the wine bar under your apartment?"

"Yeah. Nate gave me a discount. He says hi, by the way."

"I'll have to stop in."

"Anyway," she said, trying to bring the conversation back on track. "I think...I think I want to keep at it. It feels like it's giving me a sense of purpose. Maybe I can do some good while I work through my own stuff." Tears misted her eyes again. Her stomach clenched as the visions of Brad lapping up the blonde came rushing back.

Mae hugged her, a concerned look on her face. "Maybe you're right, and that's exactly what you need to help you feel better. Listening to other people's problems and giving back is super noble. But what about you? Maybe you can tell me about *your* problems." Mae shrugged her tiny shoulders.

Elena swiped away a tear, feeling grateful for her friend. The unlikeliest of pairs, her mother would say, but they balanced each other out beautifully. "You're great, you know that?"

Mae moved to the kitchen and uncorked a bottle of wine. She took a gulp straight from the bottle before handing it to Elena. "Now I'm an even better friend. C'mon. Let's sit, and you tell me what happened. In detail."

As expected, the next couple of hours were full of talking crap about Brad and even more wine—more wine than she should have had. As she wandered back home with

Marley, well-past buzzed, she somehow found clarity in the booze-induced fog.

After her vent session with Mae, she saw a glimmer of hope. Maybe tomorrow would be the start of the healing process. It would take some time to get over the betrayal, and it might take even longer to trust her instincts again, but the promise of a new beginning blossomed something inside of her.

It was the blog.

Maybe she hadn't set it to private, but she never advertised it either. In a world where an insane amount of content is produced every second, her blog was somehow discovered in the sea of digital noise. To her, it felt like a sign. People found it, read it, and now turned to her for help.

As she got back to her apartment and tucked herself into bed, she grabbed her phone to set her alarm. Squinting with one eye to reduce the double-vision, she saw another ten alerts from the blog pop up.

Mae had urged Elena to sleep on it because this wasn't normal Elena behavior, and it really *had* been a shitty day. Diving into this might not be healthy, she had warned, and Elena might see that after her emotions had evened out.

But Mae didn't understand there was something more to it. Sure, it was great to help people, but the blog offered Elena something she hadn't felt in a very long time.

She saw a glimpse of her old self, of what could be. And she liked it. As her finger hovered between the button to delete the blog or to reply, her gut told her what she needed to do.

3

ELENA

 *ne year later.*

"AND THAT'S how you're going to stand out from your competitors, plain and simple." Brittany shined a blindingly white smile before taking her seat. Elena tried not to roll her eyes.

Mark, head of advertisement, walked to the front of the room. "Thank you, Brittany. Very compelling presentation." He addressed the two prospective clients sitting at the end of the table. "Now that you've gotten a glimpse of what our two top copywriters have to offer, do you have any thoughts or feedback?"

Mary, an executive for a prestigious restaurant group that owned and operated some of the finest dining establishments in Charleston, nodded. "I have to say, very impressive work, ladies. As you know, we have meetings with two other agencies next week. Once we meet with them, Chuck and I will weigh our options and get you an answer. We'll make our decision before the end of the month."

Mark's stance shifted into what Elena recognized as his way to exude confidence. "Fair enough. We look forward to hearing from you. And please, don't hesitate to reach out with any questions."

Elena shuffled out of the conference room with the rest of the group and beelined it to her desk, trying to get away from Brittany as soon as humanly possible. If she thought Brittany had been bad before, she'd been sorely mistaken. In the past year, Brittany had managed to undermine most of Elena's projects, causing a boatload of extra work. It had been hell, and despite her complaints to Mark, he did nothing to intervene. Brittany's methods were locking in clients, and that's what mattered to him, even if it was causing friction between colleagues.

"That could have gone better," Mae commented as she took a seat on the edge of Elena's desk.

Although Mae owned her own graphic design business, Elena's company often contracted with her. Those weeks were Elena's favorite. Something about having her friend in the office eased her murderous tendencies when it came to Brittany.

"Leave it to Brittany to diminish all my hard work into nothing. She somehow makes *me* look like the amateur here. I should feel lucky Mark hasn't demoted me to the junior position with how things have gone lately." Her smile was self-deprecating. She tucked her hair behind her ear. "Your design was awesome, by the way," Elena added.

"Let's hope they see through Brittany's bullshit and choose you. That's one of the best campaigns I've seen you do."

"A lot's riding on it. Mark said whoever lands this

account will automatically get a promotion. It's a brand-new role that oversees the creative direction for all the agency's copywriting projects. It's a pretty big deal."

Mae's eyebrows shot up. "And if Brittany gets it, that means…"

"That I'd technically report to her and she'd have a say on what projects I can take? Yeah." Elena pursed her lips and shivered at the thought. It would be hell.

The truth was Elena had struggled to find the right words to put into the campaign, and she worried it would cost her the promotion. Mae's design was eye-catching, but it took Elena longer than normal to think of the copy that would wow anyone who saw it but also stay within the parameters of what their clients typically liked.

Writing had always come easy for Elena, which is why she became a copywriter in the first place nearly seven years ago. She was excited about writing for a living, especially after she learned novelists didn't usually earn enough to pay the bills. But within her first year of writing in a professional setting, she quickly found that's where creativity went to die.

She thought she would have *way* more freedom to push the envelope and write something compelling. Revolutionary. *New*. However, she learned clients just wanted something stable, which was another word for unoriginal. Writing to appeal to the clients' needs sucked her soul dry.

Sure, they had loved her creative pitches at the beginning. And, for a moment, she felt a glimmer of hope that she'd get free rein to see what she could do. But by the time the campaign went from concept to production, they had picked it apart, taking out every creative twist and replacing it with a rehash of whatever they were doing before.

They wanted to play it safe. It disappointed her every time.

After experiencing it as many times as she had, it became a struggle to create new pitches. It was hard to stomach how much it would get watered down to the point of being unrecognizable.

There was nothing wrong with working at Holy City Advertising Agency. It was a fine job. Paid the bills. Offered steady work. Had a cool office space in downtown Charleston. *Most* of her coworkers were awesome. But with corporate copywriting, she found herself with limitations.

At least she could flex her creative muscles on her own projects, like the novel she had started a couple years ago.

And *that* blog.

It had taken on a life of its own, making her both terrified and proud. Elena had made a choice a year ago, rather than shutting it down, she had embraced it head-on as a way to help others and herself. Then a post went viral, her subscribers skyrocketed, and along with the dozens of help requests she received every day, she was getting requests from news outlets and magazines to write articles.

Elena had needed to create a whole new presence. Email address, social media, swanky new *Always, Ella* website, her beautifully designed logo—thanks to Mae's expertise. Turns out, moonlighting as an advice columnist during her free time was both exhausting and energizing.

Even with so much attention on her, she'd managed to keep her identity under wraps, only allowing herself to be referred to as Ella.

But that was about to change, and it scared the shit out of her.

Mae dipped her mermaid-dyed head down, keeping her voice low. "Are you ready for your other meeting?"

Elena swiveled her head, checking to see if anyone was

listening. Brittany's cubicle was next to hers, and it had gone awfully quiet.

"You know, Elena, if you spent less time slacking off with your friend, you might have a real shot at winning this account. Maybe," Brittany chimed in. "If I were you, I'd be using every spare moment to step up my game."

Elena gritted her teeth, her nostrils flaring.

Mae raised an eyebrow, a look of fire filling her eyes, one that Elena knew all too well. Mae was ready to go to battle for her, a role she'd taken on early in their friendship. She may be tiny, but she wasn't one anyone should trifle with.

Elena gripped her hand. "Don't you dare," she whispered.

"Wouldn't it be nice to finally put her in her place?" she whispered back, her voice rough with anger. "She would lose it if she knew you're not only you-know-who but that you're about to be published."

Elena shook her head, trying to snap herself out of picturing Brittany's stunned face when she dropped that bomb. She nodded her head towards the break room where they both wandered off to.

Her viral blog was about to become a book, and after work, she was meeting with her team to discuss the launch plan. For the first time in her life, she felt like she had some sense of control and that people actually appreciated her for who she was. Which was a ridiculous notion because she'd hidden behind her pseudonym, but that just went to show how powerful it was. The idea of coming forward caused a flurry of doubt. What would people think? Would revealing Elena discredit the all the good she'd done as Ella?

What if it all went away?

No. She couldn't stomach that thought. *Always, Ella* had become everything to her.

"I'm a little nervous," she finally answered when the last person making their late-afternoon coffee had filed out.

"Christopher will take care of you, don't worry," Mae said with confidence. "You've wanted to be a published author since we were kids. Celebrate this."

Christopher Adams was Elena's agent and a friend of Mae's old college roommate. When a massive publisher had reached out to her only a couple months after the blog had taken off, Mae had suggested Elena get an agent to watch her back.

And he had. As a well-respected agent in New York's publishing scene, Christopher not only helped Elena navigate through the ins and outs of publishing, but he also negotiated a two-book deal rather than the one the publisher had initially pitched.

It may not be the type of book she had intended on writing when considering becoming a novelist, but it was a start and a pretty good learning experience. Hopefully, this deal would help her move from self-help to fiction.

"I know. He's been great. I just don't understand why my editor is flying down here from New York. She left me a voicemail this morning saying her marketing director would be attending too." Elena shook her head, trying to release her knotted stomach, a natural reaction whenever she thought of her books finally being published.

Mae shrugged and grabbed an apple from one of the fruit bins on the counter. "No idea."

"Rachel said she wanted to meet face to face because she was excited about the launch. Something about how it would be bigger than anything she's done for any of her authors."

"Oh yeah, no pressure at all." Mae smirked and took a bite of the granny smith.

Elena sighed and leaned a hip against a nearby table. "Once this book comes out..."

"Everyone is going to know that *you're* Ella," Mae finished for her.

"Shhh." Elena looked over her shoulder. "Keep your voice down. God."

Mae rolled her eyes. "Your identity is about to come out, Elena. You're going to have to get used to it."

"Ladies, excellent meeting," Mark said as he entered the break room and poured himself a cup of coffee.

Elena and Mae straightened, trying to act casual. "Thanks," they said in unison.

"Keep it up," he added before leaving as quickly as he came.

Elena let out a breath.

Mae squeezed Elena's shoulder. "I gotta get back to work. Stop by my apartment after the meeting. Okay?" Elena grimaced. "Oh my God. Relax. You'll be fine."

——

"Um. What?" Elena looked at Christopher with a silent cry for help.

Their group sat on the back patio at the Vintage Vines wine bar, enjoying the moderately warm spring day. Rachel had just given them a quick overview of the launch plan, rendering Elena speechless.

"What Elena is trying to ask is what's reasoning behind this approach? This is a pretty significant change."

Christopher, her savior. Confident, distinguished, and never takes anyone's shit. He was a true professional. Surely he could navigate this conversation in a way that would bring her editor back to reality. To share her real identity was one thing, but this? This was too much to process.

"Absolutely, Mr. Adams. I'll be happy to answer that," Celeste Merrimak, the marketing director, chimed in.

Rachel pushed a manicured hand through her impeccable red hair and leaned back into her chair with a glass of wine, indicating Celeste could take the reins.

"Studies have shown more people are in relationships during the winter months. Therefore, we've decided to launch your singles-focused advice book this summer, when more people are either unattached, or summer flings are popular. Since the second book is focused on couple's advice, we are tying that launch to Valentine's Day, and the show will air the during the week leading up to the launch. That is when we will do the big Ella reveal. We'll offer those who have purchased your first book or have preordered the second book exclusive access to behind-the-scenes footage. Really get a buzz going. It's brilliant."

Christopher looked pensive for a moment before nodding, no doubt crunching numbers in his head. "I see."

Elena swallowed and wrung her hands under the table, a bead of sweat trickling from her temple. A show. As in TV. Her freaking face on national TV. She knew the publisher was just one arm of Berkshire Media, a major media conglomerate. But this?

She was *not* prepared for this.

"And," Celeste continued, "the show will be a perfect way to illustrate the book's value. It will be shot reality-style, with three couples at varying stages of their relationships. They'll come here, to Charleston. We felt it would be a nice touch as we finally introduce the woman behind *Always, Ella*." She smiled warmly at Elena, but Elena couldn't return it.

"That's why we're here. To meet with the location scout," Rachel added.

"And you want me to coach them through their relationship challenges?" Elena asked slowly, that sinking dread weaving its way to her stomach.

Celeste nodded with an encouraging smile, her precision bob shifting with the movement. "Yes. You're going to help them rediscover their romance or fan the flame of new love just like you do in your blogs and, now, the book."

"Will you excuse us for a moment?" Christopher tapped Elena's shoulder, pulling her from her trance, and led her inside the wine bar and out of earshot. "We're doing this."

"Are you insane?" she whispered-shrieked.

"I get it. You're scared; if your white face is any indication."

She shook her head. "I don't think I can do it. It's too much."

He shot her a look that told her he was about to unleash a dose of reality, one she wasn't going to like. "You want to be a novelist? You need to prove to publishers you're worth the investment and will do what it takes to market it. *Always, Ella* worked out for you because you managed to get a cult following. You coach people every single day. You can do this."

"But a show, Christopher? You know how I feel about being in the spotlight." She swallowed. "It's not what I want."

A social media takeover and a multi-city book signing she could handle. She could even stomach some digital ads splashed across Times Square.

A reality show was far more than she was comfortable with. She was almost tempted to pull the plug on the release altogether. "Elena, you're a talented writer and one of my favorite authors, but you have to realize that this isn't a normal offering. Other authors would *kill* for an opportunity like this. It's the golden ticket to success. If you say no now, I don't think you can repair the relationship here." He paused and looked at her pointedly. "The publishing industry is small," he let the unspoken warning linger.

Elena exhaled a breath, hating how right he was. She should be beaming with joy that they'd invest this much in a debut author, not acting like a difficult diva. "I guess that makes sense."

"That's my girl. Plus, once I negotiate a big, fat contract with them for this show, it will give you a nice advance, so maybe you can quit your day job and focus on writing." He winked. "C'mon, doll, let's get back out there."

Elena trudged behind him like a toddler being forced to leave the playground. She wasn't ready to deal with this, but she knew she had to.

"We're listening," Christopher said as they retook their seats. Elena took a gulp of her wine, attempting to push down the bile traveling up her esophagus.

"Wonderful. Then the last detail I should tell you is that we want you to have a co-host."

Elena's eyebrows knitted. "A co-host? I'm not sure I'm following."

Excitement danced in Celeste's eyes. "How do you think your boyfriend will feel about being on the show with you? You two lovebirds can be a good example to show the couples how it's done."

Oh, shit.

Houston, we have a problem.

4

JACKSON

Jackson St. Julien tucked the surfboard under his arm as he waded through the water. The waves crashed against his legs, propelling him to the shoreline. May was his favorite time of year to surf in Charleston. The ocean was a refreshing seventy degrees, and as the sun beat down on his bare skin, the water was the perfect way to feel rejuvenated. He could stay out here for hours.

He was glad he came back home, timing his trip perfectly for when his parents were on their annual bullshit vacation somewhere in the Virgin Islands. Same place with the same people for the past three decades.

He shuddered at the thought. For the last ten years, he had been traveling the world to different seaside communities. Some were popular destinations, bustling with tourists and surfing enthusiasts. Others were remote lands with the most awe-inspiring, untouched landscapes he'd ever seen.

With his company's sustainable surfing products, he'd traveled far and wide to understand how he could improve the communities he'd visited and protect the world's oceans. It had been one hell of a ride. And now it was time to take a beat and figure out the next phase of his business. He sure as hell didn't need his father breathing down his neck while he considered his action plan. Hence, visiting while they were gone.

Old money. Old fashioned. Old expectations. It was all the same if you were born and raised in a well-off family in the South. His father had never really gotten over the fact Jackson hadn't followed in his footsteps of becoming a lawyer, instead opting out of graduating college during his senior year to pursue this new venture.

It had been a point of contention for them for many years. As his father became more and more vocal about it, Jackson came home less and less. He knew it wasn't fair to his sister or mother, but he needed space to breathe so he could grow his business on his own terms.

Now he was at a crossroads. He needed time to settle and regroup.

"Those were some of the best waves we've had here in a while," Mae commented as she followed him along the beach, making their way to their parents' house—a beautiful stilted home on the shore with massive windows and sprawling porches that always had the best views of the sunrise.

"It's good to be back."

They propped up their surfboards in the sand so they could get rinsed off in the outdoor shower, and wrapped towels around their bodies as they padded up the stairs to the kitchen. His mom would have a fit if she knew they were dripping all throughout the house, but thankfully the cleaners would be there tomorrow.

"Mae!" a feminine voice shouted from the front of the house, followed by erratic pounding on the door. "Mae! Open up!"

Jackson's long legs effortlessly beat Mae to the front. He swung the door open and felt like he was gut-punched.

Elena Lucia.

It had been a couple of years since he'd seen his little sister's BFF, and despite the look of sheer panic—and a bit of annoyance—she had somehow gotten even more gorgeous than he remembered.

He had always thought she was attractive with her thick chestnut hair, olive skin, sparkling brown eyes, and curves that could bring a man to his knees.

That ass. Those thighs.

Jackson fought a groan.

His eyes roved over her face, landing on her heart-shaped, kissable mouth. Lips that were most *definitely* off-limits.

Although they'd been friends when they were younger, Elena and Jackson had butted heads a lot since they were teens.

He hated the front she'd put on for other people, always desperate for approval. She would morph into someone entirely different. That version of Elena was depressing to see and frustrated the hell out of him. So what if he called her out on it from time to time? He was doing her a favor.

But she never saw it that way.

"Jackson," she scowled. "What are you doing home?"

He leaned against the door frame casually and smiled. "Miss me?" He never could resist the urge to push her buttons.

She rolled her eyes. "Hardly. Where's Mae? I need her. It's an emergency."

"In the kitchen!" Mae called out.

Elena pushed past him, the scent of flowers and peppers

hitting his senses, reminding him of the little firecracker herself: sweet and spicy all at once.

He shut the door and trailed in languidly after her, watching her flail her hands as she explained her so-called "emergency." She had a big personality whenever she was brave enough to show it. He tried not to laugh as her arms moved even faster, and he couldn't help but wonder if she was on the verge of one of her famous freak outs. She was a mess—a ball of nervous energy—but he found it endearing.

"It's a disaster!"

"It sounds like a really good thing, Elena. This could be huge for your books. Plus, your identity was going to come out eventually. At least you have some control in this. You know Berkshire Media is going to make you look like a darling and an expert. They want to sell more of your books, after all," Mae reasoned as she hopped up to sit on the granite island.

Elena put her hands on her full, grippable hips. "No, Mae. That was the old problem. It almost seems like a blip in comparison to my new problem."

Mae gestured with her hand, indicating for Elena to spit it out.

"They want me to co-host with my boyfriend."

Mae's forehead scrunched. "But you don't have a boyfriend."

Jackson sucked in a breath. "What happened to Brad?"

Elena whipped her head in his direction, her long-standing annoyance with him clear. "We broke up like a year ago."

Huh. Elena finally got rid of that shitbag. Brad had always been a douche, even when they'd been kids. But no matter how often Mae tried to tell her, Elena shut it down. She was stubborn like that, but he was glad to know that her stubbornness didn't land her in a marriage with a selfish prick like Brad Beaumont.

"The point is, you and everyone who knows me will know I don't have a boyfriend. That's the problem," she continued.

"What gave them the idea that you had one?" Mae asked.

Elena bit her bottom lip and looked down. "I kinda said I did."

"Come again?"

Elena let out a dramatic sigh. "When the blog blew up, people came to me for all sorts of advice. Lots of relationship woes, not just the broken-hearted. So, I embellished a little in my responses. I kinda shared examples of what me and my boyfriend did to keep the romance alive or overcome bumps in the road. I never expected the blog to go this far, so I didn't think it would matter."

Jackson couldn't help but laugh, which earned him a scowl from both of them. "This is good. Even though I have zero clue on what's going on."

Mae gave him a quick rundown on the blog and publishing deal. Seemed like he'd missed a lot since he's been gone.

Interesting.

"I have until tomorrow to decide. They're drawing up the new contracts and need me to sign on the dotted line by close of business tomorrow. The production schedule is aggressive." She put her face in her hands and let out a little scream.

"Okay..." Mae started, her face contorting in deep thought. "What if you had a boyfriend by the time of filming?"

Elena peeked out from her hands. "In a week?"

"A week!" Mae yelled in surprise.

"Not helping. I came here for emotional support." Elena frowned. "Apparently they had some contest going on and decided to tweak it to use it for my launch. They wanted to capitalize on the 'mystery and wonder' around my identity."

"I'll do it," Jackson offered.

Both women turned their heads in his direction again, this time in confusion.

"I'll do it," he said again. "You clearly need help, and this means a lot to you. That's what *friends* do," he emphasized, knowing it would get under her skin.

"No way," Elena argued as she crossed her arms. "You'll just embarrass me like you always did when we were growing up. I don't trust you not to mess this up."

Her immediate dismissal only challenged him more. He loved this competitive side of her. As frustrated as she was, he was enjoying this way too much. Elena's fiery personality had always been one of his favorite things about her.

He rolled his eyes and played it cool. "I wasn't embarrassing you. I was trying to save you from yourself. You tried too damn hard for people who didn't really matter."

She narrowed her eyes. "They mattered to me."

"Do you even talk to those people anymore?"

Elena glared at him, but couldn't answer. "Even if I were to say yes, it would never work. You wouldn't stick around long enough to count on. I need someone I can trust to be here. You haven't been home in months, and how long do you even plan on staying this time? A couple nights tops? You'll be gone before shooting starts."

"Actually, he won't be." Mae slipped off the counter and came to his side, wrapping an arm around his middle and staring up at him with sisterly adoration. "He's sticking around for a few weeks this time. Gonna stay in my spare bedroom."

"What? That's not like you." Elena eyed him with suspicion.

He shrugged casually. "I need to stay put a bit to plan the next phase of my business."

Hopefully, one that could allow him to set roots somewhere. Traveling had been amazing, and he never wanted to give it up completely, but he knew he needed more balance in his life. And for the sake of his business, he needed more stability in his schedule to think about growth.

Mae nodded. "Jackson might have to be your 'happily ever after.'"

A slow smile rose on Jackson's lips. "Hate to say it. But I think I'm your only shot for this not to blow up in your face."

5

ELENA

Jackson was fighting dirty with his signature smile, a slow grin, rising slightly higher on one side, before transforming into a full-on smile with straight white teeth and deep laugh lines. It was an infectious smile, one that made you want to be in on whatever it was that made his face light up, and his blue eyes sparkle.

Elena had seen how many girls had fallen over that smile. She couldn't blame them. That hypnotizing boyish grin often made her forget how much he had tormented her over the years, always humiliating her in front of the popular kids at school or new friends. Always revealing her flaws. She just wanted to be normal and accepted, but he'd go and make one tiny little comment that would have her face flaming, waiting for everyone to judge her.

She wouldn't fall for that smile.

"No."

He squinted at her, his face falling flat. "What do you mean 'no?'"

"I don't trust you." She crossed her arms and held her

head high. Inside, she was panicking, but she couldn't let Jackson see her desperation.

"Elena—" Mae warned. "I know you two didn't always get along growing up, but you need to think about this."

Elena put a hand to her chest and took a deep breath, reluctantly coming to terms. Mae was right, there was no way around this. "There has to be another option."

Jackson walked to the fridge and pulled out three beers. Elena accepted it with suspicion. Was he buttering her up?

He cracked his open with a refreshing fizz. Jackson was always the laid-back one. Of course, he would be, he had nothing to lose.

"Way I see it," he said after taking a healthy sip, "you have three choices: admit you lied, tell your publisher you won't do it, or let me help you."

She traced a bead of condensation on the can, not meeting his eyes. "There has to be someone else. *Any*one else," she said in distress.

Mae squeezed Elena's shoulder as a sign of moral support. "You need a guy in a week. Is there anyone you trust enough to keep this under wraps?"

She'd trust pretty much anyone else more than Jackson. Right? *Right?*

But when it came to something like this, her mind went blank. *Damn it.*

Her shoulders hung low as she conceded. "Fine."

Jackson held a hand to his ear. "What was that? Couldn't quite hear you there."

"Fine. You can be my boyfriend."

He held a hand to his heart. "Well, don't sound so put out by it. You're really wounding my ego."

She raised an eyebrow. "Maybe knocking your ego down a few notches would do you some good."

He let out a deep laugh. It was a good laugh, just like his damn smile. The kind that made you want to lower your defenses.

"I'm going to say this loud and clear: I think this is a horrible idea. But, I don't have any other choice. So, listen up and listen good."

Jackson took a seat at a barstool and placed his beer aside, exaggerating that she had his full attention.

God, she was going to kill him. How would that look on the show?

She turned to Mae. "You're a witness for all of this. Got it?" Mae nodded. "Jackson, if we're going to do this, I need some assurances. I need to know you're committed to this."

"Want me to get down on one knee?"

"Can you be serious for once in your life?" She scowled.

"Fine. I'm listening. For real."

"This is extremely important to me. A lot's at stake here. This needs to go per-fect-ly. No games. No trying to humil-iate me or trip me up."

"Elena, I have never tried to—"

She held up a hand. "I need you to promise me you'll be the best boyfriend."

"Yes, ma'am."

"I need you to swear you won't leave before the filming is over."

"I swear." He held up his fingers, scout's honor.

"And you need to act like the boyfriend I've been describing these last couple of months to a tee."

His eyebrows furrowed as he paused, his face growing more serious. "What's that now?"

"The boyfriend I've been referencing in my blogs. You need to be that. I'll give you a crash course before filming."

"Hold on. I never agreed to be someone I wasn't."

She shrugged. "It is what it is. I already talked about a guy, and they're expecting that guy to show up."

"This changes things. I'm going out on a limb to help you. I'm here for a reason—to work on my business. Not on some fun vacation."

"Yes. You look *very* hard at work," Elena said dryly as she eyed the towel hanging from his hips and the beer sitting on the counter next to him.

"When I'm not on the road, I like to take a few minutes of downtime. Is that a problem for you, princess?"

"You hang out on the beach for a living. I'm sure you're really 'struggling' traveling to the most exciting destinations across the globe. For us here in the real world—"

Jackson rose to his feet, his normal, carefree smile disappearing from his face. "Don't make assumptions about my life and my business, Elena. You have no idea—"

"And why would I? You left town years ago and barely come to visit. When you do, you're busy flirting your way through the women of Charleston."

His eyebrows rose as he took a step closer, a wolfish grin creeping on his lips. "Keeping tabs on me, huh?"

She put a hand against his defined chest—one she hardly noticed, of course—and kept him at bay. "You wish."

"Guys!" Mae said interfering. "Can we focus? We're all friends here." Elena and Jackson both made a face. "Jackson, you'd always help out a friend in need. And, Elena, you'd do the same. No matter what. I've seen you both move mountains for the people you care about."

Jackson looked at Elena skeptically. She glared back at him.

"Jackson, c'mon," Mae pleaded.

He huffed out a breath. "I'm willing to make some adjustments to my schedule to help you. But you want me to be some random dude you made up? No way. I have to draw the line somewhere."

"What can I do to sweeten the deal?"

He sat for a moment as he considered it. When his gaze finally locked on hers, her stomach dropped. There was a mischievousness to it that made her uneasy. "This is a huge 'save your life' kinda favor, so if I do this, you'll owe me one of the same." She went to protest. "Whenever I choose," he added.

"I can't agree to some open-ended mystery IOU." There was no way she was giving that much power to Jackson.

He shrugged a shoulder like it was no bother to him and took a long pull of his beer. His eyes never leaving hers. "Silly me. I forgot you weren't the type of woman who's open to spontaneity and adventure."

Her cheeks burned. "You can't blame me for wanting to know what I'm agreeing to, given our history."

"Elena. I think this is your only option unless you want to pull the plug on the whole thing," Mae said quietly.

Elena glared at her. "Whose side are you on anyway?" *Traitor.*

Mae held up her hands defensively. "Hey, don't put me in the middle. I'm just the voice of reason. You guys really need to get over whatever issues you have if you're ever going to be believable."

Jackson stepped closer to Elena, towering over her as he looked into her eyes. "What do you say? Do we have ourselves a deal?" His voice was quiet. Intimate.

She eyed his outstretched hand and hesitated before she took it. "Fine. But I'm not happy about it.

Elena tried to ignore the zing of electricity that shot up her arm.

Nerves. Just nerves.

6

JACKSON

"I have a bad feeling about this," Mae commented as she sipped her coffee the next morning.

Jackson ambled around her apartment's kitchen, grabbing a tumbler from an overhead cabinet to take his coffee to go. "What's that?" he asked as he poured the coffee—black—to the brim.

He needed Mae's rocket fuel. This stuff was enough to keep you wired for days, and judging by how insane his schedule was—even before his commitment to Elena—he needed all the help he could get.

"You and Elena." She shook her head. "She's not as tough as she seems, you know. I love you, and I know you mean well, but I'm worried about you two. It's not like you're exactly on the friendliest terms."

He shrugged. "Maybe this will help us get back to a good spot."

Mae barked out a laugh. "Yeah, right. For Elena, this is a test. She's going to watch your every move for a chance to point out that you're the same old Jackson who tormented her in high school."

"I wasn't tormenting her—"

"I know. I know." She waved it off. "But *she* sees things a little differently. I hope you know what you're doing."

"I've got this. Don't worry about it."

Mae placed her mug on the kitchen island and looked him dead in the eyes. "You can't just wing it, Jack. This is important."

He tried not to let his irritation show. "Can you have a little more faith in me? Out of everyone, I thought you'd be in my corner, at least."

Guilt flashed across her face. Rounding the island, she gave him a hug, squeezing until his ribs felt like they would crack. Sure, Mae was tiny, but she was strong as hell. "I'm sorry. You're right. Speaking of which," she said, segueing into a new topic, "mom and dad want to see you."

Jackson cocked an eyebrow. "Dad?" he asked, disbelief lacing his voice.

"Well, he didn't outright *say* it...but—"

"If I'm still here by the time they get back from their frolic in the islands, I'll stop by or something."

"We miss you. You know that, right?"

The seriousness in her voice pulled at his heart, almost enough to forget the family feud between him and his father. The truth was, he missed his family too. Like hell. But every time he tried to extend an olive branch, his father reminded him why he should stay away.

Jackson had done a lot of good in the world. He was proud of everything his business had accomplished, and he knew they were just at the beginning of everything they could do. Yet, every time he was around his dad, he was transported back to his early twenties. Right around the time he told his parents he was dropping out of school to build his sustainable surfing product company.

"You think a beach bum has what it takes to make it? In three months, after you blow all your money on marijuana and loose women, you'll be crawling back here. Mark my words. You don't have what it takes to make it, son."

Even a decade later, his father's words still crept into his mind, making him doubt his own abilities to make it, despite the amount of success he's had.

Jackson was back in Charleston to make a pivotal change for his company. To take it to new heights. He couldn't afford to let his father's words make him choke when it came to this.

"I miss you guys, too," he finally managed. He screwed the lid onto his tumbler, trying his best to distract himself from the pang of anxiousness coursing through him.

"Big day today, huh?" Mae commented, likely noticing his shift in demeanor. She was always good at that.

"Yup," he said, popping the p. "I'm going to give the team the rundown of the next phase of the business. There's still a lot of planning to figure out, but I want them to get up to speed so they don't feel like they're in the dark."

With all his travel, he made it a point to be as transparent as possible with his team, especially in the rare situations when he could be face to face with them.

"I'm just glad this means you're sticking around a little longer than normal. We can do stuff like old times. That is if you're not too busy with Elena." Mae wagged her eyebrows.

"Is that jealousy I hear?" he teased.

"Not at all. You have your work cut out for you with her. It's going to be entertaining to see how she hands you your balls."

He laughed. "Seems like I have a lot of work cut out for me all around. I should get going."

"See ya," she sing-songed as he left the apartment.

How did four hours feel like a lifetime?

After Jackson had gotten down to the warehouse and held his staff meeting, it felt like a flurry of activity. There was so much to catch up on, so many questions to answer. But despite it all, everyone seemed pumped by the potential expansion of their operations.

He knew his plans to grow their warehouse space, change their delivery fleet to make it more accessible to remote locations, hire more sales and production staff, and work on a new product line was ambitious. However, he also knew he had the right team behind him. Their enthusiasm only solidified he was on the right path.

With their support, he was ready to move forward. They might be fairly small still, but there was strength in numbers. He couldn't have asked for a better group of people to stand by him through this.

Now, it was just a matter of figuring out how this would all work and who he could trust to delegate to while he was on the road.

Sitting in the makeshift office near the production line, Jackson leaned back in his chair and rubbed his eyes. He'd been staring at his strategy plan for nearly two hours, and his brains felt like mush. After spending years on the road, sitting still in an office felt like a shock to his system, and it made him antsy.

His phone buzzed next to him, lighting up with a text from Mae.

Mae: To get into Elena's good graces, you might want to read up on her blog. She appreciates people who prepare.

From what he remembered, Elena was so organized that she didn't just have a plan B. She prepared all the way to plan Z. How she didn't have a brain aneurysm from stressing out that much was beyond him.

He clicked the link Mae texted and scanned through some of her more recent posts, unable to stop the smile from reaching his lips.

This is really *good.*

She was funny and kind and smart and compassionate. Through her words, he saw a glimmer of the Elena she kept hidden from the real world. He almost forgot how much he liked that side of her.

As he went down a rabbit hole of posts from the last few months, he was determined to bring that side out in her again. The world deserved to see it.

Whether she was ready to show it or not.

7

ELENA

E lena breathed a sigh of relief when Jackson strolled through the front door of the quiet wine bar located underneath her apartment. She had spent the last few nights tossing and turning, convinced Jackson would have packed his bags and left on the next big adventure without so much as a warning. And with the show officially kicking off tomorrow, they needed every moment they could get to make sure they were a convincing couple.

He shifted his sunglasses to the top of his head, pushing back his dirty blond hair that was perpetually kissed by the sun thanks to surfing. He wore tan shorts with a blue short-sleeved button-up, surfer-chic style. But it wasn't until his eyes roved across the small space and landed on her in the private corner that she realized she was in trouble.

Those blue eyes always reminded her of a photo of the salt flats from Salar de Uyuni, Bolivia her father had sitting on his desk. One of the many adventures he'd had as an archeologist.

She'd get lost looking at the alluring, bright aqua reflected in those salt flats. Jackson's eyes had the same effect on her. She tried to stop her heart from beating out of control and failed.

Just when she got it back into a steady rhythm, his slow grin spread across his face, setting her heart off again and sending a warm flush through her body. It was the specific grin she said she'd never fall for, and yet all she could do was stare dumbfounded.

Jackson St. Julien was always a sight to behold, but he was Mae's brother, and occasionally a jerk to her. So why was she suddenly acting like having his eyes on her was the only thing that mattered? The shiver up her spine shocked her.

She straightened her shoulders and twisted her head to crack her neck, something she did to relieve tension. Her reaction was only because she was surprised he'd made it this far. That had to be it. He wasn't one to stick around, so his presence was shocking.

He motioned to the bartender for a beer before making his way to her. "Hey, Ella."

"Elena," she corrected.

"You're Ella. You're *my* Ella," he said matter-of-factly as he seated himself casually into the chair, his tall frame dwarfing it. He nodded to the bartender, who dropped off his beer and took a sip. Cocking his head to the side, he looked at her expectantly. "If we're going to be a couple, don't you think we'd be less formal by now?"

Shit. He was right.

"I read some of your blogs yesterday. They were pretty good," he mentioned, surprising her. She didn't take him for a proactive guy at all.

She cleared her throat. "Did you now?"

Is it hot in here? Why does knowing that Jackson took the initiative to read my words feel so...intimate.

She knew the blog was public, there for the whole world to see. But something about him reading it felt like he had access to the deepest, most vulnerable sides of her.

"I especially like the ones where you talk about why actions matter more than words. A lot of people can forget that sometimes." The sincerity in his voice hit her straight in the heart.

Flustered, she pulled out a binder from her purse resting on the floor and flipped a few pages. "If we're going to make this believable, we need to be straight on our story. I scoured through my posts, where I referenced a boyfriend. Did you read any of those?" He shook his head. "Well, thankfully, I never mentioned how we met or his backstory."

"So, it's a blank slate?"

She scrunched her nose. "Not quite. I wrote out a backstory for you to memorize. I also printed out the blogs where he's mentioned so you could study them." She slid the binder to him and watched as he read, his face becoming more annoyed with each passing moment.

He pushed the binder away, his lips a tight line. "So, you want me to be like that, huh? All flash and grand gestures and...this seems a bit over the top. It's like your 'boyfriend' is in a competition to win Best Boyfriend of the Year award. None of this seems real." He tossed his sunglasses on the table and shoved a hand in his hair. "Are you still hung up on Brad? That has his douchiness written all over it."

She tried to keep her breathing even. "This stuff matters to me. This is how I want to be treated."

Jackson's blue gaze held hers. "Is it, Elena?"

She changed the subject, trying to defuse whatever was going on between them. It felt like his stare could strip her down and see the truth of what she needed. Wanted.

And damn if he didn't seem like he wanted to be the one to give it all to her.

"Why are you so passionate about your dislike for Brad?"

There. That should distract him enough.

He turned away, looking like he wanted to unleash fury but paused. "He just...wasn't good for you."

She laughed incredulously. "Oh? And you're such an expert on who's deserving of me? With how you treated me in high school, you don't have much room to talk." She knew she was picking a fight with him to create some distance. Sitting here with Jackson felt a little too good for her liking.

"How many times do I have to tell you I'm sorry? It wasn't like that."

"You weren't on the receiving end of it." Elena watched him with curiosity, seeing how his nostrils flared and how pink crept up his neck. The affable Jackson apparently had a sensitive spot.

He leaned forward and tapped his finger on the binder. "This isn't me. I can't be this guy. It feels like you're just trying to win over people's approval. *Again.*" The disappointment crossing his face put her on the defense.

"Is this guy not good enough for me either?" she asked sarcastically. "I made him up. He's exactly what I want."

Jackson's gaze shot up and locked on hers again, rooting her to the spot. "Do you even know what you *really* want, Elena?"

"What the hell is that supposed to mean?" She leaned forward and whispered, noticing a few patrons' eyes on them now. "What's so wrong with him?"

"He's cheesy and one-dimensional. He's too perfect."

"He's romantic. And nice."

"There isn't an authentic bone in this guy's body. C'mon. Did you look at a J.Crew catalog and dream him up?"

She crossed her arms. "Fine. What do you propose?"

"Why can't we just be who we are?" he asked, passion filling his voice. "Why fabricate any more? You're already in over your head. Why make it harder? We'll just be two people who grew up together and fell in love. Simple. Believable."

She squirmed in her seat, liking the sound of that too much.

This is all fake, Elena. He's not really suggesting he's in love with you. Get it together.

She swallowed, wondering why whether or not Jackson cared for her more than friends mattered. "It's just too normal."

He made a face. "So what? You want to say that we met in a rainstorm one evening and that a perfect stranger offered you his umbrella? That you had meet-cute?"

"Actually, yes."

"No!" He wiped a hand down his face. "This isn't a romance movie. We don't need to be those people. We can just be you and me, Elena. Who we are should be enough. That's how I've lived my life. But you—" he paused, shutting his mouth quickly.

"But me what?" she ground out.

He softened, "Love is supposed to be unique, maybe a bit messy at times, but real. It's not a highlight reel of perfect moments."

Elena cocked an eyebrow. "And you know all of this from your many successful relationships?" she asked dryly as she took a sip of her wine.

Jackson had always been undeniably true to himself. Mae was the same. It's what made her feel comfortable with them when she met them all those years ago. With the St. Juliens, she knew exactly what she was getting, and that brought her peace in a life that felt all wrong.

She shook her head, remembering who she was talking to. From what she recalled, he'd had a couple long-term girlfriends in high school and college and one right before he launched his business in his early twenties. Since then, it had been short flings, his travel schedule likely making it hard to sustain a real relationship. He had no business telling her what love should be like.

"That's not the point," Jackson argued. "The point is, I know what you have on paper isn't the real deal."

"But—"

He leaned forward, mere inches from her face. "Elena. I've known you for years now. Don't get ahead of yourself here. You want your readers to relate to you, right?" His voice was low, serious. Not typical for Jackson.

Elena sucked in a breath, trying not to be curious about the faint lines that had formed around his eyes and all the life he would have had to live to get them. He was adventure personified, so very different from her safe, controlled existence.

Way too dangerous to be face-to-face so close. And yet, his presence pulled her in.

It hadn't always been this way between them, had it? Something had changed over the years, making her wonder if this whole plan was more trouble than it was worth.

Jackson had seemed like a safe choice. Their bad blood as young adults would protect her heart from getting involved. So why was it suddenly beating erratically as his gaze dipped to her lips? A glance so quick, she thought she'd imagined it.

This felt charged. Anticipation zipped through her. She

used to think the tension between them was dislike, but now she wondered if there was something else.

Something she didn't dare to name.

She swallowed. "Right."

He leaned back again, the seriousness on his face disappearing. "Then stop giving them something to compete with. You said these people are turning to you for help. Why make them strive to achieve some whirlwind romance and series of perfect events to meet the love of their life? It doesn't have to be tied nicely with a bow."

Damn him. He was right again. Part of the reason her blog went viral was because she was relatable. Fabricating the boyfriend was bad enough, but making him into some extraordinary catch would alienate the people who trusted her to begin with.

She grabbed her glass of wine and put her lips to the rim. "You make a valid point," she admitted quietly into her glass.

"Damn right, I make a point, *Ella.*"

She rolled her eyes and took a sip. "So, you're proposing we just use our history to keep it simple?"

He slowly smiled again. "Yup."

She cocked an eyebrow. "So, does that include the time Mae and I caught you wasted when you were a freshman in high school with a bunch of dicks Sharpied onto your face that wouldn't come off for days? Or the time we epically catfished you when you were a senior?"

She brought up the memory as a way to create a little distance from whatever emotions that were surging through her, but she couldn't help fighting back the smile struggling to break through. They did have some fun memories when they were younger. Mae and Elena had "tortured" him, but he took it with good humor. It wasn't until his freshman year in college—her junior year in high school—that things got weird between them. He looked at her differently. Treated her differently. Always took a jab at her to embarrass her.

But before then, they had gotten along well. Even though he was Mae's older brother, they were all around each other enough that she'd considered him a close friend too.

Then, one day, all of that went away.

And now here they were—two semi-frenemies pretending to be lovers.

She still couldn't believe Mae backed this. Jackson had been strictly off-limits when it came to Mae's friends. Elena guessed the only reason she went with it is because she knew it was bullshit.

Jackson exploded into laughter, his head tilting back as he belted it out. Although a little louder than appropriate at the quaint bar, the few people in the place looked at him with amusement rather than annoyance. As always, Jackson had people smiling along with him.

"You and Mae were ruthless."

She held her hands up defensively. "Hey, you brought a lot of those things on yourself. We were just there to witness."

"You were opportunists. You know how many times my sister caught me doing something and held it over my head, threatening to tell my parents?"

Elena smiled. "I helped her come up with the terms."

He shook his head, an amused grin playing on his lips. "I should have figured. God, I was such a little shit back then."

"Agreed. Still are."

"Fair." Humor still danced in his gorgeous blue eyes.

Elena looked at him seriously again, capturing his gaze. "Jackson, you promise you'll work with me on this?" She couldn't help the worry that laced her voice. She was putting a lot of faith in him, and it scared her to death.

Sensing the shift in conversation and all the vulnerabilities she wasn't saying, he sobered. "I promise," he nearly whispered, sending a chill down her spine. With the intense look in his eyes, she couldn't help but believe him.

"Jackson!" a voice squealed, grating on Elena's nerves and pulling them from their private moment.

His eyes widened. "Take my hand," he murmured quickly, grabbing her hand resting on the table.

"Jackson, what the hell is going on?"

He squeezed her fingers gently, absentmindedly massaging her palm with his thumb. The heat from his hand warmed her chilled one from holding her white wine. "It's time to see if we're believable. Go with it," he said from the corner of his mouth.

"Jackson St. Julien!" a girl exclaimed as she approached the table.

Elena looked up at the woman with an offensively high-pitched voice and thick Northern accent. She eyed the girl— someone who looked to be straight from the show *The Jersey Shore*. Her skin was dark and slightly discolored, likely from self-tanner and tanning salons, her nails were long and gaudily decorated, and her dark hair was teased to a little poof on top.

"Hi, Alex," Jackson greeted coolly, squeezing Elena's hand. When she didn't get the hint, he cleared his throat.

Elena lifted her free hand into a tiny wave. "Hi, I'm Elena."

"My girlfriend," Jackson quickly added. Elena tried to hide her confusion. The woman's face dropped. "Elena, this is Alex."

Ah, another one of Jackson's flings? She didn't seem like the type he'd go for. She was just too...much.

Looking closer, she could have been pretty. But her over-processed, trying-too-hard look took that subtle prettiness away.

"Nice to meet you, Alex. How do y'all know each other?" she asked sweetly, just to make Jackson squirm a little. Served him right for all the hearts he'd surely broken in his wake.

Alex tried to hide her judgy look with a smile that came off more like a sneer. "Jackson and I hung out a couple of summers ago," she said dismissively before giving Jackson her full attention again.

Jackson coughed. "Alex and I have a few mutual friends, so we ran in the same circles," he tried to clarify, making it painstakingly clear there had been *nothing* more between them.

By the look on Alex's face, she'd hoped for otherwise.

"I didn't know you were home. You should have called!" Alex playfully swatted at him, completely oblivious to how awkward this whole thing was.

Was that a little flirtatious eyelash flutter? He's literally with his girlfriend!

He rubbed the back of his neck with his free hand. "Yeah, I haven't had a chance to catch up with anyone since I've been back. As soon as I got home, I wanted to see my girl." He grinned at Elena, and for a second, she almost believed he had real adoration for her.

Elena shrugged. "Guilty. He's been hanging with me." She reached out and stroked his jaw. "I just missed him *so* much while he was gone." It was lame, but it was the best she could come up with. She wasn't an actor skilled in improvisation for Christ's sake.

"I see," Alex said, undeterred. "Well, be sure to give me a call when you're...*unattached*. I'd love to catch up." She rubbed a hand down his arm, affectionately. Her mouth pursed as she turned to Elena. "Nice to meet you," she disingenuously added before taking a seat at the bar with a friend.

Jackson looked at Elena with a stone-cold expression and released her hand. "I'm going to be honest here. You were off your game."

"I was thrown off-guard," she argued.

"What do you think is going to happen on the show, Elena? They're not handing you a perfect script you can follow. We're going to be dealing with unexpected situations, and you are going to have to adapt on the fly. All eyes will be on us."

She crossed her arms defensively. "I know that."

He raised an eyebrow. "Do you? Because seeing Alex here was a trial run, and you failed. You think she'd openly flirt like that if she thought you were *real* competition?"

"Well, I don't know, Jackson. She could be that type of girl. Doesn't seem super classy."

"If this show fails, Elena, it's not because I wasn't living up to my end of the bargain. It's because you aren't believable." He ran a hand through his hair and let out a breath.

Every bit of self-doubt came crashing into her. Her stomach twisted. This show held the key to all her hopes and dreams, and Jackson was telling her she likely wasn't good enough.

This was a mess, and it hadn't even started yet.

"I-I don't know what I need to do," she said quietly.

He pegged her with his blue-eyed stare. "You're going to need to trust me. Okay? I know you like everything to be perfect, to have a plan figured out down to the minute detail.

To control everything. But this won't be that, and you're not the type of person that does well with gray areas. Luckily, I'm an expert in go-with-the-flow, so you're going to have to work with me to make this believable."

She swallowed and nodded her head. She hadn't trusted many people in a long time and for good reason, but the conviction in his voice made her want to put her life in his hands. In a way, she supposed she was.

"Okay. I'll trust you."

A smile lifted his lips. "Thank you. I'll take care of you. Don't worry."

Elena knew tomorrow would push her out of her comfort zone, but now she worried she wasn't thinking big enough. She just hoped she could handle all that was about to be thrown at her.

8

JACKSON

J ackson took stock of the selected couples: Maritza and Max, two youngish people in a new relationship; Ana and Zach, both career-driven and in a committed relationship of four years, but looking to bring the romance back; Natalie and Hari, nearing their fifties and in a committed relationship, but not fully on the same page for the next step.

He had to give it to the production company, they didn't pull any punches. Each couple was at varying stages in their relationship, from the honeymoon hopefuls to the ones who needed to know if it was time to shit or get off the pot.

He had spent the last few nights rereading Elena's blog, trying to get a sense of how she offered her advice, as well as researched the kind of guy she talked about in her blogs. If he was going to keep his word, he needed to know what they "did" together that she always referenced. It was the least he could do.

As much as he gave her a hard time growing up, he cared about her. She was important to Mae and, in a way, important to him too. She had gotten herself in a real mess, but he wasn't about to let her down.

"Alright, everybody. Now that you've filmed your introductions, we're going to get started on our first event," the producer announced.

Stephanie Johnson had many successful shows under her belt. A cute black woman with wild hair and a few face piercings. The tattoos that showed off her passion for film gave her an edge, which worked perfectly for her Los Angeles residence.

From what Jackson could tell, she was damn good at her job, too. Introductions felt a little awkward, but she loosened everyone up, got them doing what they needed to do, and secured her footage seamlessly.

Celeste, Berkshire Media's marketing director, clapped and smiled broadly. "Thank you all for coming. As we mentioned, this is a week full of fun adventures, designed to help bring the romance and intimacy back to your relationships." She took Elena by the shoulders for a dainty side hug. "We have our expert, Ella, here to get us started on these activities and provide guidance."

The group nodded, murmured, and smiled in response. Maritza nearly exploded with excitement as Celeste introduced Elena.

Guess she wasn't joking when she said she had super fans.

"Alrighty. Let's get started." Rachel, Elena's editor, opened the door to Ten George, an upscale experimental kitchen in downtown Charleston. "Chef James will be with us shortly. Pair off and go to your respective areas," she announced as she directed everyone into a backroom full of cooking stations.

Elena shuffled in after Celeste and took her spot next to Jackson, looking the worse for wear already. "Everything okay?" he whispered in her ear, her florally peppery scent invading his senses.

Her big brown eyes looked back up at him, causing a pang in his heart. She was scared shitless. "Do you know how many times they made me do my introduction? I think I spent thirty minutes just pronouncing my actual name alone," she whispered back. "It's bad enough the cameras are in my face, but the added pressure of my editor and agent being here isn't helping."

"They just want to support you."

"Or be a witness to my ultimate failure."

Jackson's hand reached out to hers, his knuckles grazing her soft skin before his fingers wrapped around hers. Her eyes, lined with thick black lashes, looked deeply into his, still full of worry, but now with the added hint of appreciation. Elena gave his hand a light squeeze—so gentle, he thought he imagined it—but when her lips tugged upwards, he knew it was real.

And damn if his heart didn't clench at that tiny interaction.

"We'll be okay," he assured her, reluctant to release her hand. He didn't want to push her too much. Even as he pulled away, the warmth from her lingered on his palm, a feeling he wished he could hold on to.

A boisterous man with shocking white hair and a matching mustache walked into the kitchen. His chef's whites were equally as bright as his hair. His round cheeks and excited smile showed a man who had a life well-lived and well-fed.

"I am Chef James," he said with a thick Italian accent. "Today, I will teach you the art of pasta. Reason? I believe food is a love language. It is universal. You can have a good day, a bad day, a fight you think you'll never recover from. But food? Good food? It breeds love and saves love."

The group laughed, and although the chef laughed too, he turned more serious. "Tell me a moment where food was not used to build relationships? It is used as a celebration, a tradition, to comfort, to heal, to connect. Quality food is good for the soul." He held up a finger. "But, it is not just the act of eating or offering, it is also the act of making. It is a tangible way to come together with those you love to make something you can enjoy. You can be satisfied by the fruits of your labor. And today, this is what we will do. We will create a lovely meal together for you to enjoy with your loved one."

Chef James came to Jackson and Elena's station and offered a hand. "You must be Miss Ella, yes?"

She shook it tentatively. "Yes. It's a pleasure to meet you."

"The pleasure is mine!" Chef James went back to the main station, where he would be demonstrating. He swept a hand over the supplies on the counter, the same as each of their stations. "And here, we have all the makings of a wonderful meal. Please wash your hands, and we will get started."

As the group ambled over to the sink to prep, a few of the women stopped Elena to gush over her book. "I was so excited to get selected for this!" Maritza said, her sunny disposition was infectious.

To everyone but Elena, that is.

Elena stood stiffly, her smile bordering on uncomfortable cringe. They had barely gotten started, and Elena was already choking. This was going to be over before it started.

Unless he intervened.

The thing with Elena is that she liked everything perfectly packaged and within her control. That's how she had always been. Focused on saying the right things, wearing the right things, getting involved with the right people, despite how unnatural it was in comparison to who she was.

Jackson had seen the real Elena. She wasn't perfect. Far from it. She was fiery, ambitious, funny, sometimes awkward, a little dramatic, and always passionate about the things that mattered to her. He'd take that Elena any day.

And then there was that smile. Her real smile—the one that reached her beautiful eyes—was breathtaking. Always full of straight white teeth, and so much joy that her eyes formed into little crescent moons—not quite closed, but almost. And the way her nose scrunched in the most adorable way, usually followed by a heartfelt laugh, made Jackson always want to make her laugh like that.

But later in high school, she had changed. She was too focused on what everyone thought of her, and any attempt Jackson had made to loosen her up and remind her of who she was often caused a rift between them. She hadn't always been this stiff, he'd seen the lighter sides of her growing up. But something about high school had made her become way too serious for her own good.

It wasn't *her*.

That thought gave him pause. If they had been on good terms, maybe she'd trust him for what he was about to do. However, there was a real chance it would cause their already delicate relationship to fall apart, never to recover. Underneath it all, he had hoped this week would finally bury the hatchet between them. They were adults now, and more than a decade had passed since their strained relationship had started. It was time to set things right.

He silently prayed that whatever plan he concocted to get her out of her own head wouldn't backfire. She'd never forgive him. But he'd never forgive himself if he didn't try to help. He looked at her again, her spine ramrod straight, and her posture closed off.

Yeah. I've gotta do something. And quick.

"Everything okay?" he asked for the second time as they went back to their stations.

"Fine," she lied and sucked in a breath as a camera passed by their station. Her tension was palpable, and he was sure it would translate to the footage.

"Now, everyone place your flour and salt in the bowl and make a well in the center," Chef James instructed as he did his own.

Elena grabbed the flour and salt on autopilot and did as instructed.

"Must be easy for you," Jackson commented. "With your mom being an amazing cook and all."

Elena's mother was a proud Italian woman who took cooking seriously. She and Chef James would be in good company, for sure. Jackson loved the days when Elena would bring by leftovers or would cook for the St. Julien clan. He'd tried a lot of great food through his travels, but something about Elena and her mother's cooking was hard to beat. It reminded him of home, which was a weird because he never thought of home fondly.

At least, not since the falling out with his father.

"Yeah. I can do this in my sleep," she replied, her voice flat from distraction. Her gaze darted to the different stations and trailed the camera crew.

Jackson cracked an egg and put it in the well. He dipped low and whispered in Elena's ear, breathing in her intoxicating scent again, now mixed with the scents from the kitchen. "You have to forget about that. You need to relax."

Her shoulders went to her ears in response. He forgot how much she hated being told what to do.

"I'm fine," she said defiantly, her body even more rigid than before.

"Well, it's a good thing this is a piece of cake for you then."

She turned her head and looked at him with confusion. "What?" Realization registered. "Oh, Jackson. Don't you dare. I know that look."

"Chef James," Jackson called out.

Elena grabbed his forearm in a death grip. He winced but didn't stop.

"Yes?" he responded as he helped Zach and Ana properly use a fork to mix the ingredients.

"You know, Ella over here loves to cook. In fact, her mother is a wonderful Italian cook."

He raised his bushy eyebrows. "Is that so?"

"Some of the best meals I've ever had, Chef. You should let Ella help out with the demonstrations."

She gripped harder, her fingers likely leaving bruises in their wake. She sure had some surprising strength.

"Brava. That would be wonderful!" he said with joy. "You take my position at the front, and I will work on the technique with the couples. Yes?"

"Sure," Elena answered through gritted teeth. She threw Jackson a death stare and rose to her toes to hiss in his ear, her sweet breath warm on his skin. "You know I'm going to kill you, right?"

"Go get 'em, honey," he replied loud enough for the other couples to hear.

He placed a kiss on her head and patted her ass. Her eyes shot daggers at him, but he shrugged. She was going to kill him anyway, might as well have his kicks while he can.

Elena went to the station and took a deep, shuddering breath. A sheepish smile touched her lips, not quite a cringe this time, but not a true one either. "My mother, Alma, is a fantastic cook." Her voice shook from nerves. She cleared her throat and took another breath. "Ever since I was a child, she had me in the kitchen with her. She taught me not only the most mouth-watering Italian recipes passed down in her family but the most important aspect of cooking."

"What's that?" Natalie asked as she and her boyfriend Hari worked the dough.

Elena's smile became more genuine as she thought back to her mother. "She said, 'Ella, if there's one thing you should know about cooking, it's that you have to do it with heart. Otherwise, don't bother doing it at all.'" Elena laughed. "I was four when she imparted that harsh truth onto me, but it's stuck with me. Like Chef James, my mother believes food is a love language. Whenever she could, she'd make sure my father and I were there to help her. It was our way to bond."

"It sounds like your family is very close," Ana commented.

Elena nodded. "Yes. We are. Best parents in the world."

"And I'm thankful for it too," Jackson added. "Because I get the benefit of eating amazing meals as a result."

Elena turned to him, her smile now turned evil. Her lips lifted slightly on one side as her eyes narrowed. He swallowed. Her wheels were turning, that was for sure, and he didn't know what it meant for him.

"Well, Ana," she continued, "like I said, my mother would always include us because how can you have heart in your cooking if the people you love aren't involved?" She turned back to Jackson. "Which is why I make sure Jackson is always involved too. Isn't that right, *honey?*"

Fuck. Jackson was a wreck in the kitchen, and she knew it. He stopped kneading the dough, aware that everyone was looking at him.

"Come on up, Jack. Don't be shy," she goaded.

Well, he had tried to get her to loosen up, and it clearly it worked. At his expense.

He met her at the station, awaiting her instruction.

She looked back at the crowd. "It's stuff like this that made me fall in love with Jackson in the first place."

He raised his eyebrows but nodded along.

She took his hands and shoved them into the dough where she kneaded it with him. Every so often, their fingers would get tangled up. She grinned in a way that made it clear she had a trick up her sleeve, and he'd pay dearly, but it didn't ease his racing heart. Despite the number of people in the space, this felt *intimate.*

After a few moments, Elena added, "But it's important not to be too serious. This is a way to bond, and it's important to have fun." She brought a doughy, floury hand up to his face and ran it down his cheek slowly, leaving a huge mess in its wake.

Jackson laughed in surprise and grabbed her around the waist, pulling her close and causing her to squeal. He took his cheek and rubbed it against her face, spreading the mess onto her too. Elena giggled, her body shaking against his, making him aware of all the curves pressed against him. Soft and warm and perfect.

As much as he hated cooking, if it was anything like this, he'd do it every day.

With her.

Jackson had to admit, this restaurant was so damn romantic. One of the new ones that had opened up the last couple of years, Ten George, had seating inside a beautiful historic house, plus an outdoor courtyard.

After finishing the pasta, Chef James instructed the couples to split up so they could make a surprise meal for their significant other—as per a suggestion in one of Elena's articles. Now, they were seated in the courtyard, waiting to be served.

The early-June air was warm without being stifling, which was typical in Charleston's humid summer months. If anything, it was perfect. Between the beautifully dressed table with fragrant flowers and dancing candlelight and the twinkle lights illuminating the outdoor space in an intimate glow, Jackson felt like the star of a romantic movie. And then there was the wine. More of a beer or whiskey drinker, Jackson couldn't help but enjoy the flavorful rosé that was a perfect accompaniment for the small appetizers and the sorbet-colored sunset gracing the sky.

Elena had loosened up a bit and was now chatting with the couples who were seated around the table. He wasn't sure if it was his quick plan to throw her off her game or if the wine helped ease her nerves, but she was warm and inviting as she learned more about everyone.

She wasn't quite at the level of comfort she had with Mae, but it was good progress.

Waiters started streaming outside from the open double doors that led to the courtyard, stalling whatever conversation was going on around the table. With a flourish, they whisked away empty plates and replaced them with the pasta meal they had made earlier. Each plate held something different—a way for them to try to make their loved ones happy by offering them a meal they believed they'd love.

Elena gasped next to him as her plate was placed in front of her, her eyes going wide. She licked her full lips, causing his body to respond. Jackson suppressed a groan, reminding himself the hunger in her eyes was for the food, but damn if he wasn't curious to see if that look of excitement would be the same if it were for him.

She's Mae's friend. Strictly off-limits.

He took a sip of his wine and tried to shake off the attraction. Maybe it was the setting getting to him. It would be hard for anyone sitting in this courtyard not to have the feeling of lust or love or whatever come over them.

"Is this...fennel sausage?" Elena asked on a breath.

Jackson couldn't help but grin at her reaction. You'd think she was just presented with a check for a million dollars.

"It is," he replied with amusement.

She looked up at him in appreciation and shock. "How did you know that I love fennel sausage?" She scanned her plate again as if she couldn't believe her eyes. "And with mushrooms and cream sauce too?"

His face hurt from grinning so much. She was adorable. And sexy.

Jesus, man. Relax.

"It's hard to forget that impassioned speech you gave a few years ago about the perfect fennel to sausage ratio. I never thought someone could find thirty minutes worth of material on the subject, but you sure did."

She looked at him, half-serious and half-mocking. "It's very important stuff."

A laugh rumbled through his chest. "Of course, and it

stayed with me. You made me into a believer. Hopefully, my ratio meets your high standards."

"You have my mother to thank for that. She made me into the passionate food lover I am. It's very serious business in the Lucia household."

"And even with all that eating, you still look..."

Her eyebrows rose, waiting for him to finish. "Look..."

Beautiful. Sexy. Like an erotic fantasy I never knew I had. "Fine," Jackson finally mumbled.

The amusement on Elena's face dimmed just a fraction. "Wow. *Fine,* huh? It's no wonder I couldn't help myself from falling in love with you."

With the blood in his body rushing southbound, it took his brain a moment to register that she was referring to their arrangement, not that she was *actually* in love with him. So why did that fleeting idea warm him in ways he hadn't felt before?

It wasn't that Jackson was opposed to a committed relationship, it's just that his lifestyle hadn't allowed for it once he started his business. He didn't feel right jumping into a relationship with someone he'd never be around to treat right. He didn't want to break someone's heart, feel like he was chained to something, or have them resent him.

Yet, the idea of being Elena's someone caused a stirring in him.

Pseudo-compliment forgotten, she dove into her meal and let out a satisfied moan. A moan that went straight to his cock.

She's going to kill me. This week is going to kill me.

"This is amazing, Jackson. You have to try it." She held a fork to his mouth, and he gently took it between his lips.

"I'm pretty impressed with myself," he joked. He was a horrible cook, but this wasn't half bad. Thankfully, Chef

James had been there to help him along. Otherwise, he had no idea how this would have turned out. Probably mutilated, overcooked, and unseasoned. And he most definitely would have gotten the fennel ratio wrong.

Stephanie strutted up to them and crouched down out of eyeshot of the cameras, interrupting their moment. "Hey, guys. Great work today. Your chemistry is amazing on camera."

"Really?" Elena coughed, catching herself. "Oh, that's great to hear."

"Yeah. Really digging your stuff. Can't wait to see how it goes tomorrow."

"What's on the agenda?" Jackson asked as he swirled pasta around his fork.

"We'll have some masseuses come in to teach you all how to give sensual, intimate massages."

His fork slipped from his hand, but he caught it. "Sorry. What was that?"

She gave him a strange look. "Massages. You know? You'll strip down for one another, learn the techniques, use some special oils that stimulate desire, and..." she trailed off and looked at the clipboard in her hands. "Something about erogenous zones and aphrodisiacs. Real sexy shit."

Jackson swallowed. If he could barely keep it together when Elena sent those little looks his way and let out those small moans, how was he going to handle rubbing his hands along her smooth, soft, naked body?

Agreeing to this was the worst decision I've made yet.

9

ELENA

"So, should I kill you now or later?" Elena asked as they strolled down Meeting Street to Mae's apartment.

The sun had just set, and Charleston had transformed from one charming city to another. Between the historic houses lining the streets and the flickering lanterns lighting the way when it got dark, she could see why the producer was excited about the location. It was the perfect place to fall in love or rekindle a spark that had dulled over time.

As tough as it had been to grow up here feeling like an outcast, Elena couldn't help but love it. The palmetto trees, Spanish moss, and cobblestone streets made her think of simpler times, even as Charleston continued to explode thanks to high tourism and newcomers looking to call it home.

Jackson rubbed the back of his neck, a bit of humor making his eyes sparkle in the dark. "Not sure what you mean," he said with sarcasm.

"I thought we agreed you wouldn't throw me under the bus like you did when we were younger."

"The opposite, actually. You were too stiff. I could see

one of your freak-outs on the horizon. You're a spaz. You realize that, right?"

She poked him in the shoulder, her finger feeling a sting of pain as it hit rock hard muscle. "I'm *not* a spaz!"

"I could rattle off at least five different times when we were kids where you came barging into our house with some sort of anxiety-fueled meltdown." He glanced at her from the corner of his eye as they continued to walk down the street, now bustling with college students looking for a fun night on the town.

Elena pursed her lips as she dodged a few buzzed girls from a bachelorette party teetering unsteadily on heels as they walked by. He had a point. "I wouldn't call them *meltdowns,* per se."

"How about the summer pool party leading into your freshman year? You hyperventilated because it started raining."

"I was upset because it was ruining my chances for my first kiss."

"You were already wet. It was a *pool party.*" He shook his head.

"But they made us get out of the pool. Danny Glasco and I were *this* close to sealing the deal." She held up her pointer and thumb a centimeter apart.

"I have good reason to believe that kiss wouldn't have happened."

She rolled her eyes. "And why's that?"

"Well, I ran into Danny on a connecting flight from Costa Rica to Miami. We had a good chat."

She fluttered her eyelashes. "Did he ask about the kiss that got away?"

He bit his bottom lip as if holding back a smile. "Actually, he asked me if I was staying in town long. Invited me to a restaurant that he and his *husband* own."

Elena's face fell. "Oh."

Jackson let out a bark of laughter. "'Oh' is right. You always have these crazy scenarios in your head of how things should be and get disappointed when your perfect plan falls apart. You were and still are a hot mess—an adorable one, of course," he added quickly when she glared at him. "What I did helped loosen you up. You heard what Stephanie said, the camera loved us." He shrugged in his typical not-a-care-in-the-world way.

Although she couldn't deny the fact that she had felt awkward, nervous, and scared, putting her in that position without warning wasn't fair. She was already a "mess" enough without his spontaneous hijinks. Being blindsided like that brought back all the memories of how he'd make a stupid comment, embarrassing her in front of her friends. Thankfully, she'd pivoted quickly this time because cooking was in her blood. She'd have been hard-pressed to have messed it up no matter what he threw at her, but how could he have known it wouldn't have gone horribly wrong?

"You were lucky." She eyed him as he continued to amble down the street with his easy-going stride. "But you'll pay for it."

Jackson grinned and raised his eyebrows. "Okay, Elena. Give me your worst."

Her evil smile deflated his playful mood. For a minute, he almost looked worried. "Just you wait."

After navigating the busy streets for a couple more blocks, they made it to the new apartment complex located on northern Meeting Street. Charleston had been building out the peninsula over the years, making the northern side swankier and more modern, a stark contrast from the historic sections toward the center and south.

It was a growing city and seeing structures like this, and a slew of new hotels popping up was a clear indicator of it. Although the building was only a few blocks from her apartment, the crossover from old to new was like night and day.

They walked through the clean, minimalist stark-white lobby and hopped on the elevator. Elena couldn't help but glance at him again, noting his languid demeanor. Was he always just so...relaxed?

More importantly, why did she find it so attractive?

"I can feel you ogling me," he commented without looking at her, a smile lifting his lips.

"Oh, you wish!"

The elevator came to a stop, and she darted through the doors to Mae's, needing a little space from him. He made her feel restless and something else she couldn't quite put her finger on.

All she knew was she was crawling out of her skin.

Elena let herself in and went straight to the refrigerator, grabbing herself a seltzer. She needed something to do to busy herself and expel some of this random energy coursing through her.

Jackson strolled through the front door a moment after her, looking completely unperturbed. She must have been the only one feeling amped up.

"Mae, can you please tell your friend that she needs to stop planning life down to the second?" he called out.

Mae breezed out of her bedroom, dressed like the perfect yogi. "Ha! That's impossible, even for me." She tossed Elena her gym tote. "Where have you guys been? We have yoga to get to."

"Your brother was torturing me."

He shrugged. "All I was trying to do was get you to relax. Crack that shell you were hiding in. You can't plan for things thrown at you unexpectedly. Thinking on your feet is what gave us a glimpse of the *true* Elena."

She bristled, hating how it felt like he was calling her a fake.

But it wasn't that. It was about adaptation and presenting herself as the "right" way to be so she could finally find a place in the world.

Jackson wouldn't understand. It was easy for him to relax because he was a local. People accepted him. He didn't know what it was like to be on the outside looking in.

He'd never get it.

"Go easy on her, Jack," Mae said while pulling Elena into her arms and coddling her like a child. "She's trying."

"That's the problem. She's trying too hard."

Elena pulled out of Mae's embrace and frowned. "You guys know I'm standing right here." She wagged her finger at him. "Some of us have to actually work to get ahead in life. I didn't get where I am by 'shredding gnarly waves' and making business deals with high fives." She rolled her eyes. "Have you ever had to be serious a day in your life?"

Jackson's blue eyes went dark, his face growing stone cold. "You should know that what I do isn't all sitting on beautiful beaches while having tropical drinks. I have seen some really rough places, Elena. I've had to have tough conversations with the locals. And although I love seeing the world, living out of a suitcase isn't exactly the most comfortable lifestyle. It takes its toll."

Wow. What? I didn't see that coming.

"So yeah, maybe I get to make endorsement deals and sign new clients while wearing board shorts. Maybe you see pictures on my social media surfing pristine water. But that's only part of it. What I'm trying to do here matters. I'm trying to leave the world a little better than when I found it."

She was at a loss for words. Elena had never seen him so fired up and passionate about anything. And the altruistic aspect of his work suddenly had her seeing him differently. She knew he was making sustainable surfing products, but didn't realize the lengths he had to go to make sure he was serving even the most remote and under-resourced communities of the world.

Something about the moment clicked for her. Mae had told her all about his accomplishments over the years, but Elena had dismissed them, still feeling bitter about their falling out in high school.

The man was literally salvaging her dream while simultaneously trying to chase his own, and she'd gone and insulted him like a childish idiot.

"Jackson, I'm sorry—"

He shook his head, the seriousness of his face starting to melt away. "It's fine. All I'm saying is, I learned a lot by being on the road. There are plenty of things I could never plan for in a million years. What I discovered is the most important thing is to show up, listen, and be open and honest. People want to connect with people. My business would have never survived if I hadn't put myself out there. That's the point I was trying to make with you today."

"Okay, guys. As much as I love your back and forth, we really need to get going. Elena, go get changed." Mae scanned Jackson with her gaze. "Judging by the fact that your shoulders are up to your ears, you need to get to yoga too."

"You're probably right. I haven't surfed in a few days and

already feel my muscles tightening up." He shot a look at Elena. "Do you mind?"

She did. If Elena needed space from him before on the elevator, it was needed even more now. Her stomach did flips when his hopeful eyes landed on her. "You can come."

Mae clapped her hands. "Great. Both of you get changed, and let's get going."

A few minutes later, the three of them walked into the yoga studio located in the commercial space housed on the first floor under the apartments. Mae led them to the back of the room, where there was enough space to spread out. Even with it being the last class of the evening, it was still packed.

"Wouldn't take you as a yoga guy," Elena commented as Jackson unrolled his mat next to her.

"Yoga helped me step up my surfing game. Between the stretching and the balance work, I'm able to maneuver my board a lot better."

"Jackson?" A voice came from behind them.

He craned his neck and hesitated before smiling at the woman standing there.

Not his slow smile. Interesting.

"Laura. Long time no see." Jackson hugged her quickly, and by the looks of it, the hug ended too soon for Laura's liking.

"Yeah, it's been a while. I didn't realize you were back."

"Just in town for a little bit."

Laura's face brightened. "Oh? That's great. And it's awesome that you just so happened to spend one of those days in my class."

"You're the instructor?"

"Sure am. This is my studio."

Jackson fist-bumped her. "That's awesome. Congrats."

She bit her lip shyly. "Thanks. Well, I better get class started." She nodded at Mae and Elena before taking her place at the front of the room.

Elena cocked an eyebrow. "Another one of your 'friends?'"

"Nah. We went on a few dates a couple years back. Just wasn't any chemistry there. We went our separate ways on good terms."

Looking at the front of the room, Elena caught Laura's eyes devouring Jackson. "Oh, I'd say she'd disagree with you."

Jackson peered at Laura, his face turning bright red.

Even more interesting. Not as much of a player as I thought.

"Oh God, Jackson. I can't take you anywhere," Mae complained as she moved into a sun salutation. "She and I were just becoming friends. I can't have you making things weird."

Jackson held up his hands in mock surrender. "You don't have to worry about it. She's all yours."

"How kind of you," Mae said sarcastically with a smug smile.

As class started, they went through the sequences to loosen themselves up and get centered before they tried the more challenging moves. Laura glided around the room, pushing people deeper into their positions or helping correct them.

"Oh, Jackson. You're holding a lot of tension in your hamstrings and glutes," she commented as she came around. "Do you mind if I help you get deeper into your child's pose to release some of that?"

"I think I'm good here."

Elena chimed in. "But, Jackson, weren't you *just* telling me how important it is to loosen up?"

Oh, he's going to kill me. This is too good. It's payback time for the filming earlier.

She smiled wickedly at Mae. Mae tried to hold in her laugh.

His eyes narrowed. "I did," he replied through clenched teeth.

"Don't be shy, Jackson." She turned her head to Laura. "Maybe you can help him get a little extra oomph?" Elena suggested.

"Gladly." She didn't even bother to hide her lustful delight.

Laura rested her body on top of Jackson's back, using her weight to push him deeper into the stretch. His eyes went wide as she pressed her breasts onto his back and wriggled, doing everything in her power to ensure every inch of her was touching him, and let out a sigh of contentment.

"Wow, that looks like it's doing wonders for him," Elena commented. "If you have time, you should lay there a little longer, so he really gets the benefits of that stretch."

Elena and Mae suppressed their laughs, and for a moment, it felt like old times. They always had fun messing with him whenever they could as kids.

Her laughter suddenly stopped as Jackson looked at her with disdain, mouthing something along the lines of, "You're going to fucking get it."

Uh oh.

Elena remembered tomorrow's activity: couples' massages.

Maybe her little payback wasn't the best idea, after all. Being naked and at Jackson's mercy didn't bode well.

10

ELENA

"I'm not sure I'm ready for this," Maritza admitted to the girls as they changed into fluffy robes and made their way to the spa's relaxation room the next morning.

"What's wrong, doll?" Natalie asked, plopping next to her on a plush chaise lounge, making herself right at home at the posh Dewbury spa.

Maritza fiddled with the tie on her robe as she sunk further in the cloud-like material, making her seem even smaller than her already petite frame. "Max and I are still kinda newish to dating. We've been together for like six months, but we haven't like *slept* together or whatever."

Ana handed her a cup of hibiscus tea and sat on the other side of her. "At your age, I would have been all over that. He's a cutie. What's stopping you?"

Natalie rolled her eyes. "You're what? Early thirties? When you hit my age, *then* you can say things like, 'When I was your age.'"

Maritza tried to smile, but her eyes were still filled with worry. "It's not that I don't want to, it's just that we haven't had the right moment yet. We both work at the same hospital—that's how we met. But as a nurse, my schedule can be all over the place. He's an EMT, so it's not much better. There have been some weeks where we literally only saw each other in the hospital cafeteria. Not quite a romantic place for dinner." She rolled her eyes.

"I get that," Ana said. "Zach and I are very career-driven, and both work long hours. We've had some lulls in our sex-life, too, because of it. But it ebbs and flows, you know? That's just how it goes in long-term relationships."

As a VP of marketing, Ana Yu was a force to be reckoned with. Elena had read about her career path and watched her TED Talks. She was small but mighty. Her boyfriend also had an impressive career, selling an app in his twenties that made a pretty penny. Now, he consulted on a number of impressive projects.

Both had come on this show with the idea of it being a vacation, something neither of them had taken in some time. They came with open minds, hoping to reconnect after a year of nonstop work.

Elena perched herself on the end of Maritza's chaise, nodding in agreement. There had definitely been times where she and Brad had gone through lulls of no sex.

She frowned. Maybe it was because he didn't need her since he was getting it from other women. Elena looked at Maritza's hopeful, confused face and decided to keep that little tidbit to herself. Not every man was a Brad, she needed to remember that.

Natalie took a sip of her tea and relaxed on the lounger as if she were sunning by a pool. "Honey, this is the prime time in your relationship. You should be having fun with it. And, more importantly, confirming that he's the right guy. You're too young to be wasting months of your precious life on a guy who isn't right for you." She raised her eyebrows.

"Or might suck in the sack," she added. "Love is important, but so is chemistry."

She couldn't hide the bitterness in her voice. Natalie and Hari had met two years ago on a dating site and had fallen fast and hard. But they were at a crossroads in their relationship. Natalie, a woman in her forties, was ready to settle down and get married now that she found a nice guy. But Hari, once divorced, was against the idea of marriage, arguing that they could be in a committed relationship without the legality of it.

They came on this show to remember why they were together and determine if they could work together, compromise, or figure out if the issue they were facing was a deal-breaker.

"It's just that we haven't gotten to that point in our relationship yet," Maritza explained. "I don't want to take it to the next level in this setting." She eyed the cameraman in the corner. "With all these eyes on us," she whispered despite there being a mic on her robe to capture every word.

Elena rubbed comforting circles on Maritza's back. "If you aren't ready or comfortable for this sensual massage, that's okay. Don't feel like you're going to be forced into something just because it's on the agenda. There are plenty of other ways to build trust and intimacy that doesn't require you to strip down."

Elena gulped, realizing she was about to do that with Jackson. After the stunt she pulled last night at the yoga studio, she was a little worried about his payback.

"Like what?" Maritza asked.

"Maybe it's a nice foot, hand, or shoulder massage. You can still work on making each other feel good, but it doesn't have that pressure of the full massage. You can learn some techniques here for if and when you're comfortable enough to get to that level. But for now, do what works best for you. And more importantly, be honest with Max. I'm sure he'll understand where you're coming from. You want it to be special because it's what you're ready for, not because it's for a show."

"Exactly. You're so smart, Ella. I'm so glad I got to meet you. You're so good at this."

For a second, Elena felt like she truly was Ella, the writer people had come to trust. Being here with these couples and coaching them through their challenges felt natural. And seeing how she was helping them in real-time was the most satisfying thing she'd experienced.

More importantly, she didn't *feel* like a fraud. She listened, watched, and then provided honest suggestions. Some based on her own experiences, much like the advice she gave Maritza. How many times had she felt like she had been pushed into situations she wasn't ready for? Sure, stepping out of your comfort zone helps you grow—just like she was doing now with the book and the show—but there were plenty of situations over the years that hadn't served her. Maritza was young, sweet, and had a good heart. She didn't want her to feel pressured into something that wasn't right for her.

How was it that being thrust into this crazy show had her feeling more like herself? She'd thought being surrounded by strangers, and the constant cameras in her face would only amplify the fact that she was an imposter, but instead, she felt the opposite.

Because of Jackson.

Oh no. She wasn't going to touch that with a ten-foot pole. But if she were to nudge at it with a fifteen-foot pole instead, she could at least admit she was having fun with him. He challenged her in a way that made her forget her anxieties and had her laughing more often than not. She almost forgot how his easy-going nature had a calming effect and how infectious his humor was. It brought back a ton of great memories from when they were kids, before their relationship went south.

It was *nice,* and for a fleeting moment, she tried to imagine life with a guy like Jackson. He was a far cry from the Brad-types she'd dated through her twenties, but maybe that was the point. Clearly, they were all wrong. Maybe she needed to reevaluate the type of guy who would treat her right.

She shook her head. That's as far as she'd go with those thoughts. He may be in town for longer than normal, but he was bound to leave again for one of his many trips around the world. She shouldn't entertain any thoughts of exploring whatever it was between them if there even was anything. Plus, she wouldn't do that to Mae. It goes without saying that a best friend's siblings are strictly off-limits.

Elena sighed and sank into her seat. *That damn smile.* Just thinking about that slow grin and his sparkling blue eyes that seemed to only focus on her—like she was the only thing worth looking at—made her go all warm inside. He definitely had the loving boyfriend role down pat, maybe even better than she had envisioned it.

"Ladies, we're ready for you," a woman from the spa said in a soft, soothing voice.

The women followed the spa attendant to their respective rooms, where Max, Zach, and Hari were waiting for them. Lastly, she led Elena to her and Jackson's room.

Elena tried to breathe, reminding herself that nothing would happen between them. It was just a massage. It's not like she jumped her masseuse every time she got a rub down. She needed to think of Jackson in the same way. That's all.

When she entered the room, Jackson stood and shot her the young Marlon Brando-esque smile. Toe-curling. Delicious. Sexy.

Good God, so sexy.

Heat formed low in her belly. That wasn't a reaction she'd typically had with Jackson.

It's because of the setting. Naked skin. Romance. That's it. You do not *have feelings for Jackson St. Julien. He's Mae's brother for Christ's sake.*

"Hello, Miss Ella," the masseuse greeted. "I'm Beatrice. I'll be working with you today to show you the techniques for a sensual massage with your lovely boyfriend here." Jackson turned his smile Beatrice's way, making her giggle.

Such a charmer. Which was a perfect reminder that the heart-stopping smile he just gave Elena was a dime a dozen. It wasn't special for her.

"With sensual massages, it's all about creating a mood. That includes not just the massage itself but the atmosphere, visuals, and so on." She pointed around the room. "Here, we've set the lighting to be soft and inviting. The aromatherapy candles we've chosen are scents that stimulate your desire. The music is meant to relax."

Elena gulped.

"Miss Ella, if you'd take a moment to get under the blankets here. I'll be showing Jackson how to use some of the techniques."

For the next fifteen minutes or so, Beatrice showed Jackson and Elena the tips and tricks on how to offer a relaxing, sexy massage that would feel good for both partners.

"Any questions?" she asked. Both of them shook their

heads. "Very good. I will leave you to it then. Miss Ella, since you're already on the table, it would be best to start with you."

"Is the camera crew coming in?"

"No." She handed Jackson a remote. "We have several cameras hidden in the room to give you a certain amount of privacy. Of course, we know many couples prefer to get massaged in the nude, so you need to use this call button to let the crew know when to turn the cameras on and off. For example, when you're switching out. Or for other things..." she added suggestively.

"I see," was all Jackson could muster, the sound of his swallow audible from where Elena was resting.

"It was a pleasure meeting you. There will be a soft ding that sounds when it's time for you to switch." With that, Beatrice closed the door gently behind her, leaving them alone.

The tension in the air was thick. "Are you ready for this?" Jackson asked, his voice low and deep.

"As ready as I'll ever be. And don't you peek when I'm switching positions," she half-teased with a shaky voice, trying to ease the awkwardness between them. But nothing would change the super-charged room.

"Okay. I'm going to turn on the cameras."

"Okay."

"Alright," he said again, his uncomfortableness apparent. "I'm going to put the oil on your skin and start."

Elena signed. "Jackson, I don't need a play by play. Just do what you've gotta do."

He let out a low laugh. "Do you trust me?"

"I trust you enough."

She heard him rubbing his hands together, the sound of wet slickness on his skin, the anticipation of it made her nerves fire off. His fingers grazed her shoulders tentatively, followed by a sweeping of his palms along her back. She exhaled, breathing out the tension she had held onto waiting for this moment.

His hands moved over her back, his thumbs moving down the center near her spine, the rest of his fingers grazing along her sides. He kneaded her shoulders, putting pressure on the knots residing there, helping release them.

Jackson let out a slow, unsteady breath as his hands moved down her arms to her hands. His thumbs pushed into her palms, his fingers then entwining with hers to help stretch her wrists. Her body reacted, gripping his hand for a moment to hold him there. That simple movement made time stand still.

"Are you okay?" he asked quietly. He made no motion to release himself from her grip.

"I'm...I'm okay." She reluctantly let his hand go.

His hands continued to slide along her body, moving to her hips, taking extra care to work his thumbs into her lower back, easing the pain she held there from long days sitting at work. His fingers lingered just above the swell of her ass, a tease to her. His breath and the steady way he moved with the perfect pressure stirred something in her.

For as nervous as she was to be in this situation with him, for exposing her body in a vulnerable way, she couldn't stop herself from praying his hands would dip lower. Her breathing became more labored as he slid the sheet over just slightly, so he had access to her legs. His hands roamed up her calf and thigh, working all sides.

So close to the place between her legs that was now wide awake and wanting.

Elena let out an involuntary moan, the pleasure of his hands overwhelming her.

He stilled and tensed.

"Elena," he breathed, his fingers moving further up her leg. He paused as if debating how much higher he wanted to go.

Soft music played, telling them it was time to switch.

She wanted to kill someone.

He pressed the button to turn off the cameras and turned his back while she slipped into her robe. She wobbled from lightheadedness as she stood, partly from relaxation and partly from the intense desire Jackson had instilled in her.

He knew just how to touch her. *Where* to touch her to make her go insane. Would he be that perceptive in other areas? In other situations?

She turned to him, finding his blue gaze gleaming in the flickering candlelight. With a closer look, she noticed his hooded eyes were dilated. His chest rose and fell heavily as if trying to catch his breath.

Jackson's Brando smile suddenly seemed shy. "Mind turning around so I can get under?"

She nodded wordlessly and turned away to give him privacy. A moment later, Jackson gave the okay, letting her know she could turn the cameras back on.

Elena's hands shook with anticipation as she squeezed the oil into her palms and placed them on his broad back. She had seen Jackson shirtless before—it was hard not to with him being a beach bum. But something about seeing it up close and actually *touching* it was different.

She ran her hands along the muscles of his shoulders and upper back, perfectly formed from years of paddling on his board. They were corded and thick. And manly. And *hot.*

Using her weight, she pushed into the hard, sinewy muscles, working out his tight areas. A soft groan escaped him as she rubbed her elbow in one particularly tough spot, the noise almost had her melting right there.

His hand that dangled off the side of the table grazed her leg. Her heart jumped into her throat as she wondered if it had been intentional or an accident.

Electricity crackled between them. Her emotions were on high alert. It wasn't like her to react to a man like this, especially not *Jackson*, but the feeling of his hands on her body had wound her up in ways she'd never been before. There was a dull throb between her legs, and she had half a mind to climb on top of him and take care of it.

Thank God for the cameras. She might have followed through on that insane thought had they not been there to act as a reality check.

"You're good at this, you know," he commented as she ran her hands down his tricep, now adorned with more tattoos than she'd remembered. The ink curled down to mid-forearm, full of intricate, colorful designs.

"What happened to your back?" she asked as her fingertips traced a scar slashed across his side.

"I wiped out while surfing in Belize and got pummeled by the waves. There were some shallow reefs in the area. Unfortunately, I hit one when the waves pushed me under."

"Ouch."

"Hurt like a bitch. But it gave me a new idea."

"Hmm?" she mumbled as she worked his palm, loving the feel his large hand and strong fingers.

"Creating a new product for my surfing line and donating the proceeds to protect the coral reef."

She paused, her lips tugging up into a grin. "Leave it to you to want to save the thing that sliced and scarred you. You must really love what you do. I mean, you'd have to in order to be a nomad all these years."

"I do. Honestly."

As he let out a sigh, she continued the massage. Her hands moved over the roundness of his shoulders and glided along the defined muscles of his upper back.

Elena couldn't help but admire him. Over the years, she had heard how his parents had been disappointed he'd skipped out on college and went this unstable path instead of following in his father's footsteps.

For some time, their words had tainted her view on him. Elena and Jackson had already had a strained relationship during their late high-school and college years. When he disappeared for parts unknown, it was hard to see him as anything but the man she remembered—the guy who constantly picked on her during her vulnerable moments— and what his dad had said.

Foolish. Unreliable. Flaky. Unrealistic.

She cringed. None of those words were right when it came to describing him. Maybe back then, but definitely not the man she was getting to know now.

After spending these last few days with Jackson, she wondered if maybe they'd had him all wrong. That *she'd* had him all wrong. He hadn't been home enough these last few years for her to hear what he'd been up to or to see the kind of man he'd grown into. Sure, Mae had bragged about his mission to support surfers and the environment, and how he tried to make his sustainable products more accessible. But Elena hadn't really wanted to hear it. Truthfully, she had tuned out most things said about Jackson over the years because she'd been so frustrated by how he'd treated her.

Elena had assumed he'd never grow out of his childish behavior. Yet, in spending more time with him, she realized just how much he *had* changed.

Gone was that flaky guy. He'd shown up for her. In her gut, she felt she could depend on him to see this through.

He'd gone above and beyond to save her from the mess she'd gotten herself into. He was striving to make a better world, and he cared enough to support her even when he didn't have to.

And damn if that didn't hit her straight in the heart.

11

JACKSON

Jackson had never been more relieved and frustrated than when the soft music played, telling them their massage session was over. Somehow, the thick fabric of the robe had managed to cover his hard-on, one he could thank Elena for.

Between the feel of her soft skin and how his hands raked over her body, so close to the hidden areas he was now desperate to know, to her quiet moans when he hit the right spot, to the way she moved her hands along his back—he was on fire.

For her.

She'd gotten under his skin in a way like no other woman had. There were so many moments where he wanted to flip over and pull her on top of him. He wanted to grip those full hips again, this time while he sunk deep into her. He wanted to hear those moans, his name falling from her lips.

This is bad. So bad.

Thankfully, the group had a break for a couple of hours before they were due at Bin 142 for wine and dessert pairing.

He couldn't handle another moment alone with Elena if he expected to stop himself from following through on all the dirty thoughts racing through his mind.

And what about the way her breath hitched when his hands moved up her thigh? Or the lusty look she gave him as he dressed? Was that all in his head, or was she feeling the same raging emotions coursing through his veins?

Jackson was crawling out of his skin, his adrenaline and lust coursing through him in a way that was driving him crazy.

When he got back to the apartment, he praised the gods for finding it empty. He had to blow off some of this pent-up energy before he saw her again. Jumping in the shower to wash off the oil, Jackson took hold of the erection that *still* hadn't gone away. He wrapped his hand around it, pumping back and forth, looking for a release.

But his effort to shake off the desire he had for Elena had been futile. Instead, his mind raced with thoughts of her. Her full, kissable mouth. The shapely legs that led to a grabbable ass. The way she whispered his name. And those dark eyes that were full of mischief when she had gotten him back last night at the yoga studio.

She was incredible.

He let out a roar as his orgasm came hot and heavy, pulsating through his body aggressively. And as he came down from the high of it, he realized one thing.

He still couldn't get Elena out of his mind.

———

Jackson walked into the small wine bar a couple hours later, hormones and emotions still on high alert. Scanning the group, his eyes landed on Elena. He sucked in a breath as he took her in. Dressed in a coral sundress that high-lighted her tanned skin and wearing wedged shoes that accented her toned legs, she was breathtaking. She turned to greet Maritza, her thick, curly brown hair falling in attractive layers along her cheek, jawline, shoulders, and breasts.

Beautiful.

That insatiable burn ran through his body again.

This is going to be a long night.

"Hey, you!" she greeted, wrapping him in a tight hug and kissing his cheek.

"Aw, you two are too cute," Natalie commented as she strolled by with a glass of wine and took a seat next to Hari.

"What was that for?" he asked softly in her ear, breathing in her shampoo's floral scent.

"Would look kinda weird if I didn't greet my *boyfriend* with affection, wouldn't it?"

"Then you missed."

She cocked her head. "Huh?"

"You missed. You kissed my cheek instead of my lips."

She dropped her arms and rolled her eyes. "Let's not get ahead of ourselves."

He held up his hands in mock defense. "Hey, can't blame a guy for trying." He may have been playing it cool with light teasing, but his insides screamed at him to pull her in and kiss her hard. His fingers twitched, threatening to do it.

Jackson clenched his fist to keep his body from following through on his overwhelming desire and followed her to a small two-seater table. Taking a seat across from her, he scanned the table. "What's this?" he pointed to the fabric on the table.

"Alright, everyone," Stephanie said at the back of the small space. "This evening's activity is going to continue to ravage your senses. We touched upon most of the senses during the massage today: smell, sight, sound, and touch. Now, we'll focus on taste. In a few moments, we'll be having a wine and dessert tasting with a twist. Men, we'll have you blindfold your ladies first and feed her. Ladies, you'll describe what you're tasting in detail, honing in on your sense of taste. Your partner will tell you if you're right or not. Then we'll switch."

Elena picked up the fabric and tied it around her head to cover her eyes. After everyone was secured, the sommeliers came out to the tables with wine flights and a range of mini desserts, all looking delicious.

Elena bit her lip. "What is it?"

"Well, that would ruin the point of this, now wouldn't it?" he joked. He picked up a small round chocolate truffle. "Open your mouth."

She parted her lips tentatively, and he lifted the chocolate to her mouth, his mind instantly flashing a very *not* platonic thought. For a second, he saw Elena opening her mouth just like this, her brown gaze steady on his, as she wrapped her lips around his cock.

Fuck.

Her pink tongue took the chocolate from him. He had to stifle a groan as the warm wetness from it grazed his fingertips, only making his dirty thoughts feel that much more realistic.

And if the urge to kiss her wasn't bad enough before, it now nearly brought him to his knees. He stared at her lips, the soft, plushness of them. He wanted to lean across the table and capture them, to taste the mixture of her and chocolate.

"Is it a truffle?" she asked, pulling him from his fantasies.

He cleared his throat and looked at the place card. "Yes, but what kind?"

"I'm not sure, but it's so smooth."

He picked up her hand and placed the first glass of wine in it. "Take a sip of that, maybe that will stir your senses."

She sipped the bubbling wine. Jackson watched as it traveled down her slender throat, past the steady pulse in her neck. How that managed to turn him on was beyond him.

Elena smiled. "Champagne truffles. I remember having something like this when I visited Boston a few years ago. Some little Swiss chocolate shop in one of the main shopping areas. They were delicious."

"You're right. Ready for the next one?"

"So ready."

He laughed, forgetting how much Elena loved desserts, almost as much as she loved her fennel sausage. He was glad she wasn't one of those girls who focused on eating as little as possible. Elena's love for food was endearing. Even half-covered, he could see her love for it all over her face.

He brought the next mini dessert to her mouth, and within the second it hit her tongue, she called it out. "Tiramisu."

"Too easy for an Italian, especially with your mom's cooking." He paused and looked at her lips again. "Looks like I got a little cream on you."

She touched her mouth, completely missing it. "Can you help?"

"Sure."

Reaching out slowly, the pad of his thumb wiped away the cream from the corner of her mouth. Instinctively, her tongue licked it straight off his finger. He sucked in a breath, now transfixed on her lips. As he ran his finger along her bottom lip, her mouth dropped open just a bit. She sat absolutely still, aside from her steady, deep breath—the warmth of it blowing across his hand.

"Elena," he let out.

She didn't move. Didn't protest. Instead, she sat perfectly still as if scared any movement would make him stop touching her like this. A small gesture, but intimate. He wished he could take off the blindfold so he could see her full reaction. He needed to see if there was lust in her eyes.

A camera whirled in their direction, capturing that very moment and snapping Jackson out of his trance. He needed to create a little distance. This was all starting to feel too real. Too addicting. And it would be a horrible idea to give in to whatever feelings he was having for Elena.

This was all pretend, wasn't it? All for the show.

They had a deal. He needed to remember that. These private looks, soft moans, and quiet moments were nothing more than that.

As he pulled his hand away, he could have sworn he saw her mouth drop into a frown before recovering. He cleared his throat. "How about we raise the stakes?" he said loudly, capturing everyone's attention.

Now Elena was definitely frowning, probably scared he was going to pull the rug from under her again.

"Why don't we have a little friendly competition? My Ella here always talks about how communication is important in a relationship." Well, at least that's what he read when he researched her blog. "Why don't we have a little fun with this? We'll award points to couples who guess the tastings right. Kinda like that *Heads Up* game. The non-guessing partner can give hints but can't give it away."

"That sounds like fun!" Maritza said. The others nodded and agreed.

"What's gotten into you?" Elena asked.

"Just following your lead. What better way to test communication than something like this?"

"Clever."

He breathed out a sigh of relief. Changing the focus of the night from intimate to a challenge was the right call. He knew how competitive Elena was. Rather than focus on the sensation of his hands on her mouth, she'd focus on the tasting and getting it right. Anything to stop her from feeling how his hands shook as they grazed her skin.

When the game was in full-swing, Jackson realized how good they were together. Maybe they had an unfair advantage over the other couples. After all, they'd known each other for nearly two decades. Even though they hadn't spent much time around each other these last few years, they knew the other's personality and quirks well enough to work together. Not only did they get most of the wine and dessert tastings right, but they did it in record time, blowing everyone else out of the water.

Elena pulled off his blindfold after the last round and wrapped him in an excited hug, hopping against him with pride. "We crushed it!"

"Wow. You two are on fire," Zach commented. "How did you guys get in such good sync? It's like you shared the same brain."

Elena turned back to Jackson, her arms still wrapped around his shoulders. He was relieved she didn't let go. He wasn't quite ready to let her slip out of his arms.

"We were friends before anything."

Right. Friends. Just friends, he reminded himself.

But his body and heart screamed in protest.

12

ELENA

"I'm going to kill her," Elena fumed as she paced the small balcony, her phone clutched against her ear. She had intended to spend the morning relaxing with a cup of coffee and enjoying the sunny and comfortable weather. Just a quick check-in on her work emails, respond to her clients so they stayed happy, and call it a day.

All so simple...until *Brittany*.

"Honey, you shouldn't let that stuff get to you," her mother Alma replied on the other end.

Elena knew her anxiousness wasn't all due to Brittany. Not really. She had been trying to distract herself from her unrelenting feelings for Jackson, the same feelings that had tortured her all night. Every time she closed her eyes, she remembered the feel of his fingertips on her lips during the mystery tasting. The rough pad of his thumb mixed with a gentle touch, it was enough to drive her insane.

Thank God for the blindfold. Had she had been forced to look into his endless blue eyes, she wouldn't have been able to stop herself from leaning across the table and kissing him right then and there. Something about how he had looked at her, spoke to her, and touched her these last couple of days had her out of sorts. He filled her every waking thought. As much as she tried to convince herself that it was all part of the deal they had made, her heart cracked a little at the thought.

Not good.

Thankfully, her work inbox had delivered her a brief distraction she needed to push these unusual feelings to the recesses of her mind, if only for a moment.

Elena had only been out of the office for two measly days, and somehow three of her projects had been hijacked. Brittany passed it off as being a "team player," but Elena was a writer for Christ's sake. She could read between the lines of those overly helpful emails.

"I can't turn my back for one minute," she muttered as she plopped down onto the outdoor loveseat and scrolled through another infuriating email.

"Enough about this Brittany. I want to hear all about the show. Your father and I missed you at dinner last night."

Elena's parents were her favorite people. To some, that may seem lame, but she really did love them to death. Living only twenty minutes away on John's Island, they always got together for family dinners on Monday nights. Her mom would spend Sundays making her world-famous sauce, and on Monday, Elena always left with a full heart and even fuller stomach.

Plus, it didn't hurt that her mom sent her off with several days' worth of leftovers. It had gotten a little depressing to cook for one after she and Brad had broken up.

"It's alright."

"Mija, just alright?" her father's lyrical voice came on the line. Somehow, that man always sounded like he was ready to break out in song and dance. His vibrant personality stole the spotlight no matter where they were.

"Got me on speaker, huh?" Elena smiled.

"He insisted. You know how antsy he gets when school's out."

Elena's father had been an archaeologist early in his career, but when her mother got pregnant, he settled down and became a professor—a real-life Indiana Jones. His job was the reason they were brought to Charleston nearly two decades ago, and he'd been teaching at the College of Charleston ever since.

"It's been...interesting." Elena bit her lip as she thought of Jackson's bare, muscular body on the massage table.

"Jackson is treating you well, yes?" Her father, Rodrigo, asked. "Do I need to straighten him out?" he joked with an empty threat.

"He's been a perfect gentleman, papa."

"And the couples? How is working with them?" her mother interjected.

"Surprisingly good. Coaching them felt a lot more natural than I thought it would."

A car horn sounded followed by a shout of her name. She stood from her chair, Marley trailing behind curiously, and peered over the railings. Jackson stood up through the open roof of his Jeep and smiled.

"Guys, I gotta go," she said a little breathlessly, distracted by the grin Jackson reserved just for her. "I'll come by as soon as I can. Love you!" she said quickly and hung up. "What are you doing here?" she asked, checking the time on her phone.

"Making sure you don't drown today. Can I come up?"

"Sure." Her heart thudded in her chest. Why did the idea of Jackson in her apartment feel dangerous?

Moments later, he pushed through the front door. Marley did a happy dance, rubbing against his legs for pets as her tail wagged a mile a minute.

"Hey, girl. Long time, no see."

Elena leaned against the small island in her kitchen, trying to appear casual even as her insides turned inside out. "So..." she dragged out. "It's barely nine. What's up?"

"I know we don't shoot until later this afternoon, but I couldn't sleep last night thinking about you." His face flushed, and he coughed. Elena held her breath. "I meant you and surfing," he recovered. "Mae said you haven't surfed. Is that right?"

"Yup." She tried to keep her voice from shaking. He was thinking about her?

"Well, clearly, all I do is surf."

"Uh-huh."

"And if we're going to be a believable couple, don't you think we would share our hobbies with each other?"

"You've got a point."

"Which means you can't look like an amateur during the surf lessons today. I say we get down to Folly Beach now so I can prep you on the basics."

Her eyes went wide. "You're right. Oh God. I'm totally not prepared."

There was his damn grin again, making it impossible to say no. "Get changed and meet me at the car. We'll get you ready. Don't worry."

Ten minutes later, Elena slipped into the open door of the Jeep and buckled herself in. Jackson pushed his sunglasses up and scanned her body, causing her to feel warm all over.

"What?" she asked to break the charged tension.

"Is that what you're wearing to surf in?"

She looked down at her cute turquoise bikini peeking out from her cover-up. "What's wrong with this? I wear it to the beach all the time."

He smirked. "Do you do anything at the beach other than lay out?"

"I'll take a dip in the water to cool off."

Jackson let out a laugh—one that she was coming to love—and shook his head. "Mae knows you too well." He reached behind him and tossed her some clothes.

"What's this?"

"A rash guard and board shorts. Two seconds of paddling, and you'll be falling out of that teeny bikini. I'm sure you wouldn't want that all over TV, huh?"

She held up the clothes and inspected them. "I'll never fit in these. Mae's petite." Elena looked down at herself. "I've got boobs and an ass."

"That you do," he said in a low voice, his eyes lingering on her in a way that made her shiver. He blinked a couple of times, pulling himself from whatever thought he got lost in. "It's from one of her ex-girlfriends. She said you're about the same size."

Jackson put the Jeep into drive and took the connector bridge to James Island. Elena watched the beach houses fly by as they made it to the small bridge leading into Folly Beach.

It was a beautiful day. The sun was bright and cheery, reflecting off the calm waters that filled the marshes. The air was fragrant from the colorful flowers lining the roads.

Her hair blew around wildly in the wind. Jackson slipped a hand to the seats behind him and pulled out a baseball hat. He placed it on her head, helping the hair stay in place. The act was simple but kind and reminded Elena of when they were kids. She, Mae, and Jackson would always spend long days on the beach at their parent's Sullivan's Island home, sitting out by the water until the sun had set and the air had chilled. She had always forgotten to bring a hoodie with her, assuming the warm summer air would last into the night.

Every single time, Jackson would slip his sweatshirt over his head and hand it to her, opting to be a little chilled himself so she could stay warm. How could she have forgotten that? He had always looked out for her. Taken care of her.

At least, he *used* to. When things got rocky between them in high school, it was hard for those good memories to push through. All she could see was the hurt and humiliation he had caused.

So, which Jackson was he now? The one who offered his sweatshirt or the one who called her out and embarrassed her?

Pulling down Center Street, Jackson slowed his speed to allow a hoard of tourists to stroll through the crosswalk to the bar across the road.

"Busy for a weekday," he commented.

"It's been like this a lot lately. These last few years, especially." Elena smiled at a group of girls giggling obnoxiously as they walked past the car. "Lots of bachelorette and bachelor parties too. Guess it's been a while since you've been down here."

"I usually go to the washout during off-season. I stick to my parents' place during the warmer months. Much quieter."

He took a left onto East Ashley Avenue and found a spot on Eighth Street. Hopping out, he grabbed the boards and set off to the wooden stairs leading to a quiet section of the beach.

"So, how are we going to do this?" Elena asked as she stripped off her cover-up.

Jackson paused mid-swipe of waxing his board, openly gawking at Elena in the "teeny bikini" he commented on.

"You know, I'm almost embarrassed for you," she joked as she leaned down to push his jaw back up. "Who are you? Pepé Le Pew?"

He laughed, his face flushing. He focused his attention back on the surfboards. "Take it as a compliment."

"A compliment is, 'Hey, Elena. You look good.' What you did was straight up leering, you creeper." She nudged him playfully.

He shrugged a shoulder and laughed with her. "I can't compete with my biology. We men are visual creatures, and *that* was a very good visual."

Elena shook her head with amusement before slipping on the rash guard and board shorts. She could have sworn she saw a flash of disappointment cross Jackson's face as he stood up and handed her a board.

"Alright, we're going to start with the basics. Let's get out there and learn how to catch a wave first."

She followed him into the ocean, the water refreshingly warm. She gripped the board, trying to get past the initial crashing waves without getting smacked in the face with it. Following Jackson's lead, she took the board and ducked under the waves, paddling out past the breaking point. Although she worked out regularly, the motion burned her shoulders something fierce. But she pushed forward if only to get close to him again.

Once they reached calmer waters, he propped himself up, so he was straddling the board. Elena pushed up too, trying to get comfortable but feeling a bit awkward. She looked out and watched the water gleam under the sunlight. Here, it all seemed calm.

"Ah, you must be experiencing your first surfer's high." He laughed, his blue eyes even more radiant as the water and light reflected in them. His laugh lines dipped deep into his cheeks as he grinned at her, and she could only hope he'd throw that smile at her always.

"We haven't even surfed yet."

He shook his head. "No, I mean this moment. Right here. Right before you work your ass off to catch the wave and ride it for all you've got. Sure, there's a thrill from feeling the wind against your face as you weave up and down that barrel, but this here's a moment that matters the most. It's during this time that I find the most clarity."

"Hm. Like your next 'big move' you've mentioned a few times?"

He looked out to the horizon and let out a breath. "To be determined. I think I'd need a lot more time out here to make sense of what's jumbled in my head." He fixed his gaze back on her. "And, unfortunately, I don't have that kind of time today. Not when I gotta teach you how to catch your first wave."

"Good luck."

"It's not about luck. It's about gut feeling and timing. When you feel it, you gotta go after it."

"Wise words."

He pointed at the horizon, the muscles in his arms shadowed by the harsh sunlight, making them look even more defined.

Who's the one ogling now?

"Alright. You see those waves coming?" he asked.

She drew her eyes away from him to look. "Kinda."

"You see how they look smooth on the surface?"

"I guess."

"Well, that's when you want to start digging in. Get on your stomach. Keep an eye on that moment, and when it comes, give it all you've got. Dig your hands into the water and paddle like hell."

"Oh, Jesus."

He let out a deep laugh. "You'll be okay. I promise. I've got you. We'll just practice catching the wave. Not sure if we're ready for standing."

For the next hour, Elena followed Jackson's instructions and failed over and over. Her arms killed. The skin on her stomach was irritated from rubbing against the board despite the rash guard. And she was thirsty as hell.

She was just about to give up when a wave finally came, and she dug in like Jackson had instructed just at the right moment. She felt her board catch, thrusting her forward without any effort. And it was the most amazing feeling ever. There she was, the wind against her face, feeling like she was floating at break-neck speed. It was the closest thing to flying she had ever felt, and it was instantly addicting.

Elena looked to her left and saw Jackson surfing alongside her, cheering her on as she rode it closer to shore. As the wave died down, Elena slipped off the board, her hands raised high in triumph.

"You did it!" Jackson jumped off his board and grabbed her, lifting her from the water and swinging her in a circle.

"That was amazing!" She cheered like an idiot as he raised her overhead like an Olympic ice skater.

"That's my girl!" he yelled with enthusiasm.

My girl.

She liked that a little too much. Almost as much as she liked Jackson's hands on her body and the proud look on his face. All for her.

It was all for her.

He let her down gently, sliding her along his body as if she were the most delicate thing in the world. As if he hadn't just swung her in the air.

And that's when things shifted.

No longer were they laughing, smiling, and cheering.

Now the air was too charged. Too raw.

Jackson towered over her, his hands still on her hips, holding her tight against his wet body. Instinctively, Elena wrapped her arms around his neck, not wanting to let go.

Not now. Not ever.

"Elena," he said, his voice rough as he examined her face, his own a cross between longing, lust, and discovery.

Elena weaved her fingers through his wet hair, her mind no longer in control. It was all heart, all body driving her. She pulled his face down to her with little resistance. He dipped his head low, his mouth mere inches from hers. Her heart thundered in her chest. She never wanted anything more than this. Than *him.*

"Hey, love birds!" Celeste called from the shore with a friendly wave, breaking their moment. "Looks like you two got here early for some fun. So cute."

Elena tried not to let the disappointment show as Jackson dragged his face from hers. *So close.*

And yet, she couldn't understand why that mattered. For years, she'd kept her distance from Jackson. So what changed? Was it merely because she'd spent more time with him these last couple days? Was it a sense of appreciation that he went along with this crazy scheme? Or was it because he was playing the part so well that she almost believed he actually cared about her?

She swallowed, her mouth dry. She hoped to God that wasn't the case. Maybe she couldn't make sense of her feelings quite yet. They were a jumbled mess after all. But she didn't think she could stomach knowing she *felt* something for Jackson, and it all might be a ruse for the camera.

It was poetic justice in a way, wouldn't a fraud like her deserve that?

13

BRITTANY

"I can see why you called me out here," Brittany said as she stood on the wrap-around veranda that overlooked the waves rhythmically rolling onto the shore.

Martha Bianco's house was absolutely stunning, and her fundraiser to support the loggerheads of South Carolina would be one to remember with such a perfect venue. The home was three stories with pale sea foam green clapboard. All along the backside of the home was a mix of floor to ceiling windows and accordion doors leading out to two verandas on the upper floors and a patio with a state of the art built-in kitchen and pool area on the ground level. Every aspect of the house provided an immaculate view of Folly Beach.

Martha, a fifty-something-year-old with a beautiful blonde bob and kind eyes leaned against the railing, taking in the view and breathing in the sweet, salty air. "I thought it was important for you to see it." She pointed just past the dunes to a roped-off area. "This is one of the protected areas for the loggerheads to lay their eggs. We have a bunch of them up and down the shore but could do with more. Even with these protected areas, a lot of the babies don't make it to the ocean. With more funding, we can really make an impact on this dying breed."

"How so?"

"Aside from the protected nesting areas, we'll use the funds to clean up the beaches, create watches to keep predators away, and work with the community to reduce plastic and light pollution. That's where you come in."

Brittany nodded. Piece of cake. "No problem. Our agency has had a lot of success with these fundraisers, and you spared no expense." The woman had been a success designing chic clothes for the Southern woman. Now she wanted to give back to the place where she grew up and loved.

"I'm very confident. You were referred to me by one of my friends. She said one of your colleagues had pulled together such a beautiful campaign for her fundraiser last year." She scrunched her face in concentration. "I believe her name was Elle?" She shook her head. "No, that's not it."

Brittany tried not to let her annoyance show. "Elena?"

Martha's face brightened. "Yes, that's it. My friend raved on and on about her. Do you know her?"

"We work together from time to time," she responded, her voice flat.

Not if Brittany could help it. She may be only a few years into her career, but she could run circles around Elena. She knew what people in Charleston wanted and delivered it. Elena was always trying to get crafty with her copy, and as much as Brittany hated to admit it, a lot of it was good. Brilliant, even.

But what Elena would never get is how people here liked things to be traditional. Those born and raised in the South stuck with their own. A decade ago—before all the transplants swarmed the area—it was impossible for an "outsider" to work their way into the ranks. Doing business or hiring people outside the inner circle was almost unheard of. Maybe things have changed now that the transplants had infiltrated in insurmountable numbers—especially in Charleston—but Brittany liked to tap into what she knew.

People in Charleston wanted to work with people they trusted.

Elena was most definitely *not* that, and it worked in Brittany's favor time and time again. Even if Elena's ideas were enticing or cutting-edge, more than ninety percent of the time, Brittany knew she could sway the client by tapping into that deeply ingrained need to support their roots. Their community.

And that tactic was exactly how she continued to one-up Elena. With a promotion opening up, she was doing everything she could to push Elena out. Nothing would make her happier to see the look on Elena's face when Brittany proved she was better than her.

Little Elena Lucia. Always pretending to be something she's not.

Brittany could usually see the resentment bubbling under the surface and took pleasure in pushing Elena's buttons, but somehow the frustrating woman never snapped. She'd politely nod with a hollow smile—one that showed she was dying a little on the inside—but never said anything. Never pushed back. Elena was too afraid to rock the boat. Too scared to speak up and put a spotlight on the fact that she wasn't one of them.

She was an idiot, though Brittany should be happy about that. A true Southern woman knew how to embrace tradition and still get what she wanted. Elena's goal of fitting in always *just* missed the mark, working in Brittany's favor.

Made it easy to swoop in and steal clients. Winning this promotion would be a great reminder for Elena to stay in her own lane.

She was sick and tired of these outsiders coming into the South, taking all their jobs, raising all their housing costs, and forcing everyone to change their way of life. Some days, it felt like the Civil War all over again. Maybe not as bloody, but sometimes just as hostile.

Brittany looked off to the right and stilled. As if she'd conjured Elena from her mere thoughts, she swore the woman in the distance was her. That flawless tan skin and thick dark hair. But who was she with? She knew Elena had asked for time off from work this week, but assumed she had gone on a vacation, not stayed in town wrapped up with some hunk.

God, he was hot.

Brittany examined the man who was lifting the alleged Elena in the air. He was tall with an incredible physique. Muscular without being bulky, and some colorful ink filling his arm. His boardshorts hung low on his narrow hips as if he belonged in a surfing ad. Dirty blond hair shimmered under the sunlight, and his smile could make a woman weak in the knees.

Brittany craned her head when she heard a woman's voice call out, breaking whatever trance was going on between Elena and her mystery man.

"Hey, what's going on there?" she asked Martha as more people rolled up, now some carrying video equipment.

"I completely forgot they were filming today."

Interest piqued. "Filming for what?"

"Oh, I can't remember," she waved off. "Something about a relationship writer. It's a reality-based show to promote her new book. Something Ella."

"*Always, Ella?*" Brittany choked out.

Martha snapped her fingers. "That's the one!"

Brittany didn't know much about this "Ella" person, just that she had a relationship blog that went viral. She never had the need to look too far into it since she'd been perfectly content and capable with her own love life. She wasn't a sucker like all those pathetic people clamoring for someone to tell them they'd be okay and how to fix their poor existence.

"What are they doing filming here?"

"The marketing manager from the publisher called a couple weeks ago asking if they could film here since my section is technically private due to loggerheads. They offered a nice donation, too. She said something about the writer being from Charleston."

Brittany's wheels began to turn. "Is that so?"

"Of course, I jumped right on it. I'd do anything to support one of our own here. And the loggerheads."

A Cheshire Cat smile spread across Brittany's face as she looked out to the girl who she was now certain was Elena. It was almost too good to think of Elena—poised, trying-too-hard Elena—as the writer for this crap blog.

She couldn't wait to get back to her computer and do some digging. It might be just the thing she needed to hang over Elena's head and seal the deal on *her* promotion.

14

JACKSON

He couldn't stop thinking about that near kiss with Elena the whole time they'd been surfing with the rest of the gang. His lack of concentration definitely made him eat it a few times, but he hoped could convince the producer to cut that footage out for his company's sake. It wouldn't look great if the owner of a surfing brand looked like it was the first time on his board.

Those lips.

For first half of their time in the water, he had been attached at the hip with Elena as they went through the motions of surfing. However, as the day went on, he was often pulled away to give tips on the basics to help other couples.

Reluctantly pulled away.

He liked the feel of his hands on Elena way too much. How he was "forced" to help her onto the board and keep her steady. But it wasn't just the physical part of it, it was the way her face lit up every time she caught a wave and rode it to shore. Maybe they hadn't graduated to full-on standing— she managed to get up on her knees and ride though—but it didn't matter to Elena. She looked so damn proud of herself, and he couldn't help but feel proud for her.

That's my girl, he would think. And each time the words popped into his head, he would pause. Not because he was slipping and forgetting his whole role in this charade, but because his heart would pound hard in his chest every time he thought it.

He *wanted* Elena to be his girl.

These last few days with her had opened his eyes. She was no longer his little sister's cute best friend. She was a woman who sparked something in him and had him feeling things that he wasn't used to.

She made him feel grounded. Accepted.

He craved her presence. The second he saw her face or heard her voice, all the tension in his body melted away.

Before the rest of the crew came, they had sat on their boards, the rolling waves rocking them and relaxing the pre-filming tension away. He had told her all about his business, what it meant to be the face of the company, and how important it was that his brand reflected the good he was trying to do in the world.

The way she had looked at him while he talked about the stress and fun that came with it was...*addicting.* She'd been engaged, asking endless questions. They'd compared his business meetings—usually on the beach, a couple on a surfboard, sometimes in a small local eatery—to her typical board room and business casual attire. It was like his stories had opened a whole new world for her, showing her that being successful and doing something you love doesn't need to fit into some perfectly acceptable package that society dictated.

She could do things *her* way if she were brave enough to dream it.

As they sat on those boards, the bright sun reflecting off the ocean water, making her eyes sparkle, Jackson thought maybe for the first time in a long time they were really seeing each other.

That finally, she understood.

"Have you told your parents all of this yet?" she'd asked. "It could make a huge difference in how they feel about you dropping out of school all those years ago." She'd paused as she looked out to the horizon. "It did for me."

The statement was so quiet, he had thought he'd imagined it.

"I haven't. No. My father...he and I haven't had a normal conversation in years without it blowing up within five minutes."

She'd turned to him, her gaze holding his. "Maybe it's time you weather the storm. Rather than packing your bags and leaving after the inevitable blow-up, dig your heels in and make him listen. You seem to be comfortable putting yourself out there for everyone to see except with him."

Elena was right. In his gut, he knew it.

Jackson's father may never have approved of his choice to go out and start his own business, and although his mother never outright showed her disappointment the way his father had, she had been compliant. More willing to stand quietly by her husband's side than encourage her children.

But Elena made him believe he was doing something worthwhile. The pride on her face was a high he'd always want to chase. Sure, he'd gotten great affirmation from those he's worked with over the years, including some press releases and news that came out about his company's mission, and he'd been lucky enough to travel to remote places around the world and see how he made an impact. Yet, somehow, none of that came close to Elena's approval.

Maybe it was because she knew him as the wild kid who was always stirring up trouble. Or because she was someone he'd known most of his life. Either way, it meant more to him than he would have expected, only pulling him further into Elena's orbit.

How long could he keep pretending to be her perfect boyfriend before he actually slipped and asked her to give it a real shot? As much as the idea excited him, it wasn't fair. Sure, he knew he would have to set down some sort of roots to help him grow his business, but he hadn't planned on it being in Charleston.

He didn't want to start something he couldn't finish. Not with her. He couldn't bear the thought of breaking her heart if his work made him leave again. She deserved so much more than he could ever give.

But you can give her what she deserves if you really wanted to. You don't have to leave.

"That was amazing," Elena said on a sigh as she collapsed onto the sand next to him, pulling Jackson from his battling thoughts. Still soaked from the water, Elena lifted the rash guard over her head, revealing that perfect skin that drove him wild. He snuck a glance, careful not to outright gawk at her again.

"Never thought I'd go surfing at my age, but I'm glad I did," Natalie commented as she walked up to join them.

Hari rolled his eyes and smiled as he trailed behind. "Forty-eight isn't old." Natalie's eyes shot daggers at him as if he shared a horrible secret. "We still have a lot of living to do."

Stephanie approached with her clipboard in hand.

"Great work, everyone," she commended. "I'm sure you worked up an appetite with all that surfing."

Ana held her stomach and groaned. "Starved. I thought barre was hard. This killed."

"In a few minutes, you'll jump on one of these boats." She nodded to a pair of boats resting in the wake.

"Where to?" Jackson asked.

"We have access to a private island off the coast where we'll have a nice spread laid out. A picnic on the beach, if you will."

"That sounds amazingggg," Maritza drew out. "Wine?"

Stephanie laughed. "Of course."

"Sign me up!"

"If you'll follow me, we'll have you on this boat with a driver. The camera crew and I will follow behind. We gotta get you set up with some mics before you board so we can capture the audio, though."

The group stood with pained effort, worse for the wear and likely to be sore after using muscles they hadn't used in some time...or ever. Moments later, they were situated in the small boat and cruising along the ocean, the wind blowing their wet hair wildly around.

"Oh my goodness! Is that a dolphin?" Maritza yelled over the motor and wind.

Elena carefully moved to where Maritza was standing and tapped her shoulder. "Look." Elena pointed to where a pod of dolphins jumped out of the water beside the boat. "We have a ton of them here," she said as she watched with fascination.

Maritza leaned over further, outstretching her hand. Her fingertips skimmed the top of the water as they cruised along. "They're so close, you can almost touch them."

Elena shifted to get a closer look, too, just as they hit a

choppy wave. Maritza lost her balance, instinctively reaching out and grabbing Elena's arm, sending them both over the edge and into the water.

Natalie gasped, and Ana shrieked. Without a second thought, Jackson ripped off his shirt and dove into the water, panicked that Elena was hurt. She was a strong swimmer, but he had no idea if the fall had taken her by surprise.

He surfaced, seeing her hand sticking out from the water. He dug his hands into the water and swam to her, pulling her above surface. She sputtered and gasped for air.

"You okay?" he asked.

She nodded. "Maritza?" she coughed out.

Following Jackson's lead—albeit a little delayed, and well after the driver had slowed down to a stop—Max leaned over the edge and pulled a still stunned Maritza from the ocean. Max waved to them, signaling that she was fine.

Wrapping Elena's arms around his neck, Jackson instructed her to hold on while he swam back to the boat. Natalie and Hari pulled her up by her arms and helped her in.

With a ragged breath, Elena sat on a bench to cough out the rest of the water trapped in her lungs. "Thank you," she finally said after sucking in a big breath of air.

Jackson sat behind her and pulled her into his lap, his heart still beating out of control, a side effect of seeing her go overboard. He rubbed circles on her back to help ease out whatever water was left in her lungs. She coughed again and sputtered. "Not for a second would I hesitate to go after you."

"Aw. That's too sweet," Natalie commented as she nudged Hari in the ribs with her elbow. "Isn't that so sweet?"

"Very," he agreed while rubbing his ribs and wincing.

"If my man jumped in after me all heroic like that, I would be all over him," Ana fanned herself.

"So that's all it takes, huh?" Zach wagged his eyebrows and snaked his arms around her waist, nuzzling his face into her neck.

Ana giggled and leaned into it. "But seriously, I would at least give him a kiss. That was so romantic."

The other women nodded, and soon came the chants to kiss. Elena looked at him with wide eyes mixed with uncertainty and curiosity. Jackson—selfish as it might be—wanted to take the opportunity to finish what they had started before the rest of the group came. He shot her a look that said, "Is this okay?"

She quickly nodded, a touch of shyness, and—dare he hope a bit of anticipation maybe—creeping on her face. That was all he needed.

Cupping her cheek with one hand, he pulled her tighter against his body, his face dipping down to hers. Jackson paused. One last look into those beautiful brown eyes— another chance for her to change her mind.

Please don't change your mind.

His pulse kicked up as her eyes began to close, and she tilted her chin to him. She wanted this. She wanted *him.*

He had imagined kissing her these last few days, always picturing it as a slow, tentative exploration of each other. But now that the chance was here, the idea of going slow was the last thing on his mind. He needed her. Needed to feel her. Needed her lips on his to assess how she felt for him, that he wasn't alone in this.

His fingers dug lightly into the nape of her neck as he pulled her in and crushed his lips against hers, not at all concerned with being polite as many people would be with their first kiss. He was desperate for her, and by the way her full lips were lapping up his, he would say she felt the same.

He hoped she felt the same.

Elena's body responded, only making his need for her more intense. His body was on fire, and she was fueling the flame. She dug a hand into his hair and pressed against him—every curve of her body molded to his—kissing him with raw heat and passion. She opened her mouth, allowing him to explore, to taste the mixture of her sweetness melded with the salt of the ocean. Soft. Wet. Warm. Everything.

It was everything.

He couldn't get enough. And at that moment, he knew kissing Elena would never be enough. He'd always want more.

He'd always want *her*.

Some wolfish howls came from the other side of the boat, pulling him from the crazy spell he had been under. Elena jerked away, her face bright red, her breath coming harder than when she'd been pulled from the ocean.

Jackson was tempted to pull her back in to continue the kiss he never wanted to end.

"Wow. That was hot. You have some advice in that book of yours that talks about how to get that level of passion in our relationships?" Natalie teased.

Elena let out an awkward laugh, a look of lust still crossing her features. "I guess you'll have to read and find out." She shrugged a shoulder.

"Did you practice that line? That was perfect," Stephanie commended as their boat cruised up along theirs. "Totally making the cut. Along with that kiss. My God, Celeste is going to lose it."

Elena gripped his hand, her eyes going wide with worry, likely because she realized their somewhat private moment wasn't limited to the strangers on the boat. Once the show aired, the whole country was going to see it.

Jackson took her hand and placed a soft kiss on her palm. "We'll be okay, Elena," he whispered in her ear. And with that, he felt her body instantly relax on his lap, but despite her relaxed posture, he felt the erratic beating of her heart matching his own.

Through the years, he had fleeting thoughts about what it would be like to kiss Elena. He blamed his raging hormones as a teen for those thoughts, but puberty couldn't be the scapegoat this time. Everything in his being ached to kiss her again. It was unlike anything he could have ever imagined and unlike anything he'd ever experienced. He knew the kiss was caused by a bit of peer pressure, but she couldn't have faked *that*, right?

He didn't think he could handle knowing she faked it. Not when kissing her gave him a sense of clarity that calmed him in ways he hadn't felt before. Even with the frantic racing of his heart and the way his insides heated up with every movement of her lips on his, the world became silent. It fell away.

For once, he didn't have that unrelenting urge to move. He didn't need to pack his bags and go, always looking to discover something new. He thought it was simply a case of wanderlust and curiosity that had him traveling the world, but now he knew it was something else.

All these years, he had been on a quest to find what was missing in his life.

Although the things he experienced on his travels were ones he was grateful for, he hadn't realized how unfulfilled he was as he moved on from place to place. The unsettled feeling was always lingering there, deep down, but he never knew what it was.

Now, with Elena wrapped in his arms, her face pressed in the crook of his neck, he knew. Suddenly, every fiber of his being was telling him he needed to stay. That what he'd been looking for was right there.

If he did stay, would she feel the same? Could all of this be real?

15

ELENA

Despite the little overboard accident, the private beach lunch was pleasant. Everyone had a great time, and Elena had tried to enjoy herself as much as she could muster. But Elena had felt like she couldn't breathe the rest of the day, and not because of the ocean water sitting in her lungs. She couldn't believe how Jackson dove into the water to rescue her, but it wasn't the heroics that had her heart beating out of her chest. It was the gentle way he held her after and the not-so-gentle kiss that had her insides on fire.

Never in her life had she been kissed like that.

All that heat and passion and...she let out a big sigh. She was already entering the danger zone with Jackson, her feelings getting muddled and confused as she tried to figure out what between them was real and what was for show.

She didn't think she could handle knowing that the kiss—the best kiss in her whole freaking life—was an act. Her insides twisted as she thought of never having that kiss again. When the show wrapped up at the end of the week, would he disappear from her life as quickly as he came barreling in it again?

Going back to how it was before they agreed to this whole charade was a distant, empty memory. One she didn't want to revisit.

Her insides twisted again as she thought about what that meant. Leave it to her to have feelings for a guy who was completely off-limits, not just as her best friend's brother and her fake boyfriend, but because he'll likely be on some grand adventure across the world before she could even make sense of the emotions exploding throughout her body.

Maybe they could be friends. They could stay in touch. Texts, emails, and phone calls could be her lifeline.

But would that be enough? Despite him coming home here and there these last few years, their paths rarely crossed. She couldn't stomach knowing it might be years before she saw him again.

His face with the smile and laugh that centered her. And those blue eyes that pulled her in like a rip current, one she would happily float away in even if it meant her demise.

This is bad. So very bad.

Elena waved goodbye to the rest of the group as they jumped into a rideshare, excitedly chatting about where they'd explore downtown after they got cleaned up.

"Hey," Jackson said, startling her from her internal dilemma.

Elena turned to him, her gaze instantly zeroing in on his full lips that hitched into his signature panty-dropping grin.

She forced herself to look at his eyes, those eyes that reminded her of clear skies on a comfortable spring afternoon. She stared at them, getting lost in their rip current effect.

My God, I'm never going to survive.

"Elena?" Jackson asked, his eyebrows knitted in confusion.

Busted.

She shook her head and casually swiped at her mouth in case she had drooled over the sight of him. "Sorry. What's up?"

"Now that we're wrapped for the day, I asked if you wanted to get dinner with me?"

Was it just her, or did he seem nervous when he asked her? Almost shy.

"Sure, what did you have in mind?"

"My friends live on Folly Beach. Not too far from here. They're having a BBQ."

A rush of nerves and excitement coursed through her. Their fake date was suddenly starting to feel real. "Sounds good. I'll meet you back down here in a couple of hours."

He laughed and ran a hand through his hair, pushing it back in a way that looked like he'd participated in an all-nighter sexcapade. The muscles of his chest and bicep flexed with the movement, and she did everything she could to remember to breathe. "Elena, come as you are." The comment was casual, but his voice made her wonder if there was some deeper meaning behind it.

"I'm all gross from the sand and saltwater." It had been a long day at the beach, and she could use a shower to wash away the sticky, gritty feeling on her skin. God only knows what her hair was doing. She was almost scared to think of it.

Yet, Jackson wasn't looking at her wild hair in fear. If anything, he was looking at her like she was some sort of sea siren, ready to lure him into the depths of the ocean, and he'd gladly take that risk.

He reached out, an amused smirk on his face, and took an unruly wave of her hair between his fingers, tucking it behind her ear. "Elena, we're at the beach. The people we're hanging out with were likely surfing all day and most definitely didn't shower before they cracked open a beer and hung out. Don't worry about being perfect. Go with the flow."

She hesitated.

"Trust me?"

She exhaled, slightly uncomfortable at the thought of meeting his friends looking like a mess and likely smelling worse, but the hopeful gleam in his eyes made her reconsider. "Okay."

He grinned and held out his hand. She took it, enjoying the warmth of his large hand as it engulfed hers, the simple feel of it making her already frazzled hormones go insane. They walked along the main road and continued down a quiet side street.

His hand still firmly holding hers, as if they'd done this a million times.

"You know, the cameras have packed it in for the day."

"I know," he said with certainty, still clutching her hand.

Her heart raced. "So, you don't need to do all this," she commented as she squeezed his hand.

Jackson turned, piercing her with his gaze. "I know, Elena."

"Oh, okay," she said dumbly while trying to put one foot in front of the other. Her legs felt like jelly, the rush of emotions overwhelming her.

What does this mean?

Elena followed him to the bungalow a couple blocks from the beach. In the dusky light, she could see the house was small but well cared for. Several surfboards sat on the porch next to a swinging hammock. Jackson pushed through the front door without knocking, "Brandon, Shua, we're here."

"Hey, dude," a tall guy with shaggy red hair said. He pulled Jackson into one of those high-five-handshake-hug things guys do.

"Long time, no see."

"Glad you could make it. Got some time to surf with us while you're home?"

"I should."

"Sweet. Just like old times."

Jackson pulled Elena forward and tucked her to his side. "This is Elena Lucia."

Shua nodded. "'Sup, Elena?" He took her in, still in her board shorts and rash guard. "Shred some gnarly waves today?"

She grinned. "Tried. Jackson has been surprisingly patient." She cocked her head. "What kind of name is Shua? I've never heard of it."

"Name's Joshua, but everyone calls me Shua."

She laughed. "I like it. Guess the nickname Josh is played out, huh?"

"I just felt more like a 'Shua,' ya know? Sometimes you gotta just go with what you feel."

"Where's the rest of the crew?" Jackson asked.

"We're all out back. Hope you're hungry. Mikey's on the grill."

Jackson turned to her. "Mikey's cooking is unreal. He makes his own sauces from scratch. For years, we've told him he could be selling them." He shrugged. "Mikey said he was happy spending days working at the local deli and surfing. He wasn't looking for anything more."

"I guess some people just know what makes them happy."

He gave her a meaningful look. "Yeah. I guess so," he responded after a pregnant pause.

She followed Shua and Jackson to the backyard, where several people were drinking beers by a bonfire.

"My dude!" a gangly guy with sandy hair called out when he saw Jackson walk through the backdoor. The guy grabbed a couple beers and thrust them into Jackson and Elena's hands.

She cracked open the beer, taking a long pull from the bottle. Had beer always tasted this good, or was it that much better after a long day on the beach?

"Grab a plate. Mikey's dishing it out."

Elena and Jackson grabbed a plate of varying meats and took a seat on a chopped log by the fire. The sun had fully set now, casting darkness around them aside from the twinkling stars and glow from the fire.

"Today was fun," Elena said, feeling nervous. She took a bite of rib and moaned.

Jackson cocked an eyebrow. "You know, I love how you appreciate good food, but those noises are going to kill me."

"Sorry. This sauce is unbelievable."

"Told you. Mikey's the real deal."

Shua waltzed over to them and plopped down. "Bro, so glad you're here. Feels like old times seeing you around the fire." He nodded at Elena. "You know this dude is a legend, right?"

She cocked an eyebrow. "How so?"

"He went out to surf during Hurricane Charley like a mad man. Those waves were vicious." He laughed in awe.

Jackson casually took a bite of his burger as if it were no big deal. "We don't get waves like that here very often. Had to seize the chance while I could."

Shua jabbed at him playfully. "Jackson threw on a suit and took on the waves. They were massive. Deadly. And what did he do? Stayed out there for hours, catching one wave after another, taking on barrels like a mofo. No fear."

Elena gasped. "You could have been killed."

"That was back in high school. You know I was a little *wilder* in those days."

"That's a word for it." Shua laughed again. "Some of my greatest memories are with this dude."

For the next twenty minutes, Shua and Brandon talked about growing up with Jackson, sharing fond memories of their epic stories, idiotic moments, and everything in between. Each story had Elena smiling, laughing, or looking at Jackson with pure shock at his antics.

And with each memory, she couldn't help but see Jackson in a new light. Hearing about this part of his life gave her a full view of who he was when they were younger. She found that she liked it. Even more, she liked how easy it was to be around his friends. They made her feel like she was one of them, including her in all their chats and refilling her beers when she was done.

"Jackson!" a cute girl wrapped in a hoodie and a tiny pair of board shorts called out as she took a seat opposite him. "I'm so happy you're here. How long until you leave us again?"

"Hey, Katie." He gave her a quick side hug. "Not sure. I'm thinking I might stick around for a while."

"What do you mean? Like an extra week or something."

He took a sip of his beer, stalling for time. "I'm thinking longer. Like, permanently."

Elena nearly dropped her plate. "What?"

He looked at her from the corner of his eye. "I told you I'm trying to expand the business. I need to have a home base to do that effectively. I'm thinking of setting roots here. Again."

She shook her head. "But I thought you hated it here. You were so desperate to leave."

"And stay away," Katie added with an eye-roll before rushing into the house to greet newcomers, leaving just the two of them.

"I didn't *hate* it," he explained. "I just knew I needed some space to be my own man. I couldn't do that here."

"Because of your father," Elena supplied.

He took another long drink of his beer. "Yup. Good ol' dad."

"So, what changed? What's making you want to stay here now?"

Jackson's gaze held Elena's for a beat. He opened his mouth to speak, but before he could answer, Brandon interrupted.

"Yo, man. Come check out my new board. It's sickkkk."

Jackson and Elena shared another look before he stood and disappeared into the house, leaving her reeling from the news.

Jackson was staying?

"Hey, I'm Riley," a freckle-faced woman greeted her as she took Jackson's spot. She pointed to the blonde girl who sat on Elena's side. "That's Ashley."

"Nice to meet you, I'm Elena. "

The girls spent the next few minutes getting to know each other. Elena learned they all had known Jackson for years, either from surfing, working at the beach, or through friends of friends. In the few moments she chatted with them, she couldn't help but feel at ease. The women were welcoming and open and extremely down to earth. For the first time in a long time, Elena didn't feel the need to be "on." She could just be herself.

"Yeah, I grew up with Mae and Jackson. I've known him since I was about ten," she responded to Katie's question.

Katie snorted.

"What?" Elena asked with confusion.

"In all the years we've known Jackson, he hasn't been one to bring girls around. Aside from Mae."

"Yeah, we've known Jackson for a long time. Him bringing you here means something," Riley leaned in and added as if she were sharing a secret.

Jackson strolled out with Brandon, now carrying an acoustic guitar.

"Gather 'round, all, and feast your ears on the magical musician that is Jackson St. Julien," Shua joked in a phony medieval accent as he took a seat.

Jackson sat opposite Elena, the fire flickering between them. He tuned the strings and grabbed the pick, starting to strum a soft song that sent tingles down her spine.

"It's not like that between us. We're just friends," Elena told the girls, all of whom gave her a disbelieving look.

"You're the only one that thinks that," Ashley said. "You've been here barely an hour, and it's clear as day that you're *definitely* not just friends."

"How could you ever think you were just friends when he looks at you like *that?*" Riley questioned.

Elena turned back to him, catching his gaze. In the dark with the fire flickering in his eyes, something sparked between them. His lips parted, and he blinked slowly, never missing a beat as he continued to play the beautiful song.

Jackson's eyes stayed locked on hers as if he was playing every single note just for her. That it was just the two of them there by the fire. His eyes, slightly hooded now, never left her face. He took her in as if she was the only thing in the world worth looking at. And he played the song like everything was riding on her hearing it.

His lips tilted upward into a peaceful smile, a private one he meant for her only.

Maybe the girls were right. Maybe their kiss today wasn't part of the plan. Maybe it wasn't all an act.

Her heart thudded in her chest with the realization that the overwhelming feelings she had for Jackson might not be one-sided.

And as his blue eyes watched her with lust and adoration, she knew her muddled feelings weren't so muddled anymore.

16

ELENA

E lena was reeling. Although Jackson had kept things relatively friendly between them the rest of the evening, she couldn't unsee what the girls had pointed out.

Every look held a new meaning. Small touches like the way his fingers would accidentally graze hers or his hand on the small of her back were now charged. The quick glances he gave her on the ride home were packed with unspoken emotion.

And if she had any questions about whether those glances meant anything, he reached out and took her hand.

The gentle kisses on her knuckles confirmed it.

Like the Southern gentleman that he was, Jackson walked her to her door. Elena's pulse spiked with each step, and when they stood there to say goodnight, his gaze drifted down to her lips.

"Elena, can I ki—"

The door swung open, interrupting the moment she was sure he was going to ask to kiss her. "Hey, guys," Mae greeted, killing the moment.

"I didn't know you'd still be here." With a long day of

filming and the stop at Jackson's friend's place, Elena had asked Mae to pop by and walk Marley.

"Marley and I got sucked into one of those unsolved mystery shows. Been binge watching it all night. Sorry if it messes up your Netflix algorithm." Mae shrugged as if she wasn't sorry at all and turned to Jackson. "Wanna give me a ride home?"

Jackson looked murderous. Elena was happy to know she wasn't the only one who felt sexually frustrated, thanks to Mae's interruption.

"Sure," he managed to get out.

Mae was utterly oblivious to the situation. "Cool. Oh, and you might need to buy more popcorn," she called out to Elena as she made her way down the stairs to his Jeep.

Jackson pulled Elena into a hug and kissed the top of her head. "See you tomorrow."

"See you."

She couldn't help her disappointment as she watched him slip into his Jeep and drive off.

After a quick shower, Elena got into bed, finding it impossible to sleep with the endless questions looping through her head on repeat. What would it mean if Jackson really did have feelings for her? What would happen?

They were starting to repair their friendship. Did she want to complicate it by exploring what was growing between them?

Sure, she'd fantasized about it a couple times these last few days, but knowing he might feel the same changed things. Made it tempting. That thought alone was dangerous.

She wasn't sure she could handle losing him again if it didn't work out.

——

The next morning, Elena sat at her computer, trying to burn through work emails, but the effort was futile. Every few seconds, her mind went right back to the questions swarming in her mind. Her hand involuntarily touched her lips where she could still feel that kiss from the boat ride. His mouth had been hot and demanding. And perfect. And addicting. Slamming her laptop shut with a little more force than necessary, she melted into her couch as she replayed that kiss over and over.

She still had a few hours to kill before she had to get ready for the next segment of the show: the date. Apparently, the men would pull together a romantic date they thought their ladies would appreciate. It was a way to show how well they paid attention to the little things. After the date, they would meet up for tango lessons.

She grinned at the thought of seeing Jackson struggle with the dance. Dance was a love language in her household, and after years of growing up with it, she would be surprised if he could keep up with the sway of her hips.

Her body tingled at the thought of getting up close and personal with Jackson on the dance floor. The tango, with him, would be extremely erotic. She already felt like she was going to explode from the sexual tension simmering between them just below the surface. She didn't know if she could survive rubbing her body up on him without being tempted to rip off his clothes.

Clothes that would reveal that unbelievable body. All tall and muscular and agile.

Flashes of memories from last night flooded her mind. He had looked at her so intensely, like seeing into the deepest parts of her, uncovering all her secret wants and desires.

Would his eyes look just like that if they'd crossed that line and gotten intimate?

Or would he touch her carefully like he had during the massage, paying close attention to her reaction and responding in ways that made her feel like she was in heaven?

His hands all over her...just the thought of it drove her wild.

Resisting him was getting harder by the day. There was so much more beneath the surface than she'd ever realized. Sure, he'd always been a good-looking guy, but he wasn't just a pretty face. He was smart, kind, and thoughtful. How did she miss all of that before?

Elena picked up a throw pillow and held it against her face to scream. Marley ambled over and nudged her arm, a look of worry etched in her precious chocolate eyes.

"Sorry, girl." Elena stroked the soft hair on Marley's head. "Just going through something."

Marley disappeared and came back a moment later with her leash. She sat by the couch, her tail thumping with excitement.

"You're right. A walk could do us some good. You always know just what I need."

The two of them left the apartment and walked through the quiet streets of downtown Charleston. It was just before eight in the morning, and the city was still asleep. Despite being on the cusp of summer, the morning was comfortably warm without being stifling. The sun hadn't quite hit its peak when it would blast the city with its rays and make everyone feel like they were melting.

A short time later, Marley and Elena walked through

Hampton Park, taking in the colorful flowers lining the path they strolled along. Every few minutes, Marley would run up to an interesting flower for a sniff, the adorableness melting Elena's heart.

They finally reached the gazebo and took a seat in the shade for a moment of rest. "Marley, what do I do?" she asked as she smushed Marley's face in her hands, placing little kisses on her snout. "Things got *really* complicated."

She was desperate to talk to Mae, always her go-to person for things like this, but how could she admit she had feelings for her brother? That would not only break the girl-code, but she also wasn't sure how much damage it would do. Feelings for your best friend's sibling? That's a big no-no. Mae was the only person who she could count on—aside from her parents—and she worried about losing her. And for what? A harmless crush that probably was nothing?

It's not just a crush, and you know it.

She sighed and rubbed her eyes. How could she *not* have feelings for Jackson? At first, it seemed like he was pushing all her buttons to get a rise out of her like he did when they were younger. But once she embraced it rather than being scared of it, she found herself having fun. *A lot* of fun.

Jackson pushed her, sure. But all that pushing was forcing her to test new stuff. In the last few days, she found herself trying things she never would have. Engaged and entranced by this exploration, she realized she wasn't working as hard to fit in or be like everyone else. She wasn't worrying as much about their approval or perception of her. Elena was comfortable in her own skin, something she hadn't felt in so long, except when she was around her parents and Mae.

And now, Jackson.

He liked it. He liked *her*. And as she thought about it, so did the rest of the couples. They didn't treat her like some outsider. They treated her like one of them and damned if she didn't feel like she belonged for once.

A pang of guilt hit her in the gut. She felt terrible for lying to them after they'd been so accepting and open with her.

Jackson's friends were the same too. She had felt relaxed while around them, and enjoyed swapping childhood stories of Jackson. He'd been a good sport about it, even when she shared some of his most embarrassing moments. Rather than being humiliated, he had sat there quietly with a grin on his face, laughing along with his friends when Elena delivered the punchlines.

Come as you are. Jackson's words from last night sounded in her head. Maybe he didn't have a double-meaning for it, but it suddenly felt like there was.

The last few days felt so right. No pretenses. No worrying whether she said or did something wrong. No practiced responses or anything. That person she buried deep inside had taken over, and it was amazing. She felt lighter, freer. All the stress that came from worrying about what people thought of her had vanished. The heavy burden it created was noticeably gone.

And she didn't want to have it back.

It was all because of Jackson. She didn't know how she could have survived this week without him. It would have been a disaster. But with him by her side, making her believe in herself, she felt like she could handle anything.

Except maybe addressing these feelings she had for him.

A memory of his slow smile crept into her mind, making her body flush. She had it bad. Real bad.

"C'mon, Marley. Let's go visit mom and dad. Maybe they can help me not feel like a freaking psycho."

A quick walk back to the apartment and a short car-ride later, Marley and Elena pulled up to her parent's house on John's Island. Although it was early on a weekday, she knew her parents would be home. Her mom was semi-retired, and her dad only taught classes part-time during the summer.

She pushed open the front door and heard the sound of pots and pans moving in the kitchen and some light Spanish music floating through the air.

"Anyone home?" she called out.

"In the kitchen," her mom responded.

Elena followed the short hallway off the foyer to the lavish kitchen, perfect for an esteemed chef. Or her mom. She propped a hip on the counter and peered into the pots on the stovetop. "Whatcha making?"

"Beef goulash," her mother said as she nudged Elena out of the way to grab spices on the counter.

"That's...different." Her mother, a proud Italian woman, usually stuck to foods from her homeland. But Hungarian? That was unexpected.

"The girls and I are experimenting. Every week for the next three months, we're tasked with making different meals from different cultures. It's been a lot of fun," she said with delight.

Her mom and a few members of the neighborhood community had weekly get-togethers where they'd drink too much wine and chat about God knows what.

"Save me some?"

"Of course." Alma was in her element when she was in the kitchen, and her expert cooking skills didn't falter even with the new recipe on hand. She puttered about, grabbing ingredients and working around Elena as if she wasn't even there, her focus solely on making the best goulash she could.

"Ah, I thought I heard my beautiful daughter's voice," Rodrigo said as he danced into the room, grabbing Elena's hand and spinning her around.

She laughed. "What's all this about?"

"I've decided to teach dance lessons during the summer. It's time to infuse a little culture into the area, mija." He twisted his hips in tempo with the vibrant, upbeat music.

Alma shook her head in amusement as she busied herself over the goulash. "He's teaching flamenco and fandango."

"And tango," he added. "You should come to the classes one day. Show the group your tango skills taught by yours truly."

Elena grinned as she watched her father dance around the kitchen. "Funny you should say that. We'll be tango dancing tonight."

"You'll make your father proud, yes?" he asked as he stopped in front of the saucepan.

Alma slapped his hand away. "Don't you dare put your fingers in that, Ro."

He held his hands up defensively. "Never get between your mother and her cooking." He took a seat at the island. "What brings you here? Not that we're complaining."

She sighed and sat on the floor, petting an elated Marley. "Oh, you know, just wanted to say hi."

Alma turned and crossed her arms, a wooden spoon in one hand. "What's going on? Spill it."

"It's nothing," she said, dodging their stern looks.

Alma waved the spoon around. "Don't make me use this," her mother smiled with the empty threat.

Elena let out an exaggerated sigh. "Okay, okay. It's Jackson."

"Do you need me to take him out back?" Rodrigo asked as he threw his hands up like a boxer, jabbing the air.

She shook her head. "No, nothing like that. It's just..."

Her mother inspected her. "You have feelings for him?"

"How did you know?"

"It's all over your face, mija. My daughter is love-struck." She clutched her chest, delighted by the idea.

"I wouldn't say *love.*"

Alma cocked an eyebrow. "Start from the beginning."

Elena shrugged. "I don't know where to start. All I know is this fake relationship doesn't feel so fake anymore. There are moments off-camera that he does these things that make me think maybe he's got feelings for me, you know? I just don't know what's real and what's not anymore." She leaned her head against a cabinet and sighed. "I feel more like myself around him than I have in a *long*, long time. That could be it? Couldn't it, Mom? Maybe it's just the rush of feeling like myself and not actual feelings."

"I believe it's one in the same," her father, the romantic, supplied. "Maybe you haven't found 'the one' because you never felt you could be yourself around them. Jackson seems to appreciate you, yes?"

"If anything, he's always trying to get me to loosen up, so I'm more like myself." As she said the words, she suddenly realized she believed him. He had argued with her that everything he'd done back in high school was to get her to drop the persona she'd put on in front of others, and not because he was purposely trying to hurt her.

She thought he was just saying that to save face. But now, after spending all this time with him, she could see his perspective. Not only that, but she wondered if maybe he'd been right all along. If she'd just been herself all those years ago, things might have been different. Harder, likely. But at least she'd feel *right*.

Her parents exchanged a look.

"What?" she asked in annoyance.

"I know you struggled for some time when we came here years ago. Your identity was hard for you to find your place. But people like Mae and Jackson are good for you. They let you be your true self with no judgment. You need that in your life. If you're open and honest with yourself about who you are, then maybe you can make sense of these feelings you're having," Alma suggested.

Her father nodded.

Elena glared at them and stood. "What are you saying?"

"We're saying that it's time you embrace who you are," her father answered. "You spent so much time worrying about what other people thought. You were constantly trying to mold yourself to fit."

"You don't know what it was like. I was tormented when I got here. Shut out. I had to be flexible, so I wouldn't be lonely. You don't get it. You came down here and fit in just fine because you were a sought-after professor."

Rodrigo stood, his tanned skin taking on a pink hue. "You don't think we know what it's like to be shut out? My family came to America when I was just a boy. Where we landed was anything but welcoming. We had neighbors lining the streets outside our house with signs *protesting* our very existence. They didn't want 'our kind' in their neighborhood. For weeks, they were relentless. But you know what your Abuelo did?"

"What?"

"He stood his ground. He went outside and talked to them. He got to know them, and he made sure they knew who we were. It wasn't easy, facing that. But eventually, most people let it go. They saw that although we were different, we weren't a threat. Did our family become best friends with everyone in the neighborhood? Of course not. But we were accepted by a handful of families. And that's all that mattered."

"And what about when you came here? I was completely ostracized when we first got here. You both settled in so easily."

Alma gave the sauce another stir and rested the spoon on a holder. "We faced our challenges too, Elena. But we never wavered on who we are." She shared a look with Rodrigo. "People were chilly towards us when we went to department events or the neighborhood parties. No one seemed to know what to say to us, so we all stood around, smiling politely." She chuckled and shook her head at the memory.

"What did you do?"

"Your father brought his intellect and charm, telling stories of all the interesting places he'd traveled to as an archaeologist and all those wonderful discoveries he made."

Rodrigo stood next to Alma, wrapping a loving arm around her shoulders. "And your mother did what she does best, she cooked unforgettable Italian meals." He kissed Alma's head. "No one could resist. The right people warmed up to us, and they were our first friends here. Over time, we met more people, and some of them became friends too. That's what counts. You don't need everyone to like you. And not everyone deserves your attention and kindness. You need to seek out those who are worthy and hold on to them. Forget the rest."

Alma crossed the kitchen and took Elena's hands, a thoughtful look on her face. "You did your best writing and helped so many people when you were being yourself, right? Perhaps you hid behind your alias, but that gave you just enough safety to be your authentic self. That's why it took off, Elena. That's why people trust you, and that's why you got this book deal. It's time for you to see that it's not so scary to be who you are. The right people will embrace it. The wrong ones won't, and they'll try to make you feel less. But why would you want those people in your life anyway?"

Elena slipped her hands away and crossed her arms. "If you both felt I was being a fake this whole time, why didn't you say anything before now? Especially you, mom. You're a therapist."

Alma nodded, a patient look on her face. "And as a therapist, I don't push people to do something they aren't ready for. They need to recognize when change is needed and be open to it. All I can do is help them discover the issue and navigate through it. When you started the blog, I know you were scared about your identity coming out, but this has been a good thing for you. Being with Jackson is a good thing. You're realizing that you can be yourself and accepted. These are all good things."

After years of trying to be perfect, she worried it would be impossible to reverse what she'd done. Did she even know how to be the person she needed—*wanted*—to be? More importantly, would she be brave enough to embrace it?

The alarm on Elena's phone buzzed, indicating she needed to get back to her place and get ready for her date. "I've gotta go."

Her mother and father sandwiched her in a tight hug, despite her sour mood. "We love you very much, Elena. Don't you forget that," Rodrigo said as he placed a kiss on her head. Always the romantic, he added, "Just be yourself and follow your heart. That's all you can do in this life."

"I will, dad. Love you too."

Elena grabbed Marley and jumped in the car back to downtown, feeling like utter crap. She couldn't believe her parents let her go on like this for nearly twenty years. They knew she was struggling, but let her try and try again.

Then again, that tracks with how her parents were. They were loving and supportive. The best parents she could ask for. But they didn't pry. They didn't push. And they didn't force her to do things she didn't want to. They stood back and allowed her to make her own decisions, supportive no matter what the outcome.

Maybe she could have used a little prying and pushing through. Twenty years of wasted effort?

She felt defeated at the thought. How would her life have been if they had pointed it out sooner? Sure, Mae had always made comments about it when they were in their teens, but her parents' perspective would have mattered. Maybe even made a difference.

She couldn't have felt worse.

Pulling into her parking spot, she and Marley raced up the stairs to her apartment, only to find Brittany waiting by the door. Elena skidded to a stop before plowing into her.

"What are you doing here?" Elena asked.

Brittany's fake smile was a cross between a scowl and a cat-got-the-canary. She flipped her tousled blonde curls over her shoulder. "Just wanted to stop by and see how my *favorite* writer was doing on her week off."

Elena eyed her suspiciously. "If it's work-related, it will have to wait until next week when I'm back from my PTO." She dug in her purse and fished out her keys, trying to subtly push past Brittany and get into her apartment.

"No, *Ella.* I don't think it can wait."

Elena's hand froze halfway to the door lock, keys

dangling from her fingers. "What did you just say?" she breathed without facing Brittany.

"I just couldn't believe we had a celebrity working with us all this time," Brittany added sarcastically.

Time stood still. Elena turned, panic coursing through her body. "I don't know what you're talking about."

Brittany cocked her head and studied her. "So full of secrets. The famous Ella from *Always, Ella*, huh? I just find it so interesting how I've sat next to you for nearly two years, and you've never told me all about your lucrative side hustle." She raised an eyebrow. "Funny. Reading your posts seems like you're a pretty busy girl. How would you juggle all your fame with the promotion we're up for?" Brittany tapped her chin thoughtfully. "Come to think of it, this might be considered a conflict of interest. Our clients like wholesome, respectable professionals. They might feel wary working with relationship guru Ella. Just doesn't quite fit our brand at Holy City Advertising."

Elena's blood ran cold as she thought back to all the posts she'd written as Ella. Although not many, there were definitely a handful providing sex advice. She hadn't even thought about how that would reflect on her company or herself as a professional once her identity was revealed. She'd been so caught up in the momentum of the blog taking off and the book deal, she didn't consider talking to her boss about it.

I've fucked up. And now Brittany's going to make me pay.

Sweat trickled down her neck. Brittany, her nemesis, was not only going to out her but was going to cause her to lose her job. Despite the contract Christopher had negotiated for her, she couldn't afford to lose her income. "It's not like that—"

Brittany pulled out her phone and started to dial. "Maybe we should get Mark to weigh in on this."

"Please. Don't do this."

"Save it, Elena." She narrowed her eyes and stuffed her phone back into her purse. "Now I'm going to give this to you straight. You're nothing but a diversity hire at the agency. Because human resources needs to hit certain numbers, they brought you on. But you know what? That's crap. You're taking good jobs from deserving people. Your writing is subpar at best, but you only get the credit and attention because of who you are, not because you're worth it."

Tears stung Elena's eyes. She swiped them away. "What do you want, Brittany?"

"I want you to bow out of the promotion we're up for. Tell Mark you don't want to move up anymore. You do that, and I won't blow up your little side project. I'll at least give you the courtesy to tell him yourself about being Ella. Maybe he won't fire you on the spot if you go to him first."

Elena stood there, speechless. Her stomach clenched, and she became lightheaded.

"You have until the end of the week to get me your answer. Either you pull your name from the pitch and the promotion, or I air your dirty laundry." She smiled sweetly. "Talk soon!"

She sauntered down the steps without a backward glance, leaving Elena absolutely shattered.

17

JACKSON

"Jackson, my man!" Rich greeted as Jackson walked through the open garage door of their small warehouse on James Island.

Rich was one of the handful of people who worked at Jackson's company, and one that proved to be an exceptional employee. Rich had been a burnout when Jackson found him, spending his days and nights living on the beach, with no real direction in life. He'd dropped out of high school, could barely keep a job, and was more than a little lost in life.

One day, a year into starting his business, he found Rich passed out in the summer heat on a quiet section of Sullivan's Island. He had been drunk, dehydrated, and the worse for wear. Jackson took him back to his place, cleaned him up, and learned his story.

Rich was a foster kid who had been chewed up and spit out by the system. Once he turned eighteen, he was on his own. With no support system or real direction, he'd floated through life for about four years before Jackson found him.

Jackson knew he was a risk when he offered him a job.

The guy had no ties to anything. No sense of responsibility. And that all stemmed from the fact that no one gave a shit about him his whole life.

Until Jackson.

Within a year, Jackson saw Rich flourish. He cleaned himself up, got sober, and took real pride in the work that he did. All he needed was someone to believe in him and offer a little faith. That was five years ago, and they were still going strong.

Jackson and Rich did a complicated high-five-hand-shake thing they'd made up years ago. "How's it going?"

Jackson wandered over to the products currently being packaged on their production line, tracing a hand on the packed boxes ready to be shipped worldwide. Maybe their space was small, but their reach was mighty. Over the years, Jackson saw the potential his business could have, and now he was in a spot to take them there.

Rich handed him a thick stack of papers. "New orders. Just from today."

Jackson flipped through them, completely floored. "This is incredible."

"It's really coming together," Rich said with pride, his chest puffing up slightly. "Between your travel and the new regional sales rep in the US, we're really building the momentum." He eyed the overwhelming boxes stacked in the back. "We're just about ready to outgrow this place."

"I'm chatting with a commercial realtor this week. He'll look into local options and spaces in neighboring states."

"Hopefully, you find something soon because we can't ship them as fast as we have them produced. Have you chosen new freight options yet?"

"I have a couple meetings scheduled for tomorrow," he replied as he flipped through the orders.

Jackson took a seat at a nearby computer, checking on inventory and sales orders. It was beyond anything he could have ever imagined when he started this business. And the one person he couldn't wait to share the news with was Elena.

"I'll admit, I'm surprised to see you in. I thought you had that video shoot or whatever." Rich took a seat opposite Jackson, busying himself with origami made from sticky notes.

Jackson swiped the pad away. "You're going to put us out of business with how much waste you produce with these." He laughed. "Yeah, I have to get going soon for my date with Elena, but I wanted to check in on things."

"What's on today's agenda?"

"The guys had to come up with a date that was meaningful to the women. Something that showed we really pay attention."

Rich placed a finished crane on the desk between them. "And what did you come up with?"

"Elena always wanted to be a writer. She talked about it incessantly since we were kids. So I plan on taking her around parts of Charleston that inspired different books or authors. I'm hoping it will encourage her to feel better about her writing. To spark something."

Rich let out a low whistle. "Wow. You've got it bad."

Jackson made a face. "What do you mean?"

"I'm just saying, that's some deep shit right there. Most guys would take a girl out to her favorite restaurant and maybe get some flowers she likes. Or a small gift he saw her eyeing. But this? You're going to ruin her for all other men. No one's going to be able to top this."

Jackson's stomach clenched at the thought of her with someone else. Yeah, he knew going into it that this was a temporary thing. Pretend. But something between them the last couple of days had shifted. He could no longer think of her as Mae's friend, the girl he grew up around. Now, he could only think about the way her lips tasted, the feel of her smooth skin, and how her eyes turned into little crescent moons when she genuinely smiled. The sweet sound of her laugh and how she looked at him in a way that made him feel like she was really seeing him.

Those brown eyes—they stared straight into his soul at times. And in those moments, he felt like he couldn't breathe.

How could he ever let her go? Let her be with someone else?

Jackson let out a small uneasy laugh. "Yeah, man. That's the plan. She's my girl."

If only it were true. Jackson's feelings for her had grown in unexpected ways. He felt out of control. Every waking moment was flooded with thoughts of Elena. He'd assumed the "can't eat, can't sleep" thing was bullshit, but was quickly realizing how true it was.

Problem was, he wasn't sure if it was one-sided. Maybe she was putting on a great act for the cameras. After all, her career depended on making their relationship believable. The stakes were high.

But what about last night at Shua and Brandon's house?

There were no cameras around then, and yet, she seemed completely at ease with him. It almost felt like bringing here there was a casual first date. That is until he captured her gaze across the fire while he was strumming the guitar. Her soulful eyes had a glint of emotion that couldn't be faked.

Nothing about the look they shared was casual.

There was *something* there. It was growing between them. He just knew it.

"So, did you think about my offer?" Jackson asked, trying to bring them back to a safe topic.

Rich rubbed the back of his neck, not quite meeting Jackson's eyes. "Yeah. I talked it over with Jen."

A few weeks back, Jackson had asked Rich if he was open to taking his spot on the world tour. Rich had always expressed his interest in traveling, especially since he never had the means or opportunity to do it as a child. He hadn't been shy about throwing his hat in the ring if and when a spot ever opened up.

With Jackson's plans to expand the business, he needed to be rooted in one spot for a while so he could focus. He finally gave Rich the green light that he could take on the community-aspect of their work if it's what he wanted for the next step in his career.

"And?"

"Listen, man," Rich started, letting out a long sigh. "You know Jen and I just got married a few months ago. I brought it up to her, and the sentiment was that she wanted to start a family. She can't do that if I'm not around to...ya know."

Jackson made a face. "Yeah, I get the picture."

"And even if I made the most of the time, I was home to...ya know..." Jackson rolled his eyes. "I wouldn't feel right leaving her for stretches of time if she did get pregnant," he continued. "This woman is my life. She looked through the piece of shit I was and saw something good."

"Hey, man," Jackson clapped him on the shoulder. "You were never a piece of shit. You were just dealt a crappy hand."

Rich nodded. "And I'm grateful for what you've done for

me. You taking a chance on me turned my life around, but..."

"But you're ready for the next step in your life, and that means family."

Rich nodded, a look of disappointment on his face. "I've never had one, and now that I have the opportunity, I want to be the best dad and husband I can be. I like knowing I have somewhere reliable to come home to each night and that someone who loves me is waiting there. You gave me a stable life I never thought I'd ever get. Selfishly, I want to embrace every single moment—even the mundane ones.

"The opportunity you've offered is a dream. Jen and I took some time to imagine all the places we could go. But as I spent these last couple of weeks thinking about it, I realized it's not *my* dream. My dream is to set down roots, start a family, and give my kids the best life growing up. I want to give them the things I never had. I'm sorry."

"It's okay." Jackson leaned back into the chair, his mind reeling with what he could do next. "It was a lot for me to ask of you, especially with Jen in the picture. From my experience, I can tell you that travel can be demanding, and for most people, even the most beautiful places in the world won't stop you from feeling homesick." He stood and pat Rich on the back to show no hard feelings. "I get it. And I'm glad you finally found a home you never want to leave."

Relief flooded Rich's face as he stood. "Thanks for understanding."

Jackson watched Rich retreat as he went to tend to the production line. A sense of panic washed over him. He hadn't lied to Elena when he said he was considering settling somewhere, and Charleston was high on the list.

Near her. With her.

He had been banking on Rich taking his place on the

travel front. Jackson thought it was a done deal. Finding out that wasn't the case nearly knocked the wind out of him.

Just a few weeks ago, Jackson wouldn't have minded. He'd been traveling for years now and loved every minute of it. In fact, the thought of settling anywhere—especially his hometown—would have had him booking even *longer* trips. Although the warehouse was here, he knew—or at least hoped—they'd grow out of it. And now that they were, he realized he could relocate his expanding business anywhere.

Normally, being in one place for too long sent a shiver up his spine. It was unfathomable. But now, the thought of *not* being able to set roots created a heaviness in the pit of his stomach.

It wasn't just the plans for the business growth that weighed on him. Now, it was the thought of not being here to see if what was building between him and Elena was the real deal.

The thought of not seeing her everyday crushed him in a way he didn't think possible.

How did this happen?

18

ELENA

"She said what?" Mae screeched mid-bite of her sandwich. A tomato slipped from the bottom and plopped onto her plate.

"She basically said that the only reason I was hired was because I'm Hispanic." Elena leaned over the island in Mae's kitchen and snagged the tomato, chewing it before Mae could protest.

As soon as Brittany left, Elena and Marley walked directly to Mae's apartment. When Mae was in between contracts, she typically worked on freelance projects at home. Thankfully, Jackson was at his warehouse when Elena burst through the door in tears. She wasn't ready to share that humiliation with him.

"That bitch," Mae muttered, slapping Elena's hand away from another fallen tomato. "That's a horrible thing for her to say."

"Am I really that talentless? Maybe I deserved to be fired." Elena dropped her face into her hands. "God. I made such a mess of things," she groaned.

Anger flashed across Mae's face. "Do you really believe

that? Because if you do, I may have to smack you again." Mae put down her sandwich and locked eyes with Elena, her expression serious. "Listen, you know that Mark and the rest of the team don't think that, right? You can't let people like her get to you. There will always be shit people with small minds like Brittany in the world. But just because their perception is wildly skewed doesn't make a single word of what she said true. Knowing her, she's probably just trying to throw you offer your game, so you'll back down from the promotion. Seems like a sneaky move she'd pull."

Marley nudged Elena's hand as if to say, "Listen to Mae. She knows what she's talking about."

"Every time I think I'm ready to let it all go and just be who I am, someone or something comes around and reminds me that I'm not good enough. It's hard, you know?" Elena's shoulders sunk as she exhaled a breath. Her gaze darted away, not feeling quite comfortable looking into Mae's eyes as she spoke the little truth that always ate away at her.

Mae slid her plate over, knowing Elena's love language was food. "I know. We all have our insecurities and hang-ups."

"You never did. Even when you very dramatically came out to your parents."

Mae laughed at the memory. "Yeah. I don't think they were expecting me to bring my girlfriend at the time to their very upscale dinner with dad's associates, especially after they'd been trying to pawn me off on one of his colleague's sons all summer."

It had been senior year of high school, and Mae's parents had been on her about finding a nice guy who could offer her a stable future.

"I still wish I had been there to see the look on their

faces," Elena commented as she took a bite of the sandwich Mae had offered.

Mae rolled her eyes. "As if a guy was the only way to ensure a good future for myself. I was eighteen for Christ's sake. I was about to go off to college. What'd they think? It was the forties, and I was just going to school to meet myself a suitable man?" Mae scoffed. "It's been over a decade now, and they're still warming up to the idea. They aren't dicks like Brittany, but they still have their moments. Thankfully, they're getting better."

"And you seemed to deal with that just fine. Why can't I?"

Mae snatched the sandwich back before Elena ate it all, dropping a piece of turkey on the floor for Marley. "Because being bisexual wasn't a hang-up for me. If they couldn't deal with it, that said more about them than me."

"I wish I could be a badass like you," Elena said, knocking her shoulder with Mae's.

"I've been hoping after all these years my badassness would have rubbed off on you. Doesn't seem to be taking," she joked. "So, what's on the agenda for today's shoot?"

"Your brother apparently has to plan some secret date for me. Something to show he listens to the small details." She rolled her eyes. "I'm assuming he got intel from you."

Mae's eyebrows shot up. "No, not at all. He hasn't even mentioned it to me."

"Really?"

"Love my bro, but God only knows what he's going to do. As far as I know, he hasn't dated anyone in a while, let alone put together something romantic. Hopefully, he doesn't make an embarrassment of himself with some lame attempt."

Elena shrugged. "He's actually been kinda great. At first,

he was throwing me into all sorts of situations. I thought he was trying to humiliate me, but I realized he was just trying to get me to loosen up. Apparently, I was 'stiff' on camera and 'standoffish' to the group."

Mae snorted.

"What?" she asked defensively.

"I say this with love, but you're like that whenever you're out of your comfort zone. Which is like *always*."

"It is not!"

"Whatever you say." Mae got up to rinse her plate in the sink. "What are you doing after your date?"

"Meeting with the rest of the group after our dates to tango at that new brewery on East Bay Street."

"What time will that be done?"

"Not sure. Maybe ten?"

Mae spun around and smiled. "Great. Then you and Jackson can meet me at the bar afterward. My friend's band is playing."

Elena's eyes lit up. "Oh my God. Is it the band that does all the covers from our high school angst age?"

"You bet your ass. Every emotionally-fueled emo, punk, alt-rock, ska song teenage you could possibly dream of."

"I've been dying to see them."

"Well, now's your chance. Bring Jackson, too. He used to play with those guys."

"We'll be there." Elena grabbed Marley's leash and headed for the door. "I gotta get going. I have to meet Jackson in a couple of hours."

"Have fun," Mae sing-songed as she sat back at her laptop to work.

—

"When they said romantic date, I wasn't expecting it to start in a graveyard," Elena commented.

Despite the bright late-afternoon sun, the overgrown Unitarian Cemetery had a mix of beauty and creep factor. Elena could smell the fragrant flowers coming from the vines, shrubs, and trees overwhelming the space. The church wanted it this way—a way to show that everything goes back to nature. Even with the cleared pathways, something about the cemetery felt forgotten. Eerie.

Jackson laughed and took her hand in his. She flushed at the feel of it, how the roughness of his palm and strong fingers contrasted with hers. Somehow, she felt safe with his hand holding hers. He could lead her anywhere—maybe straight into the fiery pits of hell with how this cemetery looked—and she'd go willingly.

Because she was with him.

She peeked over her shoulder when she heard footsteps coming from behind. The camera crew had been paired down to only two, a cameraman and boom operator. The larger crew had been split up to follow the other couples and to give a more intimate feel to the dates. Well, as intimate as it could feel with a camera and mic hovering around.

"Just trust me," he said, leading them further into the cemetery before eventually stopping in front of an unmarked grave. "Here."

Elena scanned it, a look of skepticism crossing her face. "Okay? Is something supposed to happen?"

Jackson rolled his eyes, his signature slow grin spreading across his face. "For someone who's so passionate about writing, I assumed you knew your history. You know Edgar Allen Poe's poem *Annabel Lee*?"

"Vaguely. Why?"

"It's rumored that the poem was about a woman he met while stationed here in Sullivan's Island. Apparently, her father forbade her from seeing him, so their affair was a secret. They'd often meet here. When he got transferred to Virginia, she died from yellow fever."

"That's so sad."

He shook his head. "Gets worse. The father was so spiteful that he didn't even want Edgar to see her in death. He 'buried' her in several unmarked graves throughout Charleston—here being one of them—so Poe never knew which was hers. But he came here anyway, to this unmarked grave because it was their spot, and grieved her. It's rumored that she haunts this place."

Elena raised her eyebrows, feeling unsure. "I'm all for ghost stories. But remind me how a story about heartbreak, death, and ghosts are supposed to be romantic."

Jackson squeezed her hand. "So impatient." He gave her a quick kiss on the cheek. She did everything she could to not reach out and trace where his lips had been like a lovesick teen. "Like I said, trust me. This is just one stop on our tour."

"Tour? So, there will be more graveyards and ghosts?"

He smirked and pulled her along without answering.

Over the next couple of hours, Jackson had taken her around to several places in Charleston. Tradd Street, which was the setting for a book by Karen White. The American Theater on King Street, which was one of the locations used in the movie version of Nicholas Sparks' book *The Notebook*, followed by a stop at Boone Hall Plantation, which was Ally's house in that same movie.

"Everything okay?" Jackson asked after they wandered

the grounds, taking in the beautiful Avenue of Oaks and views of the marshes.

They had stopped in the Cotton Dock building, one of Boone Hall's buildings used for weddings, to get out of the sun. Despite it only being mid-June, the cloudless sky allowed the strong rays to penetrate her skin, making it feel much hotter than it was.

She took a sip of water from the bottle she had bought at the cafe and nodded, shooting her eyes towards the camera crew. "Fine, yeah." She shook her head slightly to indicate she didn't want to talk in front of the cameras.

Eyeing a door to a bathroom in the corner, she addressed the crew. "Hey, guys. I need a break. I'm feeling a little woozy from the sun. Why don't you take ten and grab yourself a drink or something? I'm sure you're dying in all that black clothing."

"Stephanie said you can't leave our sight. Doesn't want us to miss anything," the boom operator said.

Crap.

"Trust me, you're not going to miss anything. I'm just going to take a second." She pointed out the window. "Plus, there's a stand right there to get water and stuff. You won't *technically* be out of sight."

"I could use a drink," the cameraman commented as he dropped the camera from his shoulder and shook out his arms, sweat darkening his shirt.

"Alright. I guess," the boom guy conceded and made his way for the door, the camera guy in tow.

"What was that about?" Jackson asked, confusion crossing his face.

When Elena saw the coast was clear, she grabbed Jackson's hand and dragged him into the bathroom. She closed the door behind them and flicked a switch. Light showered them from above the vanity mirror. Her body was pressed firmly against his. She tried to inch away, but the bathroom space was tight.

How did brides fit their dresses in here?

"I didn't want to talk about it in front of the camera crew."

"Okay..." he trailed off. "So, why are we stuffed in this closet pretending to be a bathroom?"

"Just in case their magical boom could hear us from yards away."

He rubbed the back of his neck. "I don't think that's how it works—"

"Sh. Do you want to hear what's wrong or not?"

His face turned more serious. "Yeah. What's up? You seem a little more tense than usual today."

Elena bit her bottom lip. "It's my coworker, Brittany." She gave him a condensed version of their confrontation earlier this morning, leaving out some of the hurtful things Brittany had said.

"Sounds like this is Brittany's problem. Not yours," he finally said, tenderness in his voice.

Elena took a deep breath, her breasts grazing Jackson's chest in the tight quarters of the space. She looked up, finding his blue eyes staring back at her. Inspecting her. An expression on his face she couldn't quite read.

"I'm thinking of letting her have the promotion." Elena looked away and shrugged a shoulder. "I'm just tired of constantly going head-to-head with her, you know? Sure, the book deal is exciting, but it's not stable enough for me to feel comfortable losing my income. For all I know, it could flop. I need to keep my job another year or so to see how it goes."

"Hey," Jackson said, his voice low. He reached up a hand

and cupped her face, lifting it slightly so she would look at him again. A look of determination filled his features. "She only wishes she had a fraction of your talent; otherwise, she wouldn't stoop so low—push you around." He tucked a strand of her hair behind her ear. "But you need to do what you need to do. If you think she'd really jeopardize your career, then I'll support whatever decision you make."

Appreciation flooded through her. "This is a tough decision."

Jackson's free arm wrapped around her waist, and he gently pulled her closer. "We'll figure it out, Elena. Let's just enjoy today together. Just...stay with me in this moment." His voice was a whisper now, his eyes dragging from hers to her lips.

He was so close. Elena couldn't stop herself from leaning more into his hand that still cupped her face, her eyes fluttering closed at the tender way he held her. His breathing shifted to slow and deep. She wanted to give into this moment. Give into him.

She opened her eyes, seeing his blue irises darkening as he grabbed her around her waist, pulling her closer to him. The feel of his hard chest pressed against hers was addicting. Strong and steady.

Elena wanted to kiss him. She was dying to see if that heat and spark still existed between them when there weren't cameras rolling.

When the kiss was just for them.

"Hey, Ella, you alright in there?" a voice from outside the door sounded. A few knocks followed.

Their moment was over. Jackson let her go, giving her an inch of space. And within that inch of space, it felt like the whole world was wedged between them. She ached to reach out, to pull him back to her.

"Yeah. Ella just needed to splash some water on her neck. She got lightheaded," Jackson lied as he grabbed the doorknob. He flashed a quick look at her as if he wasn't ready to leave their private little space, and then opened the door.

"You okay enough to get some shots by the water?" the cameraman asked.

Elena forced a smile. "Sure. No problem."

"Great. Let's get over there. We're running behind. Stephanie will kill us if we mess up her schedule."

After they filmed additional footage and left Boone Hall, Jackson drove them for a quick stop to Isle of Palms, the setting for *The Beach House* by Mary Alice Monroe. An hour later, he finally let them settle in Waterfront Park in downtown Charleston.

"Well, that was a jam-packed date," she commented as she helped him lay out a blanket for the picnic he had prepared.

She took a seat after smoothing it out and watched as he dug into the picnic basket, pulling out different fruits, cheeses, meats, bread, crackers, and even wine he'd secretly poured into a nondescript bottle.

After making them each a plate, he settled next to her and looked out to the harbor. "I know it seemed random, but I wanted to show you something."

"What's that?" she asked in between bites of smoked gouda and crackers.

"That there's inspiration all around you. I know you said Brad wasn't supportive of your writing. Mae might have mentioned that he was likely the reason you tabled the novel you were working on."

Elena shrugged and hung her head down, but said nothing.

"I wanted to show you that Charleston has inspired so many writers. Love stories. Poems from a heartbroken man. Mysteries. Books about self-discovery. Brad was a dick, and I hate that he made you doubt your passions. But you don't need Brad. Hell, you don't need anyone. I wanted you to see that. I wanted you to know that you could simply walk down the street or go to the beach and remember all the stories and authors based here." Jackson placed a finger under her chin and gently pushed up, so she made eye contact. "And that you could be one of them too."

His words warmed her. What had seemed to be a completely random day was anything but. Jackson had taken the time to do his research, not only on the places he was showing her but also about what made her tick. And the fact that he didn't even consult Mae—someone who would have made it a hundred times easier for him to figure this all out—made this even more meaningful.

It was true. Brad had made her second-guess writing her novel. Couple that with Brittany's undermining ways, and Elena had all but given up. It had been over a year since she had opened the manuscript that was now collecting dust on her laptop. Only a quarter way in and she had abandoned it all because Brad made it seem like a silly hobby.

And here was Jackson, showing her that her writing mattered. Encouraging her never to give up and to not give in to people like Brad or Brittany. Her insides fluttered at that, and whatever murky feelings she was experiencing towards him these last few days were becoming crystal clear.

She was falling in love with him.

"Thank you," she breathed out. "This was the best date ever." And she meant it.

"Anything for my girl." He poured her a glass of wine, and they clinked glasses. Wrapping an arm around her shoulders, they looked out to the water as the sky lit up with vibrant orange-reds, leading to pinks and purples. Charleston sunsets like this were always the most impressive to watch. And as Jackson pulled her closer to him, it just made it that much better.

19

JACKSON

After the sun had set, Jackson and Elena cleaned up the picnic and dumped it into his Jeep before walking down East Bay to the nearby brewery. Jackson held open the heavy wooden door and followed in behind her, finding the space transformed.

Tables had been pushed to the sides, creating an open area on the worn wooden floors. A small band was assembling on a makeshift stage adjacent to the bar. The camera crew, Stephanie, and Celeste sat huddled in a corner, likely talking over the events for tonight.

Jackson watched Elena cross the room to where the other couples sat at the bar. Her posture was rigid, her smile wooden. He reached out and grabbed her hand, twirling her back to him. She squealed in surprise.

"What's going on?" she asked after she righted herself.

He cocked an eyebrow. "I should be asking you that. What's going on in that pretty little head of yours? You were all smiles just a few minutes ago."

Her shoulders sunk, and her lackluster smile faltered

more. She glanced quickly at the bar and back to him. "I'm just thinking about what's going to happen when I talk to my boss. We have some time to do damage control before the big Ella reveal happens, but he might not think it's worth the effort."

She peered back to the group again, who were all chatting merrily as they took shots and laughed. "I'm going to have to tell them too. It's the right thing to do. Keeping secrets and lying only give people like Brittany the ability to hold it over me. I'm never going to find my self-worth if I let people control me like that. It's time to come clean." Her lips lifted into a sad smile. "They're going to hate me," she said, her voice small.

Jackson rubbed his hands up and down the soft skin of her arms, hoping to soothe her somehow. "They're not going to hate you, Elena."

"They will. I spent this week getting to know them. All their hopes and worries. Their intimate moments. I've guided them through issues as if I was some expert in a healthy relationship. Meanwhile, I made it all up. They *trusted* me, and I lied." She shrugged and bit her lip. "If I lose their trust, I have nobody to blame but myself."

He stooped lower, capturing her tormented gaze. "You can't think like that."

"I just don't see how they could feel anything otherwise." Elena let out a dry laugh and pushed her hair behind her ears. "God, I'm going to need to talk to Christopher about this too before I tell them. This could blow up in my face. Rachel and Celeste might kill me if this gets out."

"Well, like you said. It's time to be in control of your life. If you lose their trust and it causes a rift with your publisher, it will suck. But you're coming clean now, and that's gotta count for something." He held his head up with determination. "You get to write your own story here. And no matter what happens, I'll be by your side."

He thought he saw a small glimmer of defiance in her eyes, a hint of the fiery girl he knew was deep inside of her. Maybe there was some hope for her after all.

"Ella! Jackson! Get over here and take a shot with us," Maritza yelled, waving her hand frantically as if it was hard to get their attention in the nearly empty space.

Jackson grabbed Elena's hand and gave it a squeeze. "Let's just enjoy tonight. No more worrying about Brittany or your job or telling the truth. You'll find the right moment. Okay?"

She nodded.

"What are we having here?" Jackson asked as they approached the bar.

"Tequila," Hari said while shoving a small plastic shot glass into Jackson's hand.

"At a brewery?"

"It's all part of the tango experience. Apparently, tequila is much better than beer when it comes to loosening up our hips for dancing."

"I can attest to that," Elena commented with a small laugh. "Wow. You guys look like you're having fun." She took a shot from Natalie.

"Today was great," Ana said. "The whole week has been, actually. Zach and I desperately needed a trip like this."

"Agreed," Maritza said as she and Max held out their shots.

"Ditto," Natalie added, clinking the cheap shot glass against theirs. She eyed Jackson and Elena, who still had their glasses down on the bar. "C'mon, guys. Glasses up. Let's cheers to an amazing week."

"And to Ella," Maritza added with an appreciative smile. "You've been nothing but kind and supportive this whole time."

The group nodded in agreement.

"To Ella!" they cheered in unison as they threw back their shots.

Elena shot Jackson a quick look, one of regret and panic.

Stephanie strolled up with a few members of the camera crew, her clipboard in hand. "How were your dates? The crew showed me some of the footage. Good stuff."

They all murmured something along the lines of their dates being good.

"Cool. Well, in a minute, we'll have the dance instructors Juan and Carlos get you started. Juan will take the ladies, and the guys will be with Carlos for the first part."

"Aren't we supposed to be dancing *together*?" Natalie asked as she waved down the bartender for a refill.

"Yeah. But we want to teach you a few moves before you get paired up." A slow smile spread across Stephanie's face. "Your dates were sweet. Now it's time to bring the heat."

The tango was undeniably sexy if you had the right partner. Exactly what was needed to get Elena's mind off her worries.

Jackson knew Elena could dance. It was in her blood. When they were growing up, Elena would come over to Jackson's parents' house with some new moves she'd picked up from her father, trying to get Mae to learn something.

Jackson grinned at the memory. Mae was awful. Worse than awful. In her last failed attempt, she threw up her hands and claimed she was plagued with "boring white girl hips" and would never be able to dance the way Elena did.

He pressed his lips together, trying to suppress a laugh. In his travels around the world, he would immerse himself in the local culture. After a full day of surfing and talking to the locals, they'd often invited him to their local watering holes. Many were divey, hidden holes in the wall. The drinks were strong but cheap. The crowd was lively. The music festive. And the dancing was *hot*.

More often than not, the women were eager to teach Jackson some of their sexiest dances, pressing their bodies against him, twisting around him. After years of it, he had actually gotten pretty good. No longer was he just keeping up with the basic steps, he now felt confident enough to put his own fun flair on the dances.

And Elena had no idea.

This is going to be fun.

After the couples dispersed with their respective instructor and they learned the basic steps—ones Jackson pretended not to know because he saw Elena glancing at him every so often—the instructors concluded their quick lessons.

"Alright, everyone," Carlos said, his accent strong. "It's time to tango! Grab your partner, and let's get started." He turned to the band, giving them instructions to start.

The music swelled around them, pulsing through his body, as he slowly crossed the room to Elena. He watched her body sway to the music, a soft expression on her face as she listened to something familiar. Something she loved.

He took her in his arms, holding them out the way he learned in those beachside clubs in South and Central America.

Elena gave him a surprised, but appreciative look. "You've got some great posture. Carlos must have been a good teacher."

He grinned. "Yeah. Something like that."

They started with the basic steps. Jackson took a slow

step forward, Elena followed with a step back. Another step forward. Then to the right, and a slow drag of the foot. He could tell Elena was taking it easy on him, moving cautiously as if expecting him to be new to this. She watched his feet, probably half expecting him to get the steps wrong or to step on her.

The couples around them fumbled awkwardly. Laughing as they bumped into each other. Max dramatically spun Maritza, giving up completely on trying to get the steps right.

"You're doing good," Elena commented, still watching their feet.

"Elena, look at me," he said quietly.

As soon as her brown eyes locked on his, he let her have it. No longer were the steps stiff and measured. Now he put his body into it. His heart.

He moved fluidly, pulling her closer to him as he did so. His hands ran along her body as he dipped her and brought her back up, their faces only millimeters from each other. A look of surprise crossed her face.

"Jackson?"

He grinned slowly and spun her, pulling her back against him again. He licked his lips and cocked his head. "What's wrong, Elena? Do I have more rhythm than a Spanish girl?"

Her mouth dropped open. "How?" she choked out.

"I picked up a few things while traveling. Think you can keep up?"

She lifted an eyebrow, her confidence flaring as she made the decision to rise to the challenge. He loved that gleam in her eyes when she was feeling competitive. "Do *you*?"

Jackson brought his face closer to her, a mere whisper

between their lips. He looked her deep in the eyes, watching her swallow, her mouth parting. "I guess we'll find out."

He pushed her away slightly so she'd fall into a corte step, both of them lunging. Jackson pulled her back, and Elena wrapped her leg around his hips as he dipped her low, her back arching in his hands.

There was a fire in her eyes, every teasing look was driving him wild. Her sundress fluttered around them as she spun, dipped, and wrapped her legs around him. It was by far the most erotic thing he had ever experienced in his life.

Every movement had her body molding with his. They moved seamlessly, their bodies pulling together like two magnets. She ran her hands down his neck, along his arms. He did the same to her. They danced in unison, their fore-heads nearly pressed together as they looked into each other's eyes, trusting each other's bodies to know where to go.

The world faded away. All Jackson could hear was the music surrounding them and the sound of Elena's breath. His gaze broke from hers, watching the swell of her breasts as he dipped her low again. He leaned down, trailing his lips along the soft skin of her throat, tasting a bit of her sweet-ness mixed with sweat. Her thick hair, now affected by their exertion, transformed into beautiful wild waves.

For a moment, he could imagine it's what her hair would look like if he got her naked and made her the happiest, most satisfied woman on the planet.

The thought of her moaning his name had blood shifting south at breakneck speed.

He swung her back up, her eyes darkened in the dim bar. Her pupils dilated as she watched his mouth.

She licked her lips and let out a breath. And that's when he knew she was just as turned on as he was.

Everything in Jackson's body screamed to take her. Every time she wrapped her leg around his waist, knowing only his jeans and a thin scrap of her panties were between them was enough to make him crazy.

Their near-miss moments this week had been sweet. Innocent. Romantic, even. But this was something entirely different. It's as if every fantasy he had about Elena this week had culminated in this dance, trying to show her that he was worth it. Trying to entice her to kiss him. Feel him. To give in.

Elena was tempting him in ways he had never been. Seeing her like this, feeling her like this, sucked the air from his lungs. He wanted to throw her over his shoulder cave-man-style, drag her back to her apartment, and bury himself in her.

The music around them died, pulling them out of their private dancing foreplay. Elena's arms loosened around his neck, her body pulled away slightly.

That's when he heard it—the clapping.

Jackson dragged his eyes away from Elena and noticed they were the only ones on the dance floor. The couples, camera crew, and instructors were circled around them, amazement crossing their faces.

"Holy shit!" Natalie said, "If I knew dancing could be *that* hot, Hari and I would have started sooner."

"Yeah. You guys are 'ship goals. Your chemistry is unbelievable," Maritza commented.

Jackson turned back to her—his hand still holding hers—finding her cheeks flushed and eyes wild.

Her lips tilted upwards—just the slightest smile—something that told him she shared whatever dirty, insanely sexy thoughts were going through his head.

But as she tucked a strand of hair behind her ear, her

smile becoming full-blown and making her eyes turn into those little crescent moons, he realized something else.

He was in love with Elena Lucia.

20

ELENA

E lena was on fire. Her heart thumped in her chest at a record-breaking pace. Who knew Jackson had those moves? Every touch and every look was deliberate, made to entice. To tease. To flirt.

Normally, she would have felt embarrassed to have danced like that—dripping of pure sex—on display for all to see. But her brain couldn't even think straight to worry about it. All it could focus on was how she could get Jackson to touch her like that again. For real this time.

Alone.

The rest of the evening had gone well, even though every bit of her wanted to rip her clothes off and jump Jackson. It was erotic to be so close to him, wanting him so badly, but having to keep it together because they were in public. After a quick drink with the group after filming, they'd all gone their separate ways to enjoy a night on the town.

Finally, she had him to herself.

As he took her hand and led her down the quiet side streets of downtown on the way to meet Mae at a dive bar, she wondered what his reaction would be if she dragged him into one of the dark alleys and had her way with him.

She flushed at the thought. This wasn't like her. She wouldn't say she was *vanilla* in the bedroom, per se. But she was more of a lady in the streets sorta girl, not one for public indecency. But with Jackson, she wanted to abandon all reason. He made her feel wild.

And horny. *So* horny.

It wasn't just that, though. Sure, the dance had her feeling all sorts of things towards him, but it was the week in general. She was discovering sides of him she didn't know. He was no longer a childhood friend turned frenemy in high school. He was no longer the guy who took the hoodie off his back when she was cold, or got into trouble or picked on her.

He was something else. Someone completely unexpected.

He was thoughtful, encouraging, sweet. He challenged her, teased her, and played with her. More importantly, he got her to feel more like herself than she'd been in a long time. And when she did show that side of her, he made her feel worthy. Cared for.

Loved.

As they turned another corner, he looked back at her, his slow grin that curled her toes rose on his lips. She gave a coy smile back.

Elena wondered what was going through his head. Did he feel the same chemistry between them as she did when they were dancing? Was it all just to keep up his end of the bargain, or was it something more?

No. You can't fake that kinda stuff, right?

"Here we are," Jackson said as they strolled up to a nondescript bar on a quiet street.

She could hear the music pulsing from inside as she waited for the bouncers to check their IDs. Even though faint, she recognized the song as a cover from Something Corporate.

After tucking his wallet into his pocket, he took her hand again and led her into the bar. The space was small, tight, and packed. Aside from the colorful lights lighting up the small stage, the rest of the bar was dark.

"Elena! Jack!" Mae called out when she saw them, trying to wave her hand above the crowd.

Jackson dipped down to Elena's ear as they made their way over. "Want a drink?"

Her stomach flipped, loving the feel of Jackson's warm breath on her neck. "Vodka soda."

He nodded and headed to the bar.

Mae pulled a beautiful blonde girl towards Elena. "This is Carolina!" she yelled over the music.

From what Elena could see in the dim light, Carolina had a kind face. Her complexion was perfect, even with minimal makeup, and her smile was genuine. "Hi. I'm Elena," she said while shaking Carolina's outstretched hand.

Mae wrapped her arms around Carolina's waist and kissed her shoulder. "I figured it was time to bring her out and about." She looked at Carolina. "We've been seeing each other for what now? A few weeks?"

"About a month."

"You guys look happy," Elena commented genuinely.

Jackson strolled up a moment later, carrying a beer and her drink. He passed it off to Elena and took a long pull from his bottle. They swayed together and laughed as the band played song after song from their younger years. Third Eye Blind. Finch. Trapt. Dashboard Confessional. Taking Back Sunday.

Back to a time when things were good between her and Jackson. Back when things were simple.

"Ladies and gentlemen," the lead singer said into the mic. "We have a very special guest with us tonight." He turned in their direction. "Jackson, man, get up here."

Everyone turned to look at him as he paused mid-sip. He shrugged and grinned at Elena before making his way through a small path in the crowd. Jackson hopped up on stage and stood next to the singer, rubbing his neck as if embarrassed.

"It's a rare occurrence to have our very own Jackson St. Julien in town on a night when we have a show. But, the stars have aligned, and now we'll be able to make this a very special event. Jackson, how about you sing with us for old time's sake?"

Jackson nodded, still looking a little bashful. The crowd cheered.

The singer laughed at the reaction. "Your choice of song." He handed Jackson the mic and stepped aside. Jackson turned to the band and gave them instructions. After a few nods. He turned back to the mic and took a slow breath, his eyes flashing quickly to Elena.

And then the music started. "The Middle" by Jimmy Eat World.

Jackson grabbed the mic tightly and closed his eyes as he sang the first couple lines. He was nervous, Elena could tell, but after a few seconds, he found his rhythm again. Maybe he hasn't performed in years in this capacity, but it seemed like it came right back to him.

He opened his eyes and scanned the crowd, stopping directly on Elena as he sang the line about not giving up and just being yourself, and how it didn't matter if it was good enough for anyone else.

Elena's breathing slowed as he looked directly in her eyes and sang those words. She had heard this song a million times while growing up, but having him sing it to her now gave it a whole new meaning. He chose this song for her. She knew it. Every single lyric felt like it was written specifically for her.

The music swelled, picking up tempo and intensity. Jackson pulled the mic from the stand and moved along the stage; his stage presence a mixture of sexy and fun. The band members were smiling and laughing as they watched Jackson do his thing, making the crowd go wild. Mae and Carolina were jumping around and dancing while scream-singing the words.

He was in his element. Elena watched in awe as he sang his heart out, his voice addicting. But every time he turned back to her to sing specific lyrics, his blue eyes pierced hers, rooting her to the spot. He winked, and she swore her insides melted.

Suddenly, everything made sense. Everything clicked.

All these years she had worried so much about being an outcast, trying her hardest to blend in so people wouldn't see how different she was, she had buried every little bit of her that made her who she was. Her ambition, her passion, her humor, her flair.

Her heart.

This whole week, Jackson told her she needed to let all of that go and how important it was to share who she was with the world. His words penetrated her psyche, breaking down those walls and long-rooted expectations she had set for herself. She felt herself wearing down, yet she still wasn't ready.

Now, watching him, completely uninhibited, entirely himself—as he had always lived his life—she realized she was. As he sang with all his heart, those words finally broke through the last bit of unnecessary and unrealistic expectations she'd clung to.

She didn't want them anymore. She wanted this. Him.

He sang the final words of the song, his gaze still locked on hers.

The music stopped, and the crowd went wild. Their hands reaching out to high five and grab at him like he was the lead singer of Jimmy Eat World. But Jackson didn't notice them. His eyes were still firmly on Elena's, even as he handed off the mic back to the band.

He jumped off the stage, pushing through the crowd that was praising him on his performance and asking for an encore. He moved through the sea of people, a man on a mission, stopping right in front of Elena.

"So, what did you thi—"

Elena jumped up, wrapping her legs around his hips. Surprised, he caught her and held her up. She crushed her lips against his, putting every ounce of heart into it.

He paused for a second, trying to figure out what happened, but soon followed suit. If she thought the kiss on the boat was hot, this broke the scales. Jackson's mouth moved over hers, nipping and sucking her bottom lip. She moaned against his lips at the feel of his tongue tangling with hers.

The band kicked off the song "Hands Down" by Dashboard Confessional, giving them the perfect soundtrack to their kiss. Their first *real* kiss with no pretenses, no cameras, and no expectations.

Jackson slipped one hand from under her and placed it on the nook of her neck, holding her head in place so he could get more access. His body relaxed as he kissed her more deeply as if he had been holding his breath, waiting for this exact moment, and now he could finally let go.

Elena broke the kiss, her breath ragged, her heart pounding. She pressed her forehead against his, closed her eyes, and breathed him in. "Thank you," she said quietly, just barely heard over the music.

He stroked her hair. "For what?"

"For making me see there's another way. Showing me I can live my life the way I want to."

Jackson pulled away, capturing her gaze. He trailed his thumb along her jaw tenderly, examining her face. "Anything for my girl."

She smiled at that.

His girl.

Sure, he had said it a few times during this week, but now it held a new meaning. It was just them in this crowded bar. They didn't need to pretend. Could he be feeling the way she felt for him?

He kissed her again, deeply and desperately. The kiss went from hot and sexy—a kiss to release the sexual tension simmering between them these last few days—to one of longing. In that kiss, Elena could feel his need for her. It was more than sexual chemistry, there was something underneath all the layers.

"Aww...eww." Mae made a disgusted noise. "I was super excited because that was a pretty sweet scene, but it just dawned on me that you're my *brother* and my *best friend*. Gross. I'm conflicted."

Carolina leaned a head on Mae's shoulder and looked them over. "I think it's cute."

Mae shivered as she made fake barf noises.

Jackson reluctantly let Elena down but grabbed her

hand immediately after her feet hit the floor as if he didn't want to let her go. Not completely.

Mae leaned over to talk quietly into Elena's ear. "It's about time you let yourself go and gave into what you wanted." Mae eyed Jackson over Elena's shoulder. "Even *if* it's my brother. You look happy. That makes me happy."

"I am."

"So what are you waiting for? Get your man."

Elena didn't need any more encouragement. She looked up at Jackson and smiled before dragging him straight out of the bar.

21

ELENA

L ightning flashed overhead, cracking and sizzling the way Elena's body was for Jackson. This past week, there had been a slow burn inside of her, awakening her, reminding her of feelings she had forgotten.

Jackson took her hand, pulling her along Broad Street, stopping every few moments to duck into a doorway or alley so he could kiss her with such intensity, she was sure she would catch fire.

He pushed her against a brick wall in the privacy of an alleyway, shrouded in darkness by the lush trees and shadows of buildings. The dark clouds overhead were oppressive, save for the occasional lightning flash that gave Elena a quick glimpse of Jackson's face.

He was a hungry man, devouring her mouth with every kiss.

She grabbed him, pulling him closer, and pushed her hands under the hem of his shirt. She needed to feel his body, the warmth of his skin, and the way the muscles in his back moved under her fingertips as he kissed her deeply.

Elena paused at another rumble of thunder, putting her hands against Jackson's chest to break the kiss.

His eyes fluttered open, looking dazed. "Everything okay?"

"This summer storm is about to dump right on us."

No sooner did the words escape her mouth that the skies opened up and pummeled them with heavy rain. Within seconds, they were drenched. Elena pushed wet hair out of her eyes, watching the rain batter down on Jackson. His shirt clung to him, showing off the lean, muscled physique from years of surfing.

She ached to touch him. Bare skin against skin.

Lightning flashed, quickly followed by a clap of thunder. "That was close," Jackson yelled over the rain. "Stay here. I'm going to flag down a taxi."

Moments later, he grabbed her hand and pulled her into the backseat of a mini-van taxi. The driver looked at them, likely displeased by the fact that they were soaking wet in the back of his car. Jackson smiled, a light laugh escaping his lips as he cupped her face, pushing away her mess of hair and wiping away the makeup from under her eyes.

Elena shook her head, trying to find humor in the situation. "I look like a mess."

"You're beautiful, Elena."

Her heart raced as she took in the look on his face. Earnest. Tender. And yet mixed with hot lust.

She peered out the window, trying to make out where they were through the heavy rain. The taxi driver crawled through the streets of downtown due to limited visibility and the usual flooding. Finally, he turned down her block but stopped short a few houses down. "Road is flooded down there. I have to drop you off—"

"No problem," Jackson cut in, shoving cash in the driver's face.

He pulled open the door, jumping out, and grabbed Elena's hand to pull her with him. They raced through the rain and deep puddles, laughing like two idiots as sheets of rain came down even harder.

Climbing the stairs to her apartment, she gasped for air as she fumbled with her keys to unlock the door. She pushed through the front door, Jackson hot on her heels. Before she could even close it, he was spinning her towards him. He captured her body, his hands around her hips, pressing her against him. Jackson kissed her, trailing small kisses down her jaw and neck. He slipped a strap from her dress down her arm, his lips following the curve of her shoulder.

Elena reached for his shirt, undoing the buttons as fast as she could, her frantic pulse radiating through her body. His fingers massaged the small of her back, making it hard to concentrate. She needed him so badly, she thought she might pass out before she even had him. Frustrated, she pulled at the hem of his shirt, opting to pull it overhead than bother with buttons. She slipped him free, tossing the shirt to the side.

A huff sounded. Elena turned to find the shirt had landed on the head of a very disgruntled Marley.

Jackson reached out, plucking the shirt from her head, and pat her with affection. "Sorry, girl."

She gave them both a disapproving look and scampered away to her bed.

Elena let out a quiet laugh and pressed her forehead against his, breathing him in. She ran her hands along his bare skin, her fingers exploring the roundness of his pecs and the ridges of his abs.

"Elena," Jackson exhaled, a look of pleasure crossing his face as he watched her hands trail lower. "Are you okay with this?"

She nodded, biting her lower lip. "I want you, Jackson," she whispered.

The look of hunger returned to his face as he bent down to capture her mouth again. His hands reached for her ass, lifting her up, so her legs were wrapped around his waist. Her mind short-circuited at the feel of her bare thighs touching the warmth of his torso.

Teasing her mouth, he nipped and sucked her lips. He placed her on the island in her kitchen, knocking over the random mess of cups, notebooks, and pens onto the ground. Elena frantically reached back, trying to find the zipper to her dress.

Jackson reached around her, moving her hands away so he could take over. He grabbed the tiny zipper and slowly pulled down, his fingertips trailing the exposed skin. The shift from frantic to slow torture was incredibly sexy, causing her to shake with lust.

She tilted her head up, taking in the darkness of his blue eyes. He watched her, his eyes trailing over her face, mouth, shoulders, and the swell of her breasts. He was admiring her, trying to memorize every inch of her skin. Moving his hands to her shoulders, he slipped the last remaining strap off, peeling away the fabric of her dress inch by inch, freeing her.

A mixture of a groan and a growl sounded deep in his throat as her breasts were exposed. "Christ," he said. "Perfect. You're perfect, Elena."

Normally, a string of self-doubting thoughts would flood her mind if anyone said something like that. But by the way Jackson was looking at her—his raw emotion and arousal plain as day—she knew he meant every word of it.

And that only made her want him more. No man had ever looked at her like that. No man had ever made her feel like that. She needed him.

He wedged his way between her legs, pushing her dress up her along her thighs, just stopping short of revealing her soaked panties—and not from the rain. He dipped his head down, capturing a nipple in his mouth, gently nipping and licking her into oblivion. She gasped, her body arching involuntarily towards him, a silent cry for more escaped her lips. Elena shoved her hands in his hair, tugging him to her. The feel of his tongue and warm breath on her body caused goosebumps to travel along her bare skin.

The slow burn building low in her stomach grew, warming her. She sighed as his mouth moved up her neck and back to her lips. She wrapped her legs around his waist again, her arms circling around his neck.

"Bedroom. Now," she urged against his mouth.

Jackson lifted her from the counter and walked to the back of the apartment, knocking into her small bistro table and a bookshelf.

She laughed, a rough sound filled with lust. "I'd love to make it to my bed without completely destroying my apartment in the process."

He pulled away, a devilish grin crossing his features. "Don't worry. I'll get you there."

Jackson continued down the small hall, reaching her bedroom in record time without additional collisions. He pushed the door open with his foot and crossed the threshold, depositing Elena gently on the edge of her bed.

Together, they pulled her dress down the rest of her body, leaving her in only her black lace panties. Jackson sucked in a breath at the sight of her, his hands running along her curvy hips and shapely legs. She shivered as his hands perused her body, taking their time to feel their way, stopping on her sensitive spots to drive her wild.

"I want to taste you," he said, his voice low and serious, something Elena hadn't heard from him before.

And damn if it didn't turn her on even more.

She locked eyes with him as she slipped her thumbs under the thin band of her panties and slid them down, giving him permission to take what he wanted. She lay back on the bed and propped herself onto her elbows, spreading her legs ever so slightly. Her body heated as she watched Jackson's face reveal every single emotion and thought running through his mind.

He wanted her like his life depended on it.

Kneeling on the edge of the bed, he placed his hands on her knees, pulling her legs apart further. Elena relished the pressure of his fingers on her skin and how he was taking control, eager to please her. Kissing the inside of her thighs, he made his way up with painstaking slowness. It took everything in her to not beg for him to move faster. Her body ached at the thought of his tongue on her, licking her center. She pulsed at the idea.

"Please," she whispered, the anticipation nearly killing her.

Without hesitation, his mouth found the place where she wanted him the most. She nearly came undone by the unexpected feel of his warm tongue on her sensitive spot. His tongue swept in a slow circle, getting a feel for pressure and tempo, watching how her body reacted to him.

Trust me, it's reacting.

A pool of wetness flooded between her legs as he found the right rhythm. His hand moved up her thigh, and he put a finger inside of her followed by another, adding new friction to the mix. He groaned against her at the feel of all her slickness, the deep rumble vibrating in a delicious way.

Elena's breath came in spurts as each swirl of his tongue brought her closer to the edge. Her hips moved in circles with his movements, but his hands pushed her down in place, making her take every lap of his tongue, a mixture of softness and perfect pressure that hit her in all the right ways.

"Jackson, don't stop," she pleaded between moans, her body tensing around his fingers. "I'm close."

Jackson picked up his speed, moving his tongue expertly against her clit until she shattered around him. "Jackson," she called out, her body convulsing in pleasurable pulses. He continued to lick her, letting her ride it out until it was over.

"Oh my God," she said as he pulled away and stood before her, a look of arousal and satisfaction across his face.

"Doing that...God, it turned me on so much, Elena. I could do that forever."

Elena, now breathless and somehow even hornier than before the orgasm, pushed up to a seated position. She reached out to him, her hands running along the front of his jeans. She could feel his hardness outlined underneath, just begging to be released.

His breath quickened at the sight of her, naked and ready for him. He squeezed his eyes shut as her hand moved back and forth along his cock.

"I want you, Jackson. Now."

Unzipping his pants, she pulled them down enough so that he popped out. Her eyes landed greedily on him, taking in the sheer size, enjoying the fact that she made him hard and ready. He wanted her just as badly as she wanted him.

Elena licked her lips and leaned forward, bringing the head to her mouth. She wet it, allowing her lips to glide seamlessly up and down the length. He hissed out a breath as she moved back and forth, his knees buckling a bit before he steadied himself again.

"Elena," he growled.

She looked up, capturing his eyes as she slid back down the length. A look of tortured pleasure crossed his face. Jackson gripped her shoulders lightly, reluctantly pulling her away.

"As amazing as that feels, I want you in other ways. I *need* to be inside you, Elena. I can't handle it."

A smile crossed her lips as she stood, rising on her toes to kiss him. Her bare skin slid across his chest, all hot and hard and *hers*.

Never in her life would she had expected this explosive chemistry between them. Being with him this week completely transformed how she felt about him. How she *saw* him. He was the guy who pushed her boundaries. Challenged her. Supported her. And, as his lips moved along her shoulder and down to her breasts again, he was the guy who worshiped her.

He slipped a hand into his back pocket, pulling out a condom, before stripping down to all his naked glory. Elena sucked in a breath as her eyes raked him in. Tall, lean, muscular, and one hundred percent ready for her.

She moved to the bed again, lying on her back, feeling the anticipation swell inside of her as Jackson sheathed himself. She never cared much for that visual before, but somehow watching him was so incredibly erotic that she tingled all over.

Carefully, he crawled into bed, positioning himself above her. He drew in deep breaths, and Elena could see the slope of his muscled chest in flashes as the lightning brightened the room in a blue light.

Jackson's eyes captured hers as he paused, giving her one last moment to change her mind. Because once he slipped inside of her, like she so desperately wanted, everything between them would change.

As if it hadn't already.

Elena reached a hand to his face, cupping it gently before kissing him. No longer were the kisses frantic and eager, now the mood had shifted into something more intimate. Intense.

Jackson took the kiss for what it was: permission. He moved her legs apart and positioned himself at her entrance, just putting the first bit of him inside. Elena gasped, her body adjusting to fit him, the exciting feeling of pleasure mixed with overwhelming fullness. She could get addicted to this.

Could they stay like this forever?

"Are you okay?" he whispered, his voice rough from restraint.

Elena nodded. "Don't you dare stop."

Jackson pushed himself in nearly all the way, causing a loud moan to escape her lips.

Holy mother.

He felt so good. The thought of him filling her up so perfectly was almost as good as the actual thing. Once Jackson realized she was okay, he moved back and forth, building delicious friction between them. Elena was still wet and ready from the incredible orgasm he gave her only a few minutes ago, and as he moved inside her, his naked body running along hers, another one was building quickly.

Jackson kissed her as he moved a hand between them, finding her sensitive clit, and rubbed his thumb in those perfect circles that would bring her over the edge. She felt it build again, her body clenching more and more with each stroke of his finger. Her first orgasm was always more intense than any that followed, but being wrapped around him made her believe that wouldn't be the case this time. She was in pure ecstasy, wanting nothing more than to have his hands on her, him inside her, for as long as she could take it.

This week had been thick with sexual tension and new feelings. Everything had culminated in making this moment reach new heights. Every touch, groan, kiss, look. All of it hit an intensity she'd never experienced in her life. It should scare her. She liked to have a plan, to know where things were going. And Jackson—the man who traveled far and wide—was anything but a sure thing.

But she wasn't scared, *because* it was with him.

With Jackson, she was safe.

"Jackson," Elena moaned, her body tightening more in response to him.

"Say my name again." His hips moved faster, she could sense his orgasm coming close, their breaths mingled in the heat of it.

"Jackson!" His name left her lips on a scream as that last swirl of his fingers pushed her over the edge.

Another mind-blowing orgasm shook her, taking her by surprise, so intense she thought she might faint. Her body milked him, the feel of his length inside of her with each pulse only enhanced the sensation. She never wanted it to end.

Moments later, Jackson tucked his face against the crook of her neck and roared her name as he finally found his own pleasure. He rested his body on hers, sticky and slick from exertion.

He kissed her throat, panting hard as he tried to come down from what just happened.

"Jesus Christ," was all he could manage.

Elena, still pulsing and buzzing, could only nod.

Everything about their week and their faux relationship had been uncertain. Lines were blurred between what was real and acting.

But if there was one thing that was for sure in all of it, it was that the chemistry between them just now was *very* real.

And the feelings Elena had for Jackson were too.

———

Elena started at the feel of cold wetness on her hand. She opened her eyes, finding Marley resting her snout on the bed, her face a fraction of an inch from Elena's, the dog's warm breath blowing her tangled hair from her cheek. The storm had stopped, but the room was still dark, indicating it had only been a few hours since she'd fallen asleep.

She and Jackson had repeat sessions after their first time together, ranging from hot and heavy to slow and tender. She wasn't sure whose stamina was more impressive: hers or his. But after they finally wore each other out, blissfully satisfied, he had wrapped her in his arms and whispered in her ear.

"You're beautiful. You're everything."

Elena wasn't one to cuddle for long. Of course, she liked affection like anyone else, but when it was time to sleep, she needed her space. With Jackson, however, she found herself falling deeper into his arms, pressing herself against him as if she couldn't survive without feeling every inch of his body against her.

Being in his arms meant security, something she hadn't

remembered feeling in a long time. She could just be, and that was more than enough.

Although his grip on her had lessened during their sleep, Elena could still feel the weight of his arm across her middle and the heat radiating from his body. He snored lightly near her, the sound of it comforting her in the middle of the night.

Marley jumped into the bed and circled twice before finding a small nook between Jackson and Elena's feet. She let out a contented sigh before settling in.

As Elena lay there with her beloved dog pressed against her and Jackson's arm wrapped around her, she realized this was the happiest she'd been in a long time. Examining it, she noticed how light she felt. Unburdened. She wanted to blame it on the multiple orgasms and the resulting dopamine from them, but she knew that wasn't the case.

When Brittany threatened her job, reputation, and said those awful things, it didn't sting as horribly as it used to. Sure, it affected her. Elena hadn't changed overnight, that self-doubt would always linger in her psyche. But this time, it was different.

The best she could equate it to was like wearing a fancy gown and attending a lavish party. All glitz, glamour, and holding yourself in a way you wouldn't normally. Then, coming home, stripping down, and getting into those ratty, comfortable PJs, sitting on the couch, and eating leftover Chinese food with your favorite wine and TV show. It was that level of comfort and relief that was hitting her hard right now.

She felt like she could be herself. No masquerading as someone else. No worrying about other people's opinions. She was just Elena Lucia. And that was enough.

Shifting in the bed, she turned to face Jackson, who was

still sound asleep. She ran a hand along his cheek, placing a kiss softly on his lips. He stirred for a second before falling into a deep sleep again.

She knew why she felt the way she did. It was because of Jackson. At the beginning of the week, she assumed he was just giving her a hard time. Now, she saw that he pushed her and challenged her because her genuine self was so much better than whatever she was trying to be to appease everyone else.

He saw through it. He always had. Maybe it took more than a decade to realize it, but he was right.

She was better because of him. She was better as herself.

And through it all, he liked her just the way she was. Jackson supported her, championed her, cared for her. Maybe he was a rowdy kid when they were growing up, but the memories of those quieter moments came flooding back. She could remember the way he looked at her as if studying her, trying to remember every bit of her.

Or that time he had dissed a guy who made fun of Elena's outfit one day. It was subtle, but she could remember the look Jackson gave her as he passed her by in the school halls, satisfied that he'd set the guy straight.

Or how at house parties, Jackson had always found a way to her. He never let her be alone, even if it meant him introducing her to other people when she was too shy to do it herself. She remembered how annoyed Jackson's dates would be, always focusing on Elena's needs first.

For years, Elena thought Jackson couldn't care less. Now, she knew that's all he did. He had cared for her this whole time.

Elena looked at his face, highlighted by the glow of the moon streaming through her window. He looked so peaceful. How could she have missed all the signs this whole time?

How could he?

Tomorrow, she'd tell him how she felt. That she appreciated him. That she understood. That she wanted to give their fake relationship a real shot. Because of him, she was feeling brave. Hopeful.

And after, Elena would embrace her identity wholeheartedly. She would stop worrying about what happened after the show came out or what the couples and her publishers would think once she told them the truth. She was going to set things right.

She owed it to them to be the best version of herself. She owed it to herself. Come hell or high water, she was done hiding.

22

JACKSON

J ackson tried not to pinch himself. Being with Elena
last night had been unlike anything he'd ever imagined. Unlike anything he'd experienced. She was an
unexpected but welcome surprise, full of passion and play-
fulness, and heat and tenderness all rolled into one.

He knew she had a lot of heart, but seeing her come
undone last night surpassed his wildest dreams. The way
she moaned. How she bit her bottom lip as she got closer to
the edge. The feel of her wrapped around him. The way her
eyes raked his body with hunger. The sound of her voice as
she screamed his name. It was enough to make him want to
pull her into the bathroom of the café where they were
spending a lazy morning and make her do those things all
over again.

If he'd thought he was hooked on her before, he was a
fool. He needed her like an addict needed their next fix.

Elena smiled over her oversized cup of coffee, her eyes
sparkling in the warm morning light. They sat by the
window, taking in the early morning scenes of Charleston.
The café was starting to fill in but was still quiet enough.

Even over the muted noise of the coffee machines, music overhead, and chatter from the tables nearby, the sound of Jackson's thundering heart filled his ears.

"What are you thinking about? You're giving me a funny look." She laughed lightly as she put down her mug.

I love you, Elena.

"Just happy," he replied, taking her hand and kissing her palm.

On the short walk to the café this morning, he couldn't keep his hands off her. He held hers tight, stopping every few minutes to swing her around and kiss her. But she didn't protest that it was inappropriate for a public setting. Instead, she'd wrap her arms around his neck and kiss him with the same heat as the night before.

They almost didn't make it to the café.

Everything felt amazing. Natural. As if they'd been lovers for years. There was a level of comfort in being around Elena but also a sense of excitement. This was all new, but all so familiar.

She grinned. "Me too."

This moment was perfect. Last night was perfect too, but something about being here with her like this hit Jackson deeper. He could picture doing this with her every morning.

For the rest of their lives.

Right then and there, Jackson knew he'd do anything to make this work. The fact that Rich couldn't travel put a hitch in things. It would be at least a year before Jackson could afford to hire someone to take his place, plus the six months he'd need to train them. That meant the roots Jackson had hoped to set were now out of reach...for now, at least. But maybe, even with all the travel, he could still find a way to anchor himself here. If she was open to it, he'd come back to her time and time again.

Maybe it wasn't fair to ask that of her. It wasn't fair for anyone to have a boyfriend who was gone so often, but he couldn't *not* try. He had to know how she felt.

Elena's phone vibrated on the table. She clicked a few buttons and paused, her smile dropping.

"What is it?" he asked.

She slid her phone over so he could read the text.

Brittany Hale: You should really consider the deal. Last chance.

"Are you ready?" he asked, sensing her apprehension.

"No, but I know I have to. I just don't know why she's pushing it again. I have another few days. I haven't talked to Mark or my agent or the Berkshire team yet."

"I'm here for you."

She leaned across the table and brushed a soft kiss on his lips. "Thank you. For everything."

The look of appreciation in her eyes made Jackson's heart swell with pride. It meant the world to him that she trusted him to stay by her side as she faced this tough situation. He would do anything to keep her feeling as brave as she was right now.

She took her phone back, her fingers poised and ready to type. "Here goes nothing."

Elena tapped away, biting her lip, her eyebrows knitted in concentration as she deleted and retyped over and over. But before she could ever send it, her phone buzzed again. Her face turned white.

"What's wrong?" Jackson asked.

Looking stunned, she held out the phone to him, not saying a word. Jackson pulled up lengthy texts, scrolling to the top and finding the first one in a list of three.

He clicked on the link Brittany shared, leading to a popular online gossip site, and read the headline, "Will We Finally Find out Who *Always, Ella* is?" The article talked about Ella being spotted in Charleston for filming. Grainy photos taken from a distance were scattered throughout the article, mostly at the beach. Finally, he scrolled to the bottom, where he found a picture of himself pulled from his company's website.

"We may not know who Ella is—yet—but we did get a tip on her beau. He's Charleston-native Jackson St. Julien, founder of Sustainasurf. Keep an eye on him, because he'll likely lead to the woman behind the wildly popular relationship advice column and soon-to-be book." The article linked to a pre-order page for Elena's book.

"Wow," was all he could manage.

Tears misted her eyes, washing away the confidence that had been there only a moment before. His heart clenched. "Did you read the rest of the texts?"

"No, I will now." Jackson clicked back to the texts following the link to the gossip column.

> **Brittany Hale:** I don't know what's more pathetic: the fact that you lied about a boyfriend or the fact that you were so desperate, you had to recruit your best friend's brother to keep the lie up. I know you and Jackson aren't dating, Elena. What will your readers think when they know you went to such lengths to deceive them? I'm giving you two days before I share the truth with my friends at the newspaper. I guess we'll find out what your fans think about this all if you don't drop out from the promotion.

"Oh God," Elena choked out as a tear escaped from her eyes. "I fucked up big time."

Jackson put down the phone and scooted his chair closer to her, wrapping her in his arms. "It's okay, Elena. You were going to tell the truth anyway."

"In my own way, yeah. But if Brittany exposes me first, it will ruin any chance I have to smooth things over. Brittany's going to take this wide. Now it's no longer about keeping it contained to the couples on the show. *Everyone* will know." Her eyes went wide with fear. "If she does this, my writing career as I know it is over. Berkshire would never work with me again. They could even pull the plug on the books and show." She buried her face in her hands. "Oh God. And Christopher. He'd dump me in a heartbeat. I'd be black-listed from all agents and publishers. And Mark...he'd fire me. He wouldn't want this negative press to affect the company."

A few curious eyes landed on them as she quietly hyper-ventilated.

"She might be ruthless, but she hasn't done anything yet. We have some time."

"What the hell was I thinking?" A panicked expression crossed her features. Jackson could tell she was two seconds from spiraling into one of her notorious freak outs.

He took her face in his hands, smoothing her hair away, trying to soothe her. "We'll figure it out. Together. I've got you, Elena. I'll always have you."

She pulled away and shook her head, her eyes unfocused. Was he even getting through to her?

"This...this is really bad. Worse than bad."

"Elena—"

Her accusing gaze locked onto his. "This was reckless, Jackson." She pointed a finger at him. "You got into my head. You kept telling me to push off telling the truth and to 'live in the moment.' You made me think that living my life like you, careless and...and...selfish would be okay. But I'm not like you—"

"Are you kidding me right now? Selfish? Careless?"

Anger flared through him. He knew she could be unreasonable when she got overwhelmed, but her accusations gutted him. He couldn't let them roll off his back like he used to, not after he'd gone and fallen for her.

She tucked her hair behind her ears, a jerky motion, and wrung her hands, her eyes trained on the table. "There are consequences to actions. Unlike you, I can't just pack my bags and run away until it blows over. If I'd just done things my way, I would have planned better, and this wouldn't have escalated—"

"As usual, you're making up scenarios that didn't even happen. Just call Christopher. Call Rachel. They have teams that deal with this stuff." He leaned back in his chair and shoved a hand in his hair. "God damn it, Elena. You need to stop."

She stared at him for a beat, saying nothing. Finally, she pushed away from the table and stood. "This is who I am, Jackson. We were both ridiculous to think I could be anything other than this."

A muscle in Jackson's jaw ticked, adrenaline coursing through him. "This is *not* you, Elena. No one ever said change was easy. You're going to have to deal with the backlash if being yourself is important to you. Don't let Brittany's bullshit make you think you don't have control over the situation. Listen, I will help—"

"Listening to you is going to cause me to lose everything. Can't you see that? I tried it your way. I tried to just go with the flow, and it blew up in my face." She shook her head, her eyes dropping to the floor. "This was a mistake."

"What?" Jackson asked in confusion, an unsettled feeling roiling his stomach.

"Things between you and I just got really complicated. It was a nice fantasy, but it isn't real. And a lot of damage will be caused because of it."

He sprung to his feet, reaching for her. Elena dodged his hands. "You can't be serious. Don't let one bad situation ruin us."

She put a hand to her chest. "Just because we slept together doesn't mean you can tell me what I can and can't do. Or how I should feel." She let out a frustrated breath and bit her lip. "If you thought one week could change me into some dream girl of yours who can let things roll off her back, then you're mistaken. I'm not Ella. I'm just me. We're not right for each other. You'll never understand me. We're just too...too different."

Her words stung. He knew she was overwhelmed and panicking. He could see it clear as day on her face. But she couldn't really think this, could she?

"It's not about being your boyfriend, Elena. It's about being your friend. I care about you. I loved the woman you became this last week. And it's not because I'm pressuring you into being her. It's because you *are* her, whether you realize it or not. It would be a disservice to the world to hide her again just because you're scared. Please, don't hide her again," he pleaded, feeling her slipping away.

She looked pained, her mouth opening and closing as she tried to find the words to say.

Say you'll try. If not for us, for you.

Say this is just a stupid fight, and we'll get over it. Say you're not giving up on what this could be.

Say you've fallen in love with me too.

Please, Elena.

She straightened and let out another breath. "I have to fix this. Just go home or something. I'll...see you later." Elena paused, looking agonized. "We need to stop pretending that this could work. It has to be done. *We* have to be done." She didn't wait for a response before she darted out of the café.

As he watched her go, Jackson felt like he had been sucker-punched in the gut.

23

JACKSON

"*Careless and selfish...Unlike you, I can't just pack my bags and run away until it blows over...It has to be done.*"

Elena's words from this morning played in a loop in his head, cutting him deeper each time he heard it.

He was reeling.

For a moment, Jackson thought whatever had grown between Elena and him was real. That it was stronger than whatever shit life threw at them. But the second things got tough, she went back into that ridiculous shell of hers.

She'd been clear. This wasn't real. Not only that, but she also had zero respect for him and everything he had worked for.

It was all an act. And he fell for it.

Fell for *her.*

Maybe Rich's decision not to travel was a blessing in disguise after all. The sooner Jackson got the hell out of Charleston, the better. He'd keep his end of the deal. He'd finish out the remainder of the show. They had their final night of filming tonight and then the wrap party tomorrow. After that, he was done.

Gone.

He needed space from Elena and all the things that reminded him of her—which was everything in this godforsaken city. Jackson needed to mend his broken heart.

He stuffed his boardshorts into a duffle bag and laughed to himself, a dry hollow sound. Maybe she was right. She accused him of running off, and here he was, packing his stuff to do just that.

With the way it felt like a million knives were stabbing his chest, he couldn't even bring himself to care.

Mae appeared in the door of the guest bedroom and stopped short. "What the hell are you doing?"

"What does it look like?" he ground out as he grabbed clothes from the drawers and continued to fill his bag.

"It looks like you're being an idiot."

"I'm not in the mood, Mae."

She crossed the room and sat on the bed. "What's going on?" she asked softly, clutching his arm to stop him from his task.

He tried to push pass the tightness in his throat. "Gotta get back on the road for work."

Mae shook her head. "That's not it. And I know for a fact that you don't have to leave yet."

"What do you want me to say?"

"I want you to admit you're bailing. But the question is, why? You and Elena looked really happy when you left last night, and you didn't come home. I assumed everything was good with you two."

Jackson shoved a hand in his hair and leaned back against the dresser. "I assumed so too, but we were wrong." He shook his head and went back to digging into the open drawers. "Did she tell you about the gossip rag?"

"No. I haven't heard from her. What was it?"

Jackson gave her the run down from this morning's shitshow.

Mae looked at him like he was dense. "Oh, God, Jackson. You know Elena and how easily she gets flustered. Just give her some time to get her thoughts straight. She'll come to her senses."

"She seemed pretty confident in what she said about us being a mistake."

"Elena is stubborn as hell. Have you stopped to consider her perspective? She had a lot of unexpected things thrown at her all at once, of course, she acted out. You've seen her little freak-outs a *million* times. Maybe you've helped her loosen up a bit this past week, but she isn't going to change overnight. You need to be patient with her."

"Are you like her shrink or something?"

"No. I just speak Elena." She frowned. "So that's it then? You're just going to ditch her? You know how much is riding on this show."

Jackson picked up the bag and walked out to the living room, Mae trailing behind as she tried to yank the bag from his hands. He pulled it away. "No. I'll finish what we agreed on. She'll get the boyfriend she wanted—that is if Berkshire doesn't pull the plug once she talks to them—but after the wrap party, I'm out."

"I can't believe you," Mae said, annoyance in her voice. "This will crush her."

"What?" he dropped the bag by the front door as if the placement would make his exit speedier. The second the wrap party was over, he'd be ready to go. "I'll be there through filming like she'd asked."

"I didn't mean you'll crush her if you bail on your deal. I meant you *leaving* will crush her. You're never serious about any girl, but you were about Elena. I could totally see it. And yet, you made up your mind and decided to jump ship before you even let her compose herself enough to talk this out with you like an adult."

"She doesn't want me. Not like that."

"Did you ask her?"

"No," he admitted. A sliver of hope wrapped around his heart and squeezed. She'd lost it on him earlier this morning, but he didn't recall her outright *saying* she didn't care about him, only that being together was a mistake.

"Just because she said it's over, doesn't mean she doesn't feel something for you. She just put her walls up."

He shook his head, trying to forget the thought. Whether she used those specific words or not, it was clear she didn't want to continue down whatever path they'd started last night. Jackson couldn't let his heart get crushed a second time by even entertaining the thought.

Mae looked at him like he was an idiot again. "Did you at least tell her how you felt?" she pressed.

"No."

She threw her hands up in the air. "Men! This is why I lean more towards women when I date."

"It's not that simple."

Mae grabbed her purse and keys, making her way to the front door. "You telling her how you feel might make all the difference, Jack. If it were me, I would at least want to know the truth about how someone felt about me before I made any rash decisions. I wouldn't want to be sitting in some remote beach across the world wondering what if." She opened the door. "I have to meet with some clients. You need anything while I'm out?"

"No," he replied distractedly.

She shook her head in disappointment. "See you later," she said as she closed the door behind her.

Jackson took a seat at the kitchen island and rubbed a hand down his face. He was acting irrationally, but the way Elena wrote him off like that killed him inside. She seemed so resolved about it. But maybe Mae had a point—Elena had freaked out over lots of things in the past.

A memory from high school flashed through his mind. During a heated game of Truth or Dare at one of his family's many beach parties, he'd put Elena on the spot. She'd chosen Truth, as always, because she felt it was safer than their wild Dares.

But not this time. When Jackson had asked her which of one of the guys at the party would she kiss, she froze. All eyes were on her. A handful of the boys sitting around the circle leaned forward to hear her answer.

Yet, she never told them. Instead, she looked at Jackson like he'd betrayed her and stomped away and into the house. They didn't see her for the rest of the night, and Elena never played Truth or Dare with them again.

Whenever Elena was caught off guard, she'd do whatever she could to make the situation stop. That usually meant creating distance.

Just like she was doing now. In her own way, she was running away like she'd accused him of always doing.

But if someone had fought for him to stay, would he have been gone as much? If someone showed Elena she was worth loving, would she stop being so quick to shut down and push people away?

Would that have made a difference for either of us all these years?

He had thought she'd made progress this week. She'd become stronger. Bolder. But as soon as things took an unexpected turn, her old fears came rushing back. If she could dismiss him so quickly, after one text message, how was he supposed to have a real relationship with her? A switch had turned off in her while he was standing next to her, supporting her. If he was traveling, how would she react?

Maybe she wasn't wrong in pushing him away this morning. This was only going to end in heartache.

He had to let her go before they got too deep.

Elena needed more than a guy who wasn't around to remind her she was loved. She *deserved* more.

He *wanted* to be that guy, though. He *could* be that guy if she'd be willing to wait for him.

Was it right for him to ask that of her?

No, you selfish bastard.

Jackson shoved the heels of his palms into his eyes and rubbed hard, his internal war twisting him in a knot. And there was not a damn thing he could do about it.

After a quick shower and changing into the best suit— okay, the only suit—he had, he hopped into his Jeep and drove to the warehouse. With only a few hours spare, he tried to concentrate on all the high-priority loose ends he had to deal with before his trip. But his mind kept wandering to the event tonight.

He had no idea how Elena was going to act when they were together later. He didn't know what would be harder, being shut out by her or having her pretend she cared for him when she didn't.

Getting through these next two days was going to kill him. But he had to. Whatever far-fetched idea he had believing they could navigate a successful relationship while he traveled was instantly killed this morning when they could barely survive a disagreement.

It was better off letting this go. Maybe they'd be able to

salvage a friendship again when things cooled down between them.

Jackson somehow had to find a way to keep his emotions in check for both their sakes. Maybe he couldn't have her how he wanted her, but he wasn't about to lose her completely.

24

ELENA

Oh, God. What have I done?

Elena had hurried out of the café and down the few blocks to her apartment. She needed a moment to breathe and gather her thoughts. Pushing through the door and slamming it shut, she threw herself onto the sofa. As she lay there, face buried in her hands, she nearly choked on her tears. She wasn't sure what was worse: the fact that she was going to be outed in the worst way possible or how she had snapped at Jackson, the one man who was actually good to her.

Did I just lose him?

If she did, it was her own damn fault.

The morning was perfect, and she had gone and messed it all up because she let the real world come barreling into their safe love bubble. For a moment, she had almost forgotten any worries she had. Jackson had a way of making her feel like she was on top of the world and that things would be fine, even when facing adversity head-on.

And what did she do the moment she came face-to-face with her fears without warning? She went and made

Jackson feel like he was nothing, and it was all his fault, just like how Brad and the others had made her feel most of her life. She reverted to the mentality that the world was out to get her and put her walls right back up, effectively blocking out one of the very few people who accepted her for who she was.

Would he ever forgive me?

As if knowing exactly what Elena needed to do, Marley sauntered up carrying her leash. Elena pat her head. She needed to go to his apartment to talk to him and make this right.

But before she could head out the door, Mae appeared.

"Knock, knock. Anyone home?" Mae called out as she poked her head in the front door.

"Hey, Mae. Not to be rude, but I need to talk to Jackson. I really messed up."

Mae nodded. "That's why I'm here. Maybe we should take a seat?"

Elena's stomach bottomed out. It wasn't like Mae to be so serious. Her face didn't hold a hint of her normal good-natured spirit, which only worried Elena more.

"What's going on?" Elena asked as they sat together on the sofa.

"Okay, look," Mae started, taking a big breath. Her shoulders rose to her ears with tension. "I can tell Jackson really cares for you. He always has, you know?" Mae took Elena's hands. "I know you still feel like the scared outcast from when you were a kid, but you don't realize how much you've grown and changed over this last year. I also know how hard it is for you to feel safe enough to lean into that."

Elena hung her head and nodded, unable to form coherent words. This morning was full of emotions and hard truths.

"I don't know what happened between you and Jackson, but I love you both so much. I don't want you guys to go back to not talking again." Mae sank back into the sofa, her eyes trained on the ceiling. "You've been good for him too."

"I have?" Elena's voice was a whisper. That one statement made her feel a sense of pride and peace.

"Mhm. Jackson's always been a happy guy. Clearly. But there was something different about him these last few days. There wasn't that same restlessness about him. He seemed... whole. If that makes sense?"

Elena groaned as the guilt ate at her stomach. "God, I really screwed up this morning."

Mae wrapped her arm around Elena's shoulders, squeezing her in a reassuring hug. "He's hurting," she admitted.

Elena sprung to her feet, anxious to work through this. "I have to get over there and talk to him."

"You going to tell him you're in love with him too while you're there or what?" Mae cocked an eyebrow, a shit-eating grin filling her face as she settled back on the sofa like she owned the place.

She stopped in her tracks. "H-how? What?"

Mae rolled her eyes. "C'mon, Elena. I've been friends with you forever. If there was ever a time to pull your head out of your ass, it's now."

"You're right."

"Wow." Mae looked stunned. "Not even going to put up a fight or overthink everything? I at least expected a pros and cons list in typical Elena fashion."

Elena threw a pillow at her. "Shut up. If there's anything I'm sure about, it's how I feel about him. No overthinking needed for once."

Mae popped up to her feet and slapped Elena on the ass. "Go get your man. Even if he is my brother."

Just as Elena grabbed her purse, her cell phone rang. Christopher's name flashed across the screen. "Shit. It's Christopher calling me back. I need to talk to him and do some damage control."

She eyed the front door and looked back to her ringing phone, conflicted about what to do.

"Elena," Mae said, grabbing her attention. "Jackson will be there tonight. You can tell him then. For now, fix your issue with Berkshire."

"He *needs* to know that what happened between us was more than our deal. Or just sex. Or whatever other awful things I said to him this morning, Mae. I didn't mean it. I don't want to lose him."

The phone continued to ring, making her pulse spike.

"And you'll get to tell him that. Later. Promise."

Elena sucked in a deep breath and let it out. "Okay. Okay." Hitting the answer button, she prayed that she didn't blow up both her relationship and her career all before noon.

25

JACKSON

On more than one occasion, Jackson pulled off to the side of the road on his drive to the docks. He wasn't ready to face Elena. To face the fact that whatever he thought they were was over. His insides twisted at the thought.

Everything inside him urged him to turn around. To get an earlier flight and go. Maybe if he didn't see her again, he could pretend like their fight had never happened. He could rewind back to this morning when she was wrapped in his arms, her bare skin pressed against his as the early morning light streamed through her bedroom window and washed over them in a warm glow.

That moment where he thought there was nothing in the world better than being there with her.

He could live in denial a little while longer and hold onto that memory.

Hold onto the belief that they could work.

That she was still his.

He pulled himself together and put his car in drive, easing back onto the highway. He'd made a promise to her, and he was damn well going to keep it. He'd prove to her that he didn't run away from his problems.

Jackson wouldn't bail on her, no matter how much it killed him.

He made it to the harbor cruise dock on time. When Elena strolled up in a form-fitting dress that accented every curve of her body—curves he had buried himself deep in barely twenty-four hours ago—he felt like all the air had been sucked from his lungs. How was he ever going to walk away from her willingly?

He'd given himself a pep talk before arriving with the stern reminder that he needed to keep his head straight. Elena had made it clear he was *just* a stand-in boyfriend, and although they'd crossed an unspoken line in her apartment, nothing about their deal had changed. He had to remain neutral.

That's going to be fucking impossible.

"Hi," she greeted, her voice sounding exhausted and defeated. Her small smile didn't reach her eyes. "You clean up well."

"You too."

"Jackson, about earlier—"

"Hey, guys!" Maritza said as she and Max strolled up with the rest of the group. "We were just talking about going out after the events tonight. Since it's our last official night of filming, we decided to grab a few drinks and celebrate. Wanna come?"

Jackson rubbed the back of his neck and flashed a look at Elena before responding. "I can't. I have to finish packing."

"Pack?" Natalie asked.

He glanced at Elena again, seeing the ever-so-subtle furrowing of her eyebrows. If they even had a tiny chance of working things out, he knew this would be the nail in their coffin. He felt it in his gut.

"Yeah. I have another work trip. I actually leave first thing in the morning after the wrap party."

Elena stiffened.

"How long is your trip for this time?" Hari asked.

Jackson shrugged. "Indefinitely for now. My business plans fell through, and now I need to roll with it."

Natalie swatted at Jackson and laughed. "You two are such an inspiration. You manage to keep that love going despite all your travel."

"Yeah. 'Ship goals, for sure," Maritza commented as she wrapped her arms around Max and kissed him.

"We make it work," Elena murmured and forced a smile.

Always keeping up appearances for others. Still. Her half-smile gave the impression that she knew all about his travel, and she was okay with it.

He wished she could just be real. For him.

Natalie shimmied up the ramp to the cruise. "Who's ready for some cocktails?" she sing-songed.

Ana raised a hand. "Me. For sure."

"Ditto!" Maritza looped her arm through Ana's, and they followed Natalie onto the sunset cruise.

Elena took an unsteady step forward. Jackson's hand instinctively went to the small of her back as he ushered her up the dock to the boat. He felt her flinch slightly before picking up her pace purposely so his hand would fall away.

He felt like his throat was closing. His chest was caving in. She was the one who rejected him this morning, and now she had the audacity to act hurt when she found out he was leaving? Something didn't add up. He needed to get to the bottom of it. Even if she didn't feel the same about him, he wanted to clear the air.

"Elena, I should explain—"

"Hey, guys!" Stephanie welcomed, cutting him off. Jackson did a double-take. Normally dressed in a tank, ripped jeans, and her Converse sneakers, Stephanie was now in a beautiful dress with her hair and makeup styled.

"Wow, Stephanie. You're stunning," Elena commented genuinely.

"As much as I prefer sneakers to heels, we had to look the part for the symphony later. The venue warned us that we wouldn't be allowed in if we didn't meet the dress code, even if we were just filming in the lobby." Stephanie nodded to the camera guys on the ship. "Got them to dress up too, although they fought me on it until the eleventh hour." She winked. "I know how to wear them down."

"Well, you look great!"

"As do you two." Stephanie moved aside. "Come on board. The rest of the group's out on the bow for cocktail hour. It's a gorgeous day for the sunset cruise. We couldn't have asked for better weather for the final night of shooting."

"I'd have to agree," Rachel said as she strolled up with a glass of champagne in hand, Celeste alongside her. The red-headed bombshell smiled coyly. "I'll always be a city girl, but Charleston's grown on me. It's just so...*relaxing.*" She pushed her hair over her shoulder. "Whatever that means."

Rachel's gaze roved over Elena, and her casual demeanor transformed to all business again. "But before we can enjoy, there are a few things we still need to discuss."

Elena nodded, looking like a kicked puppy. "Of course."

Celeste flashed Jackson a smile. "You don't mind if we steal your *girl* for a moment, do you?"

Jackson shot Elena a look, trying to see if she were

alright, but she wouldn't meet his eyes. "Sure. Do whatever you need to."

Jackson watched them disappear into a private room on the boat, worried that the execs at Berkshire found out about their fake relationship before Elena had a chance to tell them.

"What was *that* about?" Stephanie asked.

"Not sure." His stomach turned. If the truth did come out like that, he wished he could be there to support her for what was likely to be a difficult conversation.

"Well, hopefully, Rachel and Celeste can get Ella to snap out of whatever funky mood she's in. She seemed off. Everything okay?"

"Maybe she's just a little bummed that tonight is the last night. That all of this is almost over."

"Well, we need to make sure this last day of filming really hits all the right notes. Celeste emphasized how we need to wow the execs, especially since it's the first time since we've done anything like this. If all goes well, this could be a great marketing strategy to add to our arsenal for our non-fiction writers. It will set us apart from other media companies. We can't have Ella fall flat right at the finish line."

"I'll try to loosen her up."

"Thank God for the open bar," Stephanie whispered to Jackson and winked.

He followed her to the top deck, where the rest of the crew and group were hanging out. Every few minutes, he'd eye the stairway to see if Elena was coming up. The minutes felt like hours while he waited.

Eventually, she appeared, pale-faced as she trailed behind Rachel and Celeste.

"Well, it's safe to say have a lot to accomplish," Rachel

snapped as she waved her empty flute to the bartender. She closed her eyes, took a deep breath, and smiled when she saw the cameras milling around.

"I've already made some calls," Celeste commented as she sipped her martini and eyed Elena. "You should spend time with Jackson. We already lost nearly an hour of footage talking downstairs."

"Sure. Of course. Sorry," Elena said as she made her way to him.

Jackson felt uneasy as they sipped cocktails with everyone. All night he had been torn between wanting to give Elena her space and telling her how he felt.

Something obviously went down with the Berkshire team, and judging how Elena would occasionally get lost in thought, it was clear she had a lot on her plate. He shouldn't add to it, but Mae's words kept ringing in his head.

"If it were me, I would at least want to know the truth...I wouldn't want to be sitting in some remote beach across the world wondering what if."

Even if the smartest decision was to let this go, could he live with the "what ifs" when he left Charleston again this weekend?

Tormented emotions coursed through Jackson as he thought about leaving her. Last night aside, he had fallen hard for her, deeper than he ever could explain. Every time he looked at her, every time he smelled her flowery perfume or heard her laughter fill the air, it crushed him.

What was real? What wasn't?

Images of his hands running along the smooth curves of her body flashed in his mind. The taste of her skin—a mixture of her natural sweetness mixed with the minerality from the rain-filled his mouth. The way her eyes locked on his as he moved inside her would be forever burned in his mind. He held back a strangled noise in his throat.

She had ruined him.

Elena might have made it feel like he was nothing more than a pawn in her attempt to save face, but—as a friend— he felt like he should explain why he was leaving and how he felt about her, even though it probably didn't matter.

As they cruised around the harbor while the sunset cast a beautiful orange-pink glow along downtown, he tried to find the nerve again. He needed to see her reaction, to know for sure this *really* was just about the deal.

To silence the what-ifs.

"I'll be here through the wrap party," he blurted out, startling her from whatever chat she was having with Maritza.

She turned to him, her expression unreadable. "Oh?"

Taking her by the elbow, he excused them and pulled her to the side. "This wasn't how things were supposed to go." He shoved a hand through his hair. "I *was* planning on staying. But I just wanted you to know that I'm not leaving before I see this through."

"I appreciate that."

He took in her closed off and wary expression. "That's it? After everything this week, you don't have any thoughts about me leaving?"

Say you don't want me to go. Say you'll miss me. Say anything.

"You said you didn't know how long you'd be gone for." She crossed her arms, not in a defensive way but more like she was trying to hug herself for comfort. "What am I supposed to say to that?"

He reached out to her, but she took a step back. He let his arms fall. "*Anything*, Elena."

"You're leaving, Jackson. For God knows how long." She let out a breath. "I'll apologize for what I said to you this morning. For how I reacted. It was wrong, and you didn't deserve that. But..." She looked at her feet.

His heart leapt into his throat. "But?" He stepped closer and put a thumb gently to her chin, forcing her to look at him.

"You're leaving," she repeated. "What could we possibly say to each other that would make a difference?" She shook her head, pain flashing across her face.

"Elena, please—"

"There you are," Stephanie said as she approached them. "It's time for dinner. We need you at the table." She took Elena's hand, pulling her away from him.

Jackson could have screamed. Another *fucking* person interrupted their conversation tonight. This was their moment. They were *so* close. He was going to do anything he could to get through to her. To tell her that despite him leaving, whatever they had to say to each other *could* make a difference.

His *love* for her could make the difference. And if she loved him back, then that's what mattered.

He ached to tell her, but every chance he got the nerve to pull her aside again, someone else came into the mix, ruining their chance for a few moments alone.

All through dinner, there was constant excited chatter, creating a buffer between them. And as they left the harbor on a party bus and headed for the symphony orchestra, the conversation floating around them made it impossible to talk to her about it.

Even if he couldn't have a chance to talk to her now, he had to do something. *Anything* to really confirm where they stood. He couldn't go off to destinations unknown without knowing for sure.

He put his pride and hurt aside and took her hand—an olive branch—and rested them on her thigh. She flinched just a fraction but allowed her hand to stay, doing her best to touch him as little as possible without setting off red flags for the rest of the group.

Natalie nudged him. "Here. Pass this to Ella," she said as she handed him a flute of champagne.

Rather than taking the glass with her free hand, Elena slipped her hand from his to accept it.

She didn't try to reach for him again, and that's what said it all. The knife in his heart twisted.

Telling her how he felt didn't matter anymore. She wouldn't want to hear it.

26

ELENA

E lena laid in bed with Marley early the next morning, feeling utterly hollow inside. After Jackson had parted ways with them when the symphony was over, she'd gone out with everyone for a couple of drinks. She'd gone through the motions, pretending she was completely on board with Jackson's travels and had tried to give vague responses when they asked her how long he was going for and where his travels would take him. Because a good girl-friend would know that.

Jackson is leaving?

He didn't even think to tell her. How long had he known? Did he know he was leaving before he fell into bed with her?

Before he made her fall for him?

She'd been purposely distant with him last night. She'd been pissed. And hurt. And disappointed. And...everything.

But once the anger and pain subsided in the wee hours of the morning, she realized she'd never even given him a chance to explain.

Thoughts infiltrated her mind, each of them contradicting the other. He'd talked about putting roots down, hinting at Charleston being the place where he settled down for a while. He had said there was no travel on the books for him for some time as he figured out his business. Now he was leaving tomorrow morning?

"Unlike you, I can't just pack my bags and run away until it blows over." Her harsh words haunted her, and she wondered if he was leaving just to spite her for saying it.

She was wrong for that, knowing how much calling him flaky bothered him. He had trusted her when he told her all about his business and what he was doing for the world. And there she went and threw his insecurities in his face because it was her go-to defense mechanism.

Push them away before they can see you for who you are.

But he *had* seen her for who she was, and he liked it anyway.

God, I'm such a hypocrite. Why did I push him away?

All night, visions of his hands running along her body as he whispered her name tortured her. But it wasn't the night of passion that did her in, it was all those small moments they'd shared throughout the week. In a matter of days, Jackson had shown her how she should have been treated. Not only was he supportive, but he championed her. She finally saw what it was like to have someone on her side, rooting for her.

It was unlike anything she'd ever experienced.

I love him. Please don't leave me.

She'd apologized on the cruise, albeit not nearly the planned speech she'd intended on giving, but his unexpected news threw her off. And maybe the damage had been done already.

Maybe if she hadn't waited to talk to him at the event

and just gone there in the morning, things would have turned out differently.

On top of it, she had a tough conversation with Rachel and Celeste last night. They assured her their team could spin it or get ahead of it, but it was abundantly clear they weren't pleased with her.

They had also asked her to wait to tell the group as to not ruin the last couple days of footage, which only added to her anxiety the rest of the night. All she wanted to do was come clean. Each time she looked into their friendly faces, she felt horrible.

And although Rachel and Celeste hadn't outright said it, she worried that she'd jeopardized her reputation with Berkshire for future projects. Or even worse. The publishing community is small, if any of this got out to the other publishers, she might never have another shot.

I've let everyone down. I've hurt so many people.

Being a fake cost her so much. Her sense of self. Her integrity. Her peace. Potentially her dream of being a novelist. And, now, the love of her life. She realized Jackson was right. It was worth the challenges to fight for who she was. She should have just done that from the start.

Her insides clenched, and she let out a soft whimper. Marley snuggled hard against her, resting her fluffy head on Elena's stomach for comfort.

"What have I done?" Elena asked Marley.

Marley let out a big sigh and stared at Elena with her soulful brown eyes.

As Elena stayed frozen in bed, petting Marley in soothing rhythmic strokes while her mind replayed all the twists and turns of the week, a thought came to her. A line from the very first *Always, Ella* blog: Trust the actions.

Everything Jackson had done for her this week was out

of love. His actions showed it. She wanted to argue that it was part of the deal, but as she thought back to all the years they'd known each other, his actions had always been out of love.

He had always shown her he cared for her, even when she didn't believe it. Even when she felt she didn't deserve it.

After the crappy things she said to him at the café, he still showed up, only showing her again how much he cared about her. He had every right to leave, letting her fend for herself.

But he didn't. He stuck by her side.

Elena wouldn't let him leave Charleston without telling him how she felt. She couldn't. Travel be damned. Even if he shot her down completely because she'd ruined it before it ever truly began, he deserved to know what she said in the café wasn't how she actually felt.

Shuffling out of bed—much to Marley's disapproval—she grabbed her phone from her nightstand and paced her apartment while placing a call. The phone seemed to ring forever before Jackson's voicemail clicked on. She hung up and sent him a text. Staring at the phone for ten minutes, she willed him to respond. But it never came.

Feeling like she was crawling out of her skin with anxiety, she jumped into the shower quickly and washed up. When she saw he still hadn't called after she got out, she dialed him again, only to have it go to voicemail after two rings.

He's screening my calls.

Hurt and fear swelled inside of her. "I'm coming over," she said after the beep.

Grabbing her purse and keys, she hustled out of her apartment and the short distance to Mae's apartment building. She raced inside and ran up the stairs, not bothering with the elevator.

"Please be there. Please be there," she chanted quietly to herself as she walked down the hall to the apartment. Her heart thundered in her chest.

Elena raised her hand and pounded on the door. As moments dragged on, she realized no one was there.

She pulled out her phone and texted Mae.

Elena: Do you know where Jackson is?

Mae: Nope. He left right before me but didn't tell me where he was off to.

Elena cursed. Jackson could be anywhere: his warehouse, surfing at his parents, with friends, doing errands. She could check around Charleston to find him, but with tourist traffic, it would take her forever to get back and forth in time for her scheduled hair and makeup appointment to prep for the big wrap party.

She prayed he would call her back before then, but her gut told her he wasn't going to. That only meant one thing.

Jackson had always told her to put herself out there. He'd always tried to show her that even if it was scary, it was worth it.

She knew that now.

Well, Jackson, if you wanted me to put it all out there, then that's exactly what you're going to get.

27

JACKSON

J ackson stared at the ringing phone sitting on his beach towel. It was Elena. Again. He hit ignore.

After leaving the concert hall last night, he had come back to the apartment to finish packing the last of his things. Mae occasionally stopped in his room, giving one of her signature stares that made him feel like he was making the biggest mistake of his life, but didn't say a word.

Each item he'd packed into the bag felt like it weighed a million pounds, each one taking significantly longer than the last.

When did t-shirts become so heavy?

At the end of it, he'd felt exhausted, as if he'd paddled against a raging current for hours on end. Leaving had never felt like this before. If anything, he would practically dart out the door, eager for another exciting adventure.

Now? Well, now it felt like he was leaving a huge piece of himself behind.

When he'd said he wanted to put roots down, he hadn't expected to find a place to settle on so soon. Nor had he expected his roots to cling on to Elena. But she had gone and taken a machete to it, severing the tie that kept him anchored here. He felt like he was in free-fall, with nothing to hold on to.

It was almost laughable to think a week ago, he would never have thought of Charleston as the place he'd stick around. Elena had somehow changed that for him. She showed him that staying in one place didn't mean giving up his sense of adventure. Every moment he had with her this week had kept him on his toes, wondering what would come next.

The thought of leaving again, exploring new places in the world, no longer held the same appeal. Deep down, he knew that every person who proudly talked about their home, every woman who pulled him onto the dance floor, every child who was excited to share their story, and all the incredible food, cultures, and surf spots he could discover would no longer fill his life like it once did. Elena had left a void in him that nothing but her could fill.

Jackson stared out to the horizon, watching the ebb and flow of waves roll onto the shore. He'd often come to the private spot on Sullivan's Island to reflect, as he always had while growing up. When he was in college, his reflections were about how he could forge a path as his own man without disappointing his father.

That didn't work out.

Then it was about building his company from the ground up, which was something that had made him incredibly proud. And just a little more than a week ago, he had sat here to consider the next phase of his career, which meant staying in one place for a little while for once.

That also didn't work out.

Now his ass sat firmly in the sand as he thought about the woman who stole and broke his heart.

Another thing that hadn't panned out.

If there was one thing that Jackson was, it was resilient. He's always been the type to go wherever the tides took him, never worrying about the need to adjust his sails and go down a new course. It was just his way, and it had worked well for him for his thirty-two years of life. But some things weren't that easy to float away from.

His phone rang again, showing Elena's name on the display. He ignored it once more before standing and grabbing his board. He needed a distraction, a way to step away from his phone, especially with the way his fingers itched to answer Elena's call each time he saw her name.

He had to just keep it together for one more night. He'd hold her one last time, showing the world he was the man she portrayed him to be in her blogs. He'd brush his lips against hers, a passionate kiss a boyfriend would give his lady in celebration of her success. He'd smile, say all the right things, and show the world he wasn't breaking inside.

And then, he'd let her go.

"Jackson?" A familiar voice called his name as he walked up the beach to his parent's house.

He squinted in the harsh sunlight, making out two figures sitting in Adirondack chairs. "Mom?"

She rose, closing the distance between them and wrapped her arms around him in a tight hug. "What are you doing here?"

He squeezed her back. It had been months since he'd seen her, often choosing to make visits brief to limit the strain between him and his father. "I should be asking you the same thing. I thought you were supposed to be on vacation?"

"We're always back at this time." She gave him a little pat

on the cheek. "I guess you never realized since you're typically gone by now."

Jackson followed her to where they were seated on the patio. His father stood, and they shook hands. "Son."

"Dad."

His mother took a seat again as Jackson rested his surfboard near the outdoor shower. "I'm surprised to see you're still here. Mae said you'd come home a couple weeks ago," his mom commented as she took a sip of her coffee.

Jackson shrugged. "I needed a little extra time to figure out some business changes."

His father snorted and eyed his boardshorts. "Another busy day at the office, I see."

Jackson glared at him, his blood starting to boil. Not even one minute into seeing his father, and he was already minimizing all of Jackson's work. He didn't need this, not when he was already feeling like shit.

"What kind of changes?" his mother asked with interest, likely to defuse the obvious tension rising between Jackson and his father.

Jackson dragged his gaze from his dad and focused on her, trying his hardest to pretend like his father wasn't there. He could still feel the judgment radiating from his dad, though.

"We're going through a high-growth stage, and it's time to mature the company's business plan to match the demand. I had planned to look into new production and office space." He paused. "And I was going to cut down on my travel."

Her eyes widened. "You're staying? Here? In Charleston?" She couldn't hide the excitement in her voice. His heart squeezed. Had his mother really missed him that much?

Jackson shuffled. "Unfortunately, not anymore. Some things didn't work out. I leave again tomorrow."

She looked crestfallen.

"Never thought you had the head for business. Maybe if you took things more seriously rather than slack off at the beach, it would have actually worked out," his father muttered into his coffee cup.

"Are you fucking kidding me?" Jackson blew up.

God, he couldn't deal with this right now. Not after Elena—one of the few people that made him feel like what he was doing mattered—basically said his life was a joke. He was so tired of people assuming he was just skirting by in life.

"Do you know how many businesses fail within the first few years? My business not only withstood the odds, but it's thriving, and I'm damn proud of it."

Jackson took a deep breath, trying to calm his outrage. He was so sick of his dad putting him down when he didn't even have a clue what it takes to keep this business running.

"You don't realize how much goes into what I do," Jackson continued, trying to restrain another outburst. "It takes creativity, grit, and determination to stay current on the surfing industry, as well as understanding regional changes, climate change, and how what we put out in the world can affect the environment. What I'm doing matters. I've never worked so hard in my life. I might even be working harder than *you*."

His father scoffed. "I highly doubt that. Always a pleasure having you home," he said dryly before he stood and walked back into the house.

Jackson's head hung down in defeat. "I'll never be good enough for him."

"Honey." His mom's voice was soothing and quiet. "Your father is a...difficult man sometimes."

Jackson shook his head, lost for words. She patted the empty chair for him to sit.

"Ten years, mom. He's never forgiven me for not following in his footsteps for ten years." Emotion filled his voice, and Jackson was surprised by how badly the realization stung.

"And despite his comments, he wants you to come home," she shared. "We both do. It's great that Mae was able to join you on some of your trips, and we appreciate the video calls between your visits, but it's not the same. I miss my baby boy," her voice cracked. "It's been too long since our family was truly together. This can't keep going on. We won't be around forever, you know."

"Oh, mom." Jackson wrapped her into a tight hug, guilt weighing him down. He'd been so focused on staying away from his father's criticisms all these years that he didn't stop to realize how it affected his mother and sister too.

She swiped at her errant tears and pulled away, waving a hand like it was nothing. "I'm sorry, honey. I figured by keeping this all bottled up, I was being supportive. I didn't want you to give up your dreams because you felt bad about leaving your silly mother behind."

"You always pasted a smile on your face but never said anything. I assumed you felt the same as dad."

"Oh, goodness. No. I just wanted to keep the peace, so maybe you'd want to stick around longer on the rare occasions you were home." She placed a hand on his cheek, pushing his hair aside. "A mother always wants her babies around, even if they're grown. Maybe if I'd said something sooner, this family wouldn't have lost so much time together."

His heart squeezed. How could she think this was her fault? "This is between me and dad. You did *nothing* wrong, mom. Okay? Don't you ever think that."

A hopeful look crossed her face. "Maybe it's time for the two of you to sit down and have a *real* conversation. This family needs to come together again and heal."

"Every time I try, he does *this,*" Jackson said, gesturing at the house.

"And he's wrong. But you're your father's son. Both of you think it's easier to avoid your disagreement than to deal with it. You're both so stubborn. Someone needs to make the first move, Jackson," she said, her eyes pleading.

He blew out a breath. "Fine. *Fine.*"

She squeezed his hand, appreciative tears misting her eyes again. "And you won't give up until he listens to you, right?"

"I mean, I can't force him to absorb and accept what I'm saying, but I'll try, mom."

"You should know that during these last ten years, he's read every newspaper article about you, kept magazine features about your business, and recorded every news segment."

"Then...why...what?" His mom's admission came as a shock. After all these years antagonizing Jackson, he never once thought his dad cared enough to keep up with the business.

"As I said, your father is a difficult man. He's stuck in the traditional thoughts he grew up with, and sometimes it's hard for him to battle that with his actual real feelings: that he's proud of what you've done and wants you to succeed. Before you go in there, I just thought you should know."

Better late than never.

Jackson ran a hand through his hair, his mind completely blown.

There it was: the silver-lining in his bleak day. He could feel the resentment for his father ease. His family wanted him home. And he wanted to be there with them. To patch up the hole torn between them. To make up for lost time.

As if the irony wasn't lost on him. Now, he finally had a reason to stay, but he couldn't. Not yet, at least.

He stood, ready to face his father. "Thanks, Mom."

If he couldn't stay for now, at least he could set things right so that when he did return home for good, they'd be in a better spot.

He wouldn't give up, even if it took all night to get through to his father.

28

ELENA

"Where's Jackson?" Christopher asked as he passed Elena a glass of champagne.

"He's running late. Last-minute packing for his trip tomorrow."

The wrap party had officially started half an hour ago. It was a beautiful affair, taking place at a swanky rooftop bar overlooking downtown Charleston. The space had been outfitted with decor that reminded Elena of an upscale New Year's Eve party, full of sleek black, silver, and gold. It was all so glamorous.

Even Elena looked the part with her sweeping updo, classic makeup, and a floor-length shimmering black gown that highlighted all her best features. She had picked it out days ago, hoping Jackson's beautiful blue eyes would scan her slowly, the sight of her leaving him breathless. But as she stood there alone on what should have been one of the happiest days of her life, she just felt like the pathetic girl playing dress up as she'd always been.

Elena slipped away from the crowd to look out to the city, finding comfort in the rising church steeples and the warm glow from the gas lanterns lining the buildings below. All night, everyone had asked her about Jackson, and she'd give them the same response. As the minutes ticked by, she wondered if he was going to show up at all. She'd waited all day for his call, but heard nothing.

She feared maybe silence was her answer. He wanted nothing to do with her anymore.

But he said he'd be here.

She hoped he'd follow through.

Everyone was at the party. All the couples, crew members, Celeste, Rachel, Christopher, and bigwigs from Berkshire Media. They also allowed select members of newspapers, digital news, and magazines to attend. Celeste had called all her contacts, offering them the scoop on the upcoming *Always, Ella* TV mini-series, and books. The media had to sign NDAs, promising not to expose Elena's true identity before the TV reveal.

That, of course, had them buzzing. Maybe they couldn't write about it yet, but the excitement of knowing the woman behind the viral relationship advice blog was enough to get them there. Connecting with Elena would get them on her radar so they could call on her for interviews prior to the launch, capitalizing on the book and show promo when they could finally share the news.

Celeste sauntered over to where Elena stood alone, a look of absolute self-satisfaction across her face. "Ella, quite a turnout, huh?" She lifted the champagne flute to her lips.

"Yeah, it's all pretty exciting." As much as she tried to muster up the energy she was supposed to have for such an important moment in her writing career, she couldn't. It felt meaningless without Jackson there.

Elena looked at the growing crowd, spotting Maritza,

Natalie, and Ana all taking shots and giggling, their boyfriends staring on with complete adoration.

Guilt tugged at her. Tomorrow she'd tell the couples the truth at the farewell brunch. Rachel and Celeste had been right about making her wait. She couldn't take this moment from them, not when they looked so happy.

Rachel joined them. "Looks like your 'beau' finally showed up," she said while ogling him over her champagne glass. "Well, if you were going to pick a fake boyfriend, thankfully, it was him. He's absolutely gorgeous."

Celeste nodded. "He was perfect for the show. I watched some of the footage earlier, and he's got a face for TV. I bet we'll get even more viewers because of him."

Elena wrung her hands. "So, I didn't mess this all up?"

Rachel rolled her eyes. "You didn't exactly make our jobs any easier, that's for sure. But we've got a good team at Berkshire. We're confident your little faux pas won't get out."

"The couples will have to sign an NDA before you tell them, of course," Celeste added and leaned in closer. "And besides, fake boyfriend or not, there's no denying the chemistry between you two. *That* certainly wasn't a lie."

"Elena." Jackson's voice was low behind her, sending her nerves on overdrive and a chill down her spine.

Rachel raised an eyebrow, a small grin lifting her lips. "Have fun," she said before she and Celeste went to mingle with the rest of the crowd.

Elena slowly turned to face him. Her gaze traveled up the length of him, pausing on the lips she ached to kiss before resting on his guarded eyes.

"You look beautiful," he breathed out, the tension on his face relaxing a fraction.

"I didn't think you were coming."

"I made you a promise. I would never break that." A

pained look crossed his face. "I'm sorry I was late and made you worry. I got caught up at my parents' house and accidentally left my phone there, so I couldn't give you a heads up."

"It's okay, Jackson. You're here now." She sucked in a breath, trying to find the nerve to finally put herself out there and tell him how she felt. "I need to talk to you about what I said at the cafe." She touched his arm and looked into his eyes. "You have to know I didn't mean it. I know I already apologized, but it wasn't enough.

"I reacted badly to the gossip site and Brittany's threat," she continued. "I'm so sorry for shoving you away and blaming you for it. More importantly, I'm sorry for downplaying your business success, just like your father did. It was wrong. It was awful of me to make you feel like you didn't matter. If anything, it's the complete opposite. You've shown me I deserve so much more. That I could *be* so much more. I know it's too late though," she rambled, "you're leaving and—"

A tap on the mic sounded, pulling their attention to the makeshift stage across the space. "Ladies and gentlemen, may I have your attention."

Elena froze. That voice was so familiar.

As the crowd parted just enough to give Elena a clear view of the speaker, her stomach dropped.

Brittany.

29

ELENA

She was going to throw up. How did Brittany get in? More importantly, why was she at the mic?

When Brittany's eyes scanned the crowd and stopped on Elena, a slow smile spreading across her lips, Elena knew exactly why Brittany was there. The sinking feeling in her stomach somehow got lower as Elena waited for Brittany to completely blow up her life in the worst way possible.

In all the madness of fighting with Jackson and doing damage control with the Berkshire team, she never gave Brittany her answer.

And now she was going to pay for it.

"Ah, *Ella*. There you are," she cooed into the microphone while raising her drink in a toast. Turning back to the audience, she continued. "I want to say how *privileged* I am to have worked under such a talented writer. Ella—or as I know her, Elena Lucia—is a senior copywriter at the ad agency where we work together and has taken me under her wing these last two years. In seeing her quality of work, which was mediocre at best, you can imagine my surprise when I found out she was the woman behind the ever-so-popular *Always, Ella* blog."

Some members of the crowd gasped while others whispered to the person next to them. A few people held up their phones and started to record.

"Of course, I was so shocked." Brittany put a hand to her chest, feigning surprise as she continued. "I thought I knew everything about Elena since we worked closely and all. But as I read through the responses she'd shared to build such a loyal fan base and to afford her this *amazing* opportunity, I learned something else about dear ol' Elena."

Jackson took Elena's hand and squeezed. "We'll be okay," he whispered in her ear, the phrase he'd used all week to ground her, and every time he'd been right.

Just like now. She held her head high, ready to face what Brittany was going to share. Elena would get through it, she knew she would.

The crowd, now both confused and captivated by Brittany's mysterious story, hung on to her every word. "You see, Elena got this book deal because of the success with her blog, especially in regards to relationship advice." Brittany pointed at the couples sitting near the bar. "For people like you, right?"

Christopher saddled next to Elena. "How did she get in?" she asked.

"She has a press pass."

Elena realized Brittany must have tapped her contacts at the newspaper for it.

Christopher leaned closer. "Do you want me to take care of her? I'll pull the mic out of her hand."

Elena shook her head in resolve. "Thank you, but no. You can take the mic away, but she won't stop until she says what she has to say."

"I could understand why Elena would hide this side of her," Brittany continued. "A lot of writers aren't confident enough to share their work with the world when they first start out. But that wasn't it." She laughed dryly. "It's because she's a liar."

Christopher left Elena and moved through the crowd, whispering into the ear of the security team standing nearby.

"Elena Lucia is a fraud. She pretended to be an expert in love and relationships when she didn't even have a successful one herself. Her *real* boyfriend ditched her a year ago for other women because she didn't have what it takes to keep him happy. And that guy standing next to her," Brittany pointed at Jackson, "is *not* her boyfriend. It's pathetic that she'd made up a boyfriend for the advice column, but it's a whole other level of pitiful when she has to convince her best friend's brother to keep up the charade. There you have it, folks. You've been duped." She raised her glass up before swallowing the rest of her champagne.

The crowd went utterly silent as everyone turned to look at her. Elena wanted to die. Disappointment from the execs. Hurt from the couples. And smug expressions from the press all surrounded her. She knew it would be bad, but going through it, and the mixed reactions, made it feel so much worse.

Everything in her screamed to turn and run, but before she could take a step, Jackson gripped her hand harder. He looked down at her with determination and pride. Even after everything that happened between them, he was still in her corner. He still believed in her.

It was enough to give her the courage she needed to face this head-on. Her worst fears had just come to light, and now everyone was looking for answers.

Elena gave Jackson's hand one last squeeze before letting go. She slipped away from him and walked towards the stage. The audience parted like the Red Sea, eagerly awaiting her response. Would she bolt? Would there be a catfight? Would she try to explain it all away?

This was her moment.

Elena took the microphone from Brittany, who still looked pleased with herself. "You didn't win," Elena whispered to her, causing Brittany's smile to falter just a moment before she stepped to the side.

All eyes were on her.

"I'm not going to deny what Brittany said. And for that, I'm sorry," she said, addressing the couples. It pained her to see the tears in Maritza's eyes. "*Always, Ella* started by accident, really. It's true that my boyfriend cheated on me with other women, and I turned to writing as a way to make sense of it all. I had no intention of sharing it with the world and had no way of knowing people would write to me looking for help. But they did, and I felt compelled to respond.

"I thought it would fizzle out. The world is full of content, and things like blogs die in an instant. Somehow, it continued to grow. No longer were only the heartbroken writing in, but those in committed relationships were also looking to hold on to the love they had. Again, I felt obligated to respond."

Christopher's nod encouraged her to keep going.

"It's also true that the boyfriend I wrote about to provide examples didn't exist. Not entirely anyway. He was a man formed from good memories I'd had with my ex, examples of my friends' boyfriends, and what I believed would be an ideal man and relationship. After being treated badly for years, I wanted the people coming to me to look at their own relationships and make sure they were not only being treated right but that they were treating the person they cared for right, too." She laughed quietly to herself. "I just didn't truly realize what that meant until this week."

She looked at Jackson, relief warming her body. "Jackson St. Julien is my best friend's brother, yes. He was also a childhood friend growing up. I'll admit, he was probably one of the last people I would have chosen to be my stand-in boyfriend for this show. But you need to know that I care about the people who I write to, or in this case, coached live. I didn't want my personal failures to make them lose faith in me when all I wanted to do was help. I can see how wrong that was now. Maybe I should have taken my own advice about honest and open communication for once. I should have just been upfront about my relationship with him."

Maritza wiped a tear away and listened with renewed interest. The hurt on her face was no longer there, now replaced with a flash of understanding. Elena turned to the other couples who all offered her slight nods or smiles.

Elena's gaze swept back to Jackson. He stood tall, the look of adoration in his eyes gave her the strength to continue. If she was going to tell the truth, it was time to tell the *whole* truth. Maybe this wasn't the setting or the way she wanted to go about it, but this might be the last chance she got. She wasn't going to waste it.

"In going through the exercises with the couples this week, something happened. It was incredible to watch them grow and connect with their loved ones. But I, too, have fallen in love again. When Jackson first agreed to go along with this, I had asked him to fall into the role of the man I described in the blog. He immediately said no, of course, because that's Jackson—utterly and completely self-confident. And I'm glad he refused because he showed me how a real relationship could work.

"They're messy and unpredictable. They aren't made to be put in a nice neat box, tied with a perfect bow." She smiled to herself, thinking back to the beginning when Jackson had said something similar.

"The person you're meant to be with should push you to grow and celebrate you for who you are, no matter how imperfect that is. More importantly, they'll be by your side to support you and hold you up even on the days when you don't feel like you deserve it. This week made me fall in love with Jackson St. Julien." Elena watched his face drop in shock. Keeping her eyes trained on him, she continued. "Every situation we went through on the show not only let me learn more about him and how good relationships work but showed me who I really was too."

"Oh God, you're not going to believe this bullshit, are you?" Brittany said, rolling her eyes.

Elena glared at her. "Hiding behind the name and the blog meant I wasn't being fully authentic. And I'm sorry for the pain I might have caused because of it. I was just trying to be perfect. To be worthy of the people who turned to me for help. But whether you believe it or not, this week has shown me how to be comfortable in my own skin and love myself, and that in by being imperfect, I can connect with and help others even better. A huge part of that realization was because of the people I was surrounded with and because of Jackson."

She turned back to him. "I know you're leaving, and it's too late, but I need you to know that I love you, and I appreciate everything you've done for me. I'm sorry, I got scared. I know it will take work to find the courage to be myself when life wants to challenge me, but I'm going to fight for it every day. I couldn't have gotten to this point without you. I'll forever be grateful for that, Jackson."

Before Jackson could speak, Natalie pushed her way onto the stage. "Ella—Elena—I think I could speak for the rest of us when I say that boyfriend or not, you helped us all significantly."

Elena turned to the couples, all who nodded in enthusiasm.

"You helped me and Max see that we need to make more time for each other. We want to take our relationship to the next level, so we're going to work to coordinate our work schedules better. And if all goes well, we'll consider moving in once my lease is up at the end of the year," Maritza said before laying a big kiss on Max.

"Same here," Zach added while pulling Ana to his side. "Being here reminded us of the early days in our relationship before we got so focused on work. We had a ton of fun. It renewed the spark between us."

"Yeah. I actually felt a little more like myself this week," Ana confirmed. "I didn't even check my email more than once a day! That's insane." Zach shot her a look. "Okay. Okay. *Twice* a day."

Natalie shared a sheepish smile with Hari across the space, tears misting her eyes. "And Hari and I have decided to call it quits." The crowd gasped. "Oh, no, no. This is a good thing. As much as we love each other, it became clear that we wanted different things, and neither of us is willing to budge. As much as it hurts to have to say goodbye to such a wonderful man, we both owe it to ourselves to be happy. Hopefully, we can find what we're looking for." She turned back to Elena. "This couldn't have happened without you. You need to know that."

Excited chatter surrounded them, further pissing off

Brittany. She stomped her foot down. "How are none of you furious that Elena lied to you?" She pointed at Rachel. "You signed with a fraud. How will that affect your brand? Maybe these people are fine with it, but what about the rest of her followers? They could easily ban you and her books."

Stephanie muscled through the crowd with a cameraman in tow. "I highly doubt that if they see this footage." She grinned at Rachel and Celeste. "It's honest, raw, and is going to work beautifully with the launch if we decide we need to use it."

Rachel crossed her arms, looking satisfied as she addressed Brittany. "I should remind you that you signed an NDA to be here tonight, as did the rest of the media. If any of this gets out without our approval, we'll sue the shit out of you."

Brittany's jaw dropped. "But—but—"

Christopher pushed through the crowd with two security guards in tow. The guards grabbed either of Brittany's arms, escorting her off the stage. The room erupted in applause as they pulled her away and disappeared down the stairs.

Elena turned to the crowd, appreciative tears filling her eyes. They were still here. They were still willing to support her, even after everything.

She started when a hand touched her arm and spun around to find Jackson, his eyes boring into hers. "Did you mean what you said?" he asked breathlessly as if he had been running for miles.

She reached a hand up to his face. "Every word. I love you, Jackson St. Julien."

He pulled her into his arms and lifted her, his lips crashing down onto hers in a passionate kiss. Everyone cheered around them.

"When you didn't answer my calls and were late, I thought we were over," she shared as she reluctantly broke the kiss.

"I told you that I got caught up at my parents." She nodded. "It was because I was talking to my dad."

Her eyes widened. "Like *talked* talked?"

"Yeah. Once he got over the initial hurt of me not wanting to follow in his footsteps, I learned he was hurt because he felt I didn't want to include him in my life and my business. I didn't think he ever respected what I did. I've avoided him for so long because of it, but I think...I think we're going to be okay in the end."

"Wow."

He slid her down to the ground, his hands still resting on her waist. "He offered to help me with my business as I continue to scale. He wants to invest so I can hire someone sooner to take over travel. Said he wouldn't mind having me home more often. I still have to leave, but if all goes well, it won't be for nearly as long as I'd expected.

"We got deep in discussion—catching up for lost time—and I didn't realize I was running late. Otherwise, I would have been walking into this party with you." Emotion filled Jackson's face, his blue eyes sparkling. "And I would have had time to tell you that I fell in love with you, too, Elena Lucia. Maybe I always have been. But this week showed me you're home to me. You're someone I'd miss when I was gone and would be elated to come back to every time. I've never felt like this. Not until you.

"I know me leaving tomorrow isn't ideal. I'm sure your blog boyfriend wouldn't be the type to jet-set across the world after professing his love to you," he half-joked. "But I want to make this work," he said, his tone more serious now. "I know this won't be easy, and it may take some time to figure out the whole travel thing, but I will commit to making this work. It's not the perfect relationship you envisioned, I'm sure, but I promise to love you fiercely to the ends of the earth. Every day. Always."

Her heart swelled to its bursting point. He was everything she didn't know she needed in life, and she'd do whatever it took to keep him.

"Jackson, even if I could only have you for one day a year, it would be enough for me. So, yes. My answer is yes," she answered.

A slow smile spread across his face, showing off those deep laugh lines she'd come to love. "Yes? You're mine?"

"Absolutely."

She reached up and kissed him again, her heart beating erratically in her chest. The crowd went wild, cheering once more as he wrapped his arms around her and held her close.

Here in his arms, Elena suddenly felt like she could take on the world...exactly as she was.

EPILOGUE
ELENA

It had been a year since the famous outing of *Always, Ella*. Although everyone who had attended the wrap party had signed an NDA, someone had filmed the whole ordeal on a cell phone and leaked it wide that evening. They managed to make it untraceable, so Berkshire Media was never able to figure out who did it.

After that night, Elena's life had taken a dramatic turn.

For the better, much to Brittany's dismay.

Rather than *Always, Ella* fans completely cutting Elena off, they had embraced her whole-heartedly. After watching the leaked video and the footage Stephanie's team had filmed, her fans supported her, commenting on her realness and bravery. Now, *Always, Ella* had taken on a whole new subset of people seeking advice—those looking to find their authentic selves and how to embrace it.

After going through the experience herself, their questions helped her build the confidence she needed to accept the woman who had been hidden inside all along. With each response she wrote, she felt more like herself, messy mistakes and moments of self-doubt included. And, of course, the popularity of this new blog topic had landed her another book deal Rachel was all too happy to move forward with.

The show had come out six months ago, which created a whole new flurry of superfans. Elena was thrilled to keep up with the couples after production. Maritza and Max had officially moved in together and were in talks of getting engaged soon. Ana and Zach had tried to spend more time with one another, even stopping in Charleston again for a spontaneous weekend trip. Natalie and Hari had managed to remain friends after some time apart for "soul-searching." Natalie had started to date again and found a wonderful man she clicked with only a few months ago. Hari was enjoying a bachelor's life. He'd decided to go back to school to make a career change, finding a new passion in software development.

And, as Celeste and Rachel had expected, *Always, Ella* fans instantly fell in love with "heartthrob" Jackson St. Julien. So much so that sales of his surf products spiked, affording him enough profit to hire a handful of new people to reach far and wide and bringing his vision to life in ways he never could have dreamed.

As of three months ago, Jackson had stored his duffle bag in the closet and officially set roots in Charleston, now building his business with his father by his side.

Brittany was still Brittany, desperate to see Elena fail more than ever. Soon after the whole wrap party fiasco, their employer had caught wind of Brittany's embarrassing and unethical behavior and threatened to fire her. However, Elena had convinced him to hold off so they could finally settle the score.

That big project they had worked on for the promotion? Elena suggested that Brittany finally prove she was better than her. Elena had asked their boss to allow them to pull together a campaign for the client and to submit it blind to the decision-makers. No names on the project, no pitches in person.

In the end, the clients unanimously chose Elena's pitch over Brittany's. Rather than accepting the promotion she deserved, Elena decided to quit to pursue her writing career.

She would always remember the look on Brittany's face when she told her boss she was leaving and to give Brittany the promotion.

"Don't forget, I gave this to you," Elena whispered to her as she left the office with a box filled with her things.

Maybe it was petty, but after all the horrible things Brittany had said to Elena over the years, she had hoped this experience would humble her. Knowing Brittany, though, it likely wouldn't.

As for Elena's writing career, it had skyrocketed in unexpected ways. Not only were her *Always, Ella* books wildly successful, but she had built such trust with the publisher and a platform of readers, that they wanted to publish her first debut fiction novel, a "coming of age" story based loosely on Elena's childhood in Charleston.

Christopher was beyond elated Elena had finally found her writing mojo—something she could never grasp when she was dated Brad—and already put out feelers to find production companies open to option her book for the big screen upon its completion. It all felt so surreal.

As for her and Jackson? Life was good.

Somehow, they had managed to squeeze into Elena's beloved, tiny apartment these last three months. Thankfully, Jackson hadn't acquired much because he had been traveling for so long, so they were able to make do. Marley was more than excited to have Jackson there, sometimes making Elena feel a little tinge of jealousy whenever Marley would cozy up to him on the couch instead.

With him settling in, they decided to find a new space to make their own somewhere close to Jackson's new, larger warehouse and a place that had the perfect writing nook to inspire the many stories Elena planned to write for years to come.

As Elena sat across from Jackson at a small dive bar near the beach, she couldn't help but realize how lucky she was. It was crazy to think she had met the love of her life when she was only ten years old. He'd been there, right under her nose, this whole time. Had she not gotten herself in the crazy situation with the TV show, she may have never found him again.

"You know, I never did cash in on that IOU favor for pretending to be your boyfriend," Jackson said, taking a slow swig of his beer.

Elena cocked an eyebrow. "Oh? And what did you have in mind?"

He shrugged his shoulder nonchalantly and pulled something out from his pocket.

She gasped. A box. A jewelry box. "Jackson..."

He flipped the top open, revealing a stunning princess-cut solitaire. "Elena Lucia, every moment with you is an adventure that rivals even the most exciting destinations in the world. I want you by my side no matter where life takes us, and I want to be the man who shows you that you are enough—more than enough—every day. I'm so proud of you, baby. I'm honored to call you mine. Will you marry me?"

Happy tears filled her eyes as she popped out of her seat and wrapped her arms around his neck, kissing him deeply.

"Nothing like cashing in on a favor to get a girl to marry you. You must have been nervous you couldn't seal the deal all on your own," she teased.

He laughed and planted a kiss on her cheek. "Hey, it's the only way I could guarantee you'd say yes. You owe me, after all," he joked back.

After the whirlwind experience filming *Always, Ella*, she'd appreciated the low-key proposal. It was just so *them*. It was perfect.

She plucked the ring from the box and slipped it onto her finger, loving the way it sparkled in the sunlight. "Tell you what. I'll agree to be your wife, no favor required. You hold onto that IOU because I have some more *interesting* suggestions on how you can use it." She wagged her eyebrows suggestively.

Jackson grabbed her and pulled her flush against his body. "I like where this is going," he said as he leaned in and kissed her again.

Elena smiled against his lips as she thought about all the possibilities life had in store for them. She couldn't wait to find out.

For the first time ever, she was okay not having every detail of her life perfectly mapped out. As long as she had him by her side, she knew everything would be fine.

ABOUT THE AUTHOR

When Sofia Sawyer's fifth-grade teacher handed her a journal, encouraging her to keep writing, she vowed she always would. A lifelong storyteller, Sofia writes contemporary romances featuring tenacious women who won't stop until they get their happily ever after.

 Based in Charleston, S.C., she follows her wanderlust whenever she can to new and exciting places, often finding story ideas throughout her travels.

When she isn't reading, writing, or jet-setting across the globe, you can find Sofia playing with her dog, taking advantage of the amazing Charleston restaurant scene, hiking, or hanging at the beach.

To stay up to date with her latest work, connect with her on:

- **Instagram:** @sofiasawyerwriter
- **Facebook:** @sofiasawyerwriter
- **Twitter:** @sofia_sawyer
- **Pinterest:** @sofiasawyerwriter

Or visit sofiasawyer.com to **sign up for her mailing list.**

Made in United States
North Haven, CT
18 June 2022

20399636R00168